I0571794

FOUR IN THE HOLE

EDITED BY TW BROWN
COVER ART BY SHAWN CONN

Four in the Hole
©2011 May December Publications LLC

The split-tree logo is a registered trademark of May December Publications LLC

This book is a work of fiction. Names, characters, businesses, organizations, places, events, and incidents either are the product of the authors' imagination or are used fictitiously. Any resemblance to actual persons living, dead, or otherwise, events, or locales is entirely coincidental.

This book is protected under the copyright laws of the United States of America. Any reproduction or unauthorized use of the material or artwork contained herein is prohibited without the express written permission of the authors or May December Publications LLC.

Printed in the U.S.A.

ISBN - 978-1-936730-13-1

To Mindy

FOREWARD

I have tried to make it very well known that we do our anthology story selection just a bit differently here at May December Publications. The stories are collected by Denise, the owner of MDP, and then stripped of any information that would reveal the author. Next, the story is forwarded to be read and scored. The top scores are selected and another anthology is born. This keeps us from being total homers and picking our favorites.

The fact that you may see some of the same names occur in our anthology rests on the simple fact that he or she writes exceptional material. Believe it or not, one of the biggest thrills for me is when I see a name in the final table of contents that I am not familiar with.

This anthology has one familiar name (congrats to you, Bennie!). That means that the other three, or seventy-five percent, of the authors are new to MDP. Don't get me wrong, I have a few favorites that I am always excited to see make the cut, but this industry needs new blood. You as the reader need to meet new names and find your next favorite.

I feel that you are holding an exceptional quartet of stories. I hope that you will enjoy them as much as I did. Be sure to let the writer know. This can be a thankless and frustrating field; a little pat on the back goes a long way.

Four of a kind wins the pot!
TW Brown
August 2011

CONTENTS

THE DEADLANDS

BY BILL BLUME

The first thing Paul noticed when he woke was the silence. Richmond didn't rank up there with New York where noise pollution was concerned, but the lack of sound was oppressive. He feared he was deaf until he heard his own breathing.

Moonlight, his only source of light, spilled in through the windows, but this wasn't his house. The last thing he remembered was sitting in the den with his parents, watching the TV as they waited to see if the world was coming to an end. Now, he was lying in a bed in some hospital. He wasn't sure how he'd gotten here. His back ached as he sat up, the way it got whenever he slept in too late on a Saturday.

The room felt cold. The stupid hospital gown he was sporting didn't help. He wondered if he could get an extra blanket or put on some real clothes. That was when he saw the shape on the floor near the door. He leaned closer and strained his eyes to figure out what was there.

"Oh crap!" he whispered. Someone was on the floor, and they weren't moving.

He started hitting the buttons on the arms of the bed. He couldn't see the "call nurse" button, so he punched as many buttons as he could. Nothing happened, no beeps or lights or anything. "Hello! Help!" He stopped pushing buttons and screaming after a few minutes. No one was going to answer.

Why the hell was he even here, and where were his parents? Knowing Mom, the worrywart she was, she would have set up camp in this place. He couldn't just sit here. He needed to move. As he turned to climb out of the bed and go to the person on the floor, he realized he was wired up like a damn computer. He pulled out the IV first. The bag it attached to was flat and empty. He also had sensor pads attached to his chest; the kind he assumed went to a heart monitor. He pulled them off; glad he didn't have a lot of hair there. That's when he realized they weren't attached to the same monitor. Two heart monitors? That didn't make sense, did it? And why weren't they turned on? He looked out the window and didn't see a single light on in all of Richmond, or anything on the horizon.

He called out again, not holding out much hope for an answer this time. Still nothing.

The tiled floor half froze his toes as he climbed out of the bed. He crept closer to the person on the floor. The body was dressed in a white coat, the kind doctors wore. He rolled the body onto its back. "Oh, God!" The body fell into a ray of moonlight and he saw it was nothing but a grey, withered corpse. Its eyes were empty sockets of shadow. The doctor's body was still reaching for the door as if to pull help from beyond the room.

He scrambled back from the body and ran for the door. He flung it open, but he didn't rush into the corridor. Not a single light was on, not even the emergency lights. The moonlight coming through his windows provided him with the only light to be had. His eyes adjusted, granting definition to the dark shapes. He saw a nurses station with two more bodies behind the counter. Both bodies were dried out and eyeless like the doctor in his room.

Paul shivered, as much from fear as the cold. He tried to remember how he got in this hospital, but he couldn't force a memory where it didn't exist. The last thing he remembered was the news showing images of an ethereal, pink light enveloping everywhere on Earth. The light had passed through the walls of his house, not merely through the windows, but through the walls. Mom and Dad didn't seem to feel anything, but his body had broken out in goosebumps. Icy pain had filled the inside of his chest. Everything went all dizzy, and he'd fallen to the floor. A blast of heat, his parents' screams and then...this.

His parents.

He needed to get home. That meant getting out of here, and he wasn't doing that in the middle of winter dressed like this. He needed some real clothes. He could just make out a door behind the nurses' station and a row of lockers.

"Bingo."

He felt his way around the counter and into the locker room. He found a black turtleneck, some blue jeans and a really awesome brown, leather jacket. The turtleneck came from a women's store, but he figured at this point, he couldn't really be picky. Besides, who would know?

Now that he was winterized, Paul tried the phones. Every line was dead. He found a few cell phones in the lockers, but the batteries were drained.

He scored at least two cigarette lighters, and he needed them. Damn place's emergency lights weren't working. He singed his thumb a few times trying to keep one of those lighters burning. The first one died on him halfway down the stairs.

He wasn't sure what he expected to see outside of the hospital. Anything would have been better than what he found. Cars were wrecked along the street with the dead still in the driver's seats. It looked as if everyone died all at once, everyone but him.

He needed a car. Do that and he could get to the West End, where his house was. Bad enough to find the hospital as it was, but now he was wondering just how far all this death went. Was this because of that pink light? Had it really been the end of the world? That didn't make sense. If it had, then how had he gotten in the hospital? He decided to worry about the rest of the world after he'd found a car. He ran to the nearest corner and saw a parking garage.

He found exactly what he wanted in the garage, an emaciated body on the ground just between two cars. The man wore a suit and tie and held his car keys in his hands. "Yes!" Paul snatched the keys from the guy. Even with what little moonlight he had, he could make out the VW logo.

"Well, this just sucks." His first time stealing a car, and it was a lousy, lime green Volkswagen Bug. "You could have at least made it a Mustang or a Mitsubishi 3000GT," he said with a look skyward.

Turned out he was bitching for nothing. When he turned the key, he got more silence, not even a cough or click. "Come on, dammit!" He tried to crank it at least a dozen times. Still nothing. Then he tried to turn on the lights, but he just got more, lousy nothing. The car's battery was as dead as its owner.

Paul slammed his fists on the steering wheel. Damn thing wouldn't even honk. He got out and repeatedly kicked and hit the car, screaming every curse he knew. When his hands hurt too much to hit the car again, he dropped to the ground and leaned back against the Bug. He planted his face in his hands, wishing all of this would just go away. He wanted to go home, but a dark thought had started to whisper in his mind, *You really think your home is still there?*

"Well, I'll be damned," someone other than Paul said. "Was beginning to think I was never going to find you."

Paul jumped to his feet and scrambled between the cars. Only after he was there did it dawn on him that he'd just put himself in a corner with no way out except for climbing over the other cars.

"Who said that?" Paul looked right and left. The voice had sounded close, like the guy had been in front of him, but he didn't see anyone.

"Name's Philly."

Paul slammed back into the side of the Bug. "Holy crap!" The voice came from the top of the SUV next to him. There hadn't been anyone there a moment ago.

The guy was crouched on the SUV's roof. He was some pale-skinned guy with a buzz cut, wearing a black leather jacket.

"Sorry, kid, didn't mean to scare you."

Paul stared, unsure what to make of this guy. He was big, but the way he perched on that car made him look nimble like a gymnast. Something about him just felt...wrong, aside from the fact he was the only other person alive in a city full of dead people. Looking at Philly made Paul feel like lunch.

"You were looking for me?" Paul inched his way back out from between the cars.

Philly stayed on the SUV, canting his head as he watched Paul walk away. "Long story, kid. We'll have time to get to that later. For now, we need to get you somewhere safe."

"How did you get here?" Paul felt a bit more comfortable once he had some distance between him and Philly. He'd always been a good runner, one of the best on his high school's cross country team. He wasn't so sure he could move faster than Philly, though. The guy might be big, but he looked fast. Maybe it was that buzz cut.

"Once I got in this mess, I had to walk until I found a bike. Let me tell you, kid, I was pretty pissed when my car crapped out on me. Damn thing was a rental."

"Just how far is everything…" he paused, searching for the right words, "…like this?"

"Most of central Virginia. Lot farther than I'd expected. All the way north into Fredericksburg and south past Petersburg. Real number on the place, but at least most of the coast is still there. Suppose they'd rather get taken out by a hurricane or global warming…whichever comes first."

Paul felt as if his chest had collapsed on itself. If this grey death had made it that far, then his house was in the middle of all this. Why had it happened at all? Why here? And why wasn't he dead? He sat on the bumper of a car across from Philly's perch.

"So how long have I been out?" Paul asked.

"Out?" Philly's eyes were freaky. They reminded him of glitter, the way the light reflected off of them. Philly glanced towards the exit to the parking garage. "Ah, you were in the hospital."

"Yeah." He still wasn't sure how he'd gotten there. "What's the date?"

"The date? Damn, kid, how long you been out?"

"I don't know!" Paul slammed his fist against the car he was sitting on. "If I knew, I wouldn't be asking."

Philly focused those strange eyes on him again and grunted this quiet laugh. "January twenty-eighth."

5

"2013?" Oh, God. If that was right, then more than a month had passed since the pink light on December twenty-first.

Philly laughed even louder, which pissed off Paul. "Yeah, 2013. Would have gotten here sooner, but it's been a real bitch trying to get into the U.S."

"It has? Why?"

Philly's head dropped to give Paul the kind of stare that usually works best over a pair of glasses. "Kid, if 9/11 was some parking lot fender bender, then *this*," he reached out with his arms as if to define the borders of death with his hands, "was the equivalent of a three hundred car pileup on I-95 at rush hour. People in the U.S. been thinking it's some terrorist, bio-chemical attack, so they haven't been letting anybody in the borders. Then you got everyone else in the world thinking it's some damn plague, so they didn't want to let anyone from the U.S. near their country."

"When did this happen? Was it the same day as the pink light?"

"No, happened about two weeks later. I was in Britain. Had to wait for the borders to open back up so I could look for you."

"Wait a minute." Paul leaned forward, looking intently for Philly's reaction to his next question. "You were expecting to find me? Why would you think to find anyone alive in here at all?"

Philly didn't answer right away. He hopped off the top of the car. The way Philly stood made being upright look more awkward for him than when he crouched.

Paul got to his feet, ready to run. Everything about this guy set off all sorts of alarms in his gut.

Philly held up his hands, showing he wasn't holding any weapons. Paul didn't think that made a difference with this guy, but at least he stopped walking closer.

"Relax, kid, I'm not gonna hurt you. Hell, I'm here to save you."

"Seems like I'm the only one here who doesn't need saving."

"What's happened here isn't a danger to you or me, but here's the catch. The other guys coming here, the ones who want you dead...this place isn't a threat to them either."

Paul leaned back against the car he'd been sitting on. "Want me dead? Why would anyone want to kill me?"

"You're a threat to them. The very fact you can survive here makes you dangerous."

Paul shook his head, trying to take in all of this in a way that made some sense. "Who are they?"

"Kid, judging from the looks of you, I don't think you're ready for that."

Philly was probably right. Paul's chest hurt. His heart was racing in an unfamiliar way, and he was sweating real bad. Dead of winter, and he'd already drenched the collar of his turtleneck. Heck, just breathing was getting hard to do. He forced himself back onto his feet.

"Look, thanks for the warning. If it's all the same to you, I'm gonna find a bike and get the heck out of here."

Philly put himself between Paul and the exit to the parking garage. "Hold up, kid. The bicycle is a good idea, but you aren't going to sneak past these guys, and truth to tell...I really can't let you leave the city. Not yet."

Paul heard his mom's nagging voice in his head, reminding him not to talk to strangers. "You tell me there are a bunch of guys coming here to kill me, and then you tell me I can't leave. Convenient." He walked past Philly, going as fast as he could without looking like he was running.

"Bad choice, kid," Philly said. "You need to trust me, or you're going to get yourself killed."

Paul turned around. "Look, pal, I don't know you—" He stopped short as he realized Philly wasn't there.

"Kid, you need my help or these guys will eat you alive."

Paul jumped as he heard Philly's voice. "Crap!" The guy was between him and the exit again. "How did you do that?" Damn, as if his heart wasn't beating fast enough already. "Nobody's that fast!" *Nobody human.*

"You can relax." Philly smiled as he took a step back. "If I wanted you dead, you'd be dead. I'm here to help you. The things that want to kill you, they're not as fast as I am, but they're just as deadly."

Paul's mind felt numb. Waking up in this death zone was about the most normal thing in his life at this point. Not good. "What do you mean by 'things'?"

"You want answers, and I get that," Philly said. "For now, let's see about those bicycles."

"You don't seem like you need one," Paul said.

"I can move fast, but I can only do it for so long. If I go too far, I get tired and need to get some juice."

Score one for Paul, given he was a long-distance runner. Of course, Paul would need a massive head start on Philly.

Philly walked towards the exit to the parking garage and motioned for Paul to follow. "I stashed a pair of bikes near here. You coming?"

Paul still wasn't sure he really trusted this guy, but Philly was right about one thing. Philly could have already killed him, if he'd wanted to. Didn't take much imagination to see how Philly could just do that super speed thing and crush Paul's windpipe. With that lovely mental image, Paul started walking.

"How much time do you think we have?" Paul asked as they walked back into the moonlight. "I mean before those 'things' you talked about get here." Things more deadly than Philly. Abso-stinkin'-fabulous.

"If we're lucky, we've got until tomorrow night, but best not to assume that."

"I can't decide if you're an optimist or a pessimist, Philly."

"I like to think of myself as an optimistic pessimist, kid. Less disappointment in life that way."

Philly led them down to East Broad Street and headed west. The way Philly walked made Paul nervous, not that he didn't have plenty to make him that way already. Being with this guy was like being locked in a small room with a large cat.

What Paul wouldn't give for a car that worked. Of course, now that he was walking down Broad, one of the city's major streets, he saw the cars had clogged up the roads pretty good, one wreck after another. Even if he'd gotten that Volkswagen in the parking garage started, he probably wouldn't have gotten far. He'd need a tank to plow through this.

They didn't go very far, just a few blocks down from the hospital and past City Hall. "Put 'em in here." Philly ran up the front steps to a large building that was all grey walls and large windows.

"What's this?"

"Library, according to the sign." Philly led them through a glass door that had been shattered. From the sidewalk, Paul hadn't even noticed it. There was a small elevator lobby to the right. "Found one on the sidewalk here, so I stashed my bike and the one for you in here."

"You already had a bike here for me?" Paul found that pretty damn disturbing. "Just how did you know where to look for me? That I was even close by?"

"Could sense you were somewhere near," Philly said in a tone that made it clear he wasn't in the mood to discuss that any further. He picked up a backpack from the floor and slipped it on. Paul was startled to see a pair of swords sitting on the floor. "One of those is for you. Strap it on."

Each sword was in a sheath attached to a really long leather belt. "How fat did you think I was gonna be?" Paul asked.

"Just watch how I do it." He slipped off his jacket and wrapped the brown, leather belt around his waist several times and somehow positioned the sword perfectly on his left hip. The excess belt ran through a metal ring on the other end and down the front of his left leg.

Paul did his best to duplicate Philly's movements, but he had a devil of a time getting that sword to settle on his left hip the way it should. He noticed his belt looked new, where as Philly's wore plenty of mileage.

"Surprised you left these swords here."

9

Philly laughed. "Expected you to be freaked enough as it was without the sword on my hip."

"Oh." Paul shifted the sword a bit until it felt more comfortable. "I got this thing on right?"

"That'll do." Philly walked his bike out the door and down to the sidewalk.

Paul followed him outside, pushing his bike by the handlebars west on Broad Street.

"Whoa, kid! Where are you going?"

Paul looked over his shoulder. "I'm going home. That's where I'm going."

"Why?"

"That's where I last saw my parents."

Philly shook his head. "Waste of time. All you're gonna find is a pile of ash."

"I'm still here, so maybe my parents are, too. What makes you so sure there's nothing there?"

"Because I've already seen what's left of your home. Whole world has."

"Just because this place is like this doesn't mean—"

Philly cut him off. "No, kid, that's not what I mean. Day the Avatar Light arrived, December twenty-first, a few places got wiped out. Your neighborhood was one of them. You were the only survivor. Was checking on another site like that outside of London when Central Virginia got wiped out."

"My parents?"

"Dead...on December twenty-first. Central Virginia joined 'em on January second."

"Everyone but me?"

Philly nodded. Paul's mind was fitting the pieces together, and for the first time, he was stepping back to really look at the big picture. Two disasters...and he'd survived both of them.

"You okay, kid?"

Paul's lips shivered before he could force out another word. "You—you were looking for me. You knew I was here."

Philly stared at him, the stillness of his body as hard as the silence of this place. "Kid, I don't think you're ready to hear this."

"Yeah." Pretty much what he'd expected. Paul climbed onto his bike to ride away.

"Whoa!"

Philly suddenly appeared in Paul's path, same as he'd done in the parking garage. Paul heard Philly's abandoned bike fall to the sidewalk behind him.

"Look, we don't have the time for you to go home and see it isn't there."

Paul glared at him. "And just where am I supposed to go, Philly?"

"Eventually, we need to go to Washington, but first, we gotta make sure it's safe to take you out of the Deadlands."

"Safe? You mean those 'things' that are coming after me?"

Philly hesitated. "No, that's not what I mean. I mean that if you try to walk out of the Deadlands the way you are right now, you'll never find the borders and you'll just get a hell of a lot of people killed in the process."

The only survivor—twice. Paul didn't want to look at the picture, didn't want to hear what Philly was saying, even as a part of him already knew it.

"There are a lot people dead already, pal," Paul said, "and I don't care to join them."

"Paul, I'm going to say this as gently as I can, but I'm not sure there's anyway to do that." Philly placed a hand on Paul's handlebars. "All this started with you."

"What?" He felt lightheaded as he took in those last few words.

"You couldn't help it, and it's not something you can control. Not yet, anyway. All this...it's not your fault, but if you leave here now that you know what you might do, then what happens next will be your fault."

Paul's palms were sweating, but he couldn't make his hands let go of the handlebars. "What—what do you mean I couldn't control it? What is 'it'?"

"You remember the pink light? December twenty-first, 2012? Mayans got it right. End of the world, only it's not some snap-of-the-fingers nightmare. That light was just the start. Central Virginia, the Deadlands...that's step two. Only gonna get worse from here."

"What does that have to do with me?" He glared at Philly, which wasn't easy with the guy's strange eyes staring back at him.

"The Avatar Light changed certain people and none of them for the better. They can't help what they've become, what they're going to do," Philly said the next part real slow, like he was trying to apologize for what he was saying, "or what they've already done."

"I'm just a normal guy."

Philly laughed. "Yeah? Well then how do you explain being the only person, for a good fifty miles in every direction, to survive this shit?"

"Just shut up!"

"You're not normal anymore, kid. That's all changed. School's over for you." Philly didn't move, just kept his hands on the handlebars. Only thing moving was his mouth. His head didn't even turn. "You know your Darwin?"

"What?"

"Survival of the fittest," Philly said. "Darwinism. Kind of important to you right now, because the food chain on this world has all changed."

"Let go of the bike, Philly." He wanted to get away. He didn't care where he went, just so long as he wasn't here.

"Look, just place your hand on the right side of your chest, kid. I want you to feel for your heartbeat."

"What has that got to do with a damn thing?"

"Just do it."

Paul placed his hand over the center of his chest. He didn't feel a heartbeat. Then he remembered what Philly had said, to put his hand on the right side of his chest. He shifted his hand right until he felt his heartbeat. It shouldn't be that far right, should it?

"Good," Philly said, "now leave that hand there and put your left hand on the opposite side of your chest."

He didn't argue this time, because his thoughts went back to when he'd awakened in the hospital. They'd had two heart monitors, sensors on both sides of his chest. He put his left hand where those sensors had been placed and felt a second heartbeat, thumping at a different rhythm than the one on his right.

Philly nodded, seeing the panic on Paul's face. He'd already known.

"There's only one reason you're still alive in this place, kid, and that's because you're the one at the top of the food chain right now."

"Shut up!" Paul took his hands from his chest and tried to shake the bike loose, but Philly's grip didn't budge.

"Every bit of life in this place, every soul and more...all of it eaten...by you."

Paul's body went cold as Philly said it.

"You're a soul-feeder, kid...new top of the fuckin' food chain. The Avatar Light awakened—"

"Shut up!" Paul jumped back, off the bike. "You're lying!"

Philly lowered Paul's bike to the ground. "Kid—"

"No! You're lying!"

"It wasn't your fault." Philly stayed down next to the bike, looking up at Paul.

"I said shut up!"

"Paul, it's January twenty-eighth. For a guy who's been sleeping in a hospital for close to a month, you smell pretty damn healthy to me. Last time you probably had any food or water was more than what? Almost a month ago? You should have starved to death by now or damn close to it, but I'll bet you don't even feel hungry, do you?"

13

He didn't. He hadn't even thought of food, hadn't really needed it yet. He thought of the IV bag—wrinkled, flat and empty—hanging next to his hospital bed.

He stumbled backwards and landed on his ass. His Mom ...Dad... He looked over at a wrecked car on the library's steps, saw the driver's dried up body slumped over the steering wheel.

"Oh, God."

Paul cradled his head in his hands and screamed. He didn't want to hear the silence. He tried to drown it out, but he couldn't scream forever.

His throat hurt when he stopped. After that shout, he expected to find his life at an end, but he was still here. Only thing ended here was the world, with him left behind.

When he looked up, he found himself meeting Philly's eyes. There might have been sympathy hiding there, but Paul couldn't swear to it and wasn't even sure it mattered. All the sympathy in the world wasn't going to change that.

"Kid, I'm going to make this simple for both of us. What's coming here for you... That sword on your hip won't save you. Most that'll do is keep you alive a little longer. You want to die, I'll just walk away. Don't care to get myself killed if I don't need to, and after what I just told you, I suppose some people in your shoes might want to end it all.

"You want to live, though," Philly let the offer hang out there a moment, "I'll stick around, and we might just save your happy assets."

The possibility of dying hadn't felt this real even when he'd been sitting in front of the TV with Mom and Dad, waiting for the Pink Light to reach Earth. He'd always thought of people who committed suicide as wimps too scared to get off their ass and deal with it. He wasn't so sure of that now. Some things did seem bad enough to flip the bird at God and say, *I'm done.*

"What would they do to me?" Paul asked. "What are they, and what'll they do if I just let them kill me?"

Philly didn't nod or blink. "They're called *fördröj frånfälle.* You'd probably call them zombies, but forget that 'Night of the Living Dead' shit. We're not talking about a bunch of rotting corpses moaning and dragging their way down the street. These bastards are almost as fast as me and a lot stronger. The difference is that they don't have free will, but that doesn't mean they can't think independently. They're just servants to the one who stole their souls. That's the only reason they can survive here. If they get a hold of you, they'll eat you alive... harvest your soul for their mistress."

"Last part sounds poetic." Would hardly even the score, though. He wondered just how many times he'd have to be killed to make things right.

"Never liked poetry. Too morbid for my tastes," Philly said. "The good news? You won't become a monster like them. Doesn't work like that."

"I already am a monster," Paul said. "Isn't that what you're telling me?"

Philly smiled. "Trust me on this, kid. If there's one thing I've learned in my time, you can't be turned into a monster. To become a monster...a beast...that's something you have to choose."

Paul wanted to believe that, just wasn't sure he did.

"All right, kid, what's it going to be? I leave you to become dinner, or we get moving?"

Paul looked down at the sword on his left hip. Probably less painful to kill himself with that than get eaten alive. Could he do that? What if he screwed it up and then was too weak to finish the job? He knew himself better than that; he'd never get up the nerve to do it. He couldn't even stand the idea of getting his finger pricked at the doctor's office. The fear of the pain won out. He just wasn't ready to flip the bird at God, so he'd have to get off his ass and deal with it.

"What do I have to do to make sure I don't kill anyone else when I walk out of here?"

"Good for you." Philly stood and put Paul's bike upright for him. "First thing we need to do is find us a skull, and here's the kicker, kid. You're going to lead us to it."

Somehow, Paul didn't think he was going to like this.

"This should be simple enough," Philly said, "because you've obviously found it before."

"Found what?"

"It's a crystal skull. All this stuff here, all the damage... you couldn't do this yourself. The skull can enhance your powers, but it also gives you greater control, which is how we get you out of the Deadlands without getting anyone else killed."

"Great, but wasn't like they had one sitting in my hospital room, Philly. I think I would have noticed it."

"Wouldn't need to be. As long as you're close enough to it, you can use it. That means it's probably here in the downtown area."

"So how do I find it?" Paul looked up and down the street, expecting to see those zombies Philly had talked about.

"You just need to listen for it, kid. Same way I found you. I could probably find the skull myself, but being this close to you, you drown it out."

Paul strained to listen, but the silence was all he heard. "Everything here is just so quiet. I'm not hearing anything."

"It's not exactly a sound, more like the breathing of the spirit. Close your eyes."

Paul felt like a glorified idiot, but he closed his eyes.

"Now put that image of a crystal skull in your mind. Your soul's already touched it, explored it. All you need to do is remember its voice and find your way back."

'Remember its voice.' Easy for him to say. Paul could imagine a crystal skull. That was easy enough, but it somehow seemed wrong. He wasn't sure how to make it right. Hell, he wasn't even sure why he knew it was wrong. The shape was close. That was the easy part, but even that wasn't right. *What's missing?* He kept asking that question without even really knowing how he was sure it was wrong.

"What color is it?"

"Hell if I know, kid."

Lot of help he was. Paul tried to imagine it as different colors, beginning with the same eerie pink as the light in the sky that started all this. "No," he whispered. He tried different

16

shades of blue and green before he imagined that skull of translucent rock in a shade of vibrant red. The image settled within his mind with a whisper of something, and he couldn't think of what the sound was. He thought it was like a piano, but one note held without end, so soft he could barely hear it. *Just focus on what's wrong,* he told himself. The color was right. He knew that, but there was something about the skull that was still wrong. Then he saw the hole in the back of the skull, the fracture lines flowing from it in a spider web pattern. That lone note swelled, and Paul knew exactly which direction to take.

"Let's go." Paul turned his bike west and headed down Broad Street. They went much further than he expected. Philly had said the skull didn't need to be close, but they'd traveled more than a dozen blocks, eventually even passing the Siegel Center. Dad had promised to take him to a VCU Rams basketball game this season, but no more games were going to be played there. He tried not to think about it, tried to focus on the skull.

That note grew louder as they continued west. The same way the right word sometimes helped him remember a dream, the skull's sound made his mind drift back to his hospital room. A vague image of the room, drenched in sunlight, lifted from the debris of his mind. He saw the doctor standing by his bed, talking to him. The doctor had been a woman, a detail he'd been unable to discern from what had been left of her. He could hear her voice, but his memory failed to remember the words.

The long note of the skull dipped, shocking Paul back to the present. His bike skidded to a stop, and he realized they'd just crossed Boulevard, having passed the Science Museum.

Philly stopped just a few feet past him, not having expected the sudden stop.

"What is it?" Philly looked around them. Seeing as there wasn't a red, crystal skull in sight, he had the appropriate confusion on his face.

"Why are you here?" The distraction of Paul's memories had helped him step back enough for a moment of clarity, and all the things that were wrong about Philly being here forced their way to the front of his thoughts. "*How* are you here?"

"Came here to find you." He made that sound so damn obvious.

"Why? I mean, I killed all these people. Plenty of folks would gladly kill me, would see those zombies heading here for me an appropriate punishment. So I gotta ask. Why are you here helping me?" *Or am I helping you?* Paul didn't have a guarantee that Philly didn't want this skull for some other reason.

He could see Philly was considering his words, and that just set him off. "Answer the damn question! Don't sit there and think on it, just answer!"

To his surprise, Philly almost jumped off the seat of his bike. Son of a bitch wasn't expecting that, and he spit out the answer plenty fast, too.

"I was sent to get you, because you're not the only one who was changed by the Avatar Light. Remember the other burn spot outside of London I mentioned. That was another awakening. Quite a lot of them around the world."

"More soul-feeders?" Paul got that next question off right away. He figured he had this cocky bastard off-balance, and he needed to press for all the info he could get.

"Some, but others received different powers from the Avatar Light."

"Who sent you?"

"He's gone by plenty of names, but these days, he prefers to be called Organal."

"Or-gahn-all?" Paul said the name slowly, trying to get it straight. What the hell kind of name was that anyway? "And what does he want with me?"

"There are beings now walking this world that will make what you did here seem like nothing. They'll wipe out the people of this world as they feast on your souls. That second heart in you isn't yours. That's another life, the source of your new powers. Most avatars, they no longer have control of their bodies. Their new heart is in the driver's seat."

That was a bit hard to take, but if Paul really could do all this, then who was to say there weren't others. "And what are you?"

Philly groaned. "Shit, kid. You aren't going to like this answer."

"Haven't liked much of what you've told me so far."

"Yeah, good point." Philly sat up and scratched the back of his head, stalling for the brief moment he could. "You see, I'm a vampire."

Paul felt his blood go cold, his body rigid as he contemplated pedaling for all he was worth. Any other day, he'd have laughed and said, "Yeah, right," but this was about as far from a normal day as a guy could get.

Philly held up his hands in that 'I'm-not-packing-any-weapons' gesture that suddenly didn't mean a whole hell of a lot.

"It's all right, kid. Trust me when I say we vampires have gotten a bad rap over the past few centuries. We don't go around killing people every time we get hungry. We can't turn other people into vampires either. Hell, being a vampire is the only reason I'm able to be here to help you. Any normal humans entering the Deadlands, they all die pretty quickly. If Organal could have come himself, he would have, but under the circumstances, you've got me."

That continuous note of the skull distracted Paul. He could hear something else in there now, too, but he wasn't sure what it was. Almost like several, tiny staccato notes at a higher pitch. Did that mean he was getting closer?

He looked back at Philly and decided he didn't have any real options here. Either he worked with Philly, or he took his chances. He didn't know enough about those *fördröj frånfälle* to risk it alone, assuming they even existed. Maybe they weren't even out there, and all this was some clever lie to make him lead Philly to that skull. He didn't know enough to feel like any choice was the right one, and it was driving him nuts.

"All right, but I'm getting that skull myself. When I decide it's time for you to stay back, then you do it."

Philly nodded. "If that's what it takes to make you comfortable, then that's what we'll do."

That Philly agreed to that so easily didn't offer much reassurance, but what else could Paul do? He needed to know more about everything instead of making all his decisions blindfolded. He tried to consider what he did know...what he knew about Philly and whether he really did trust him. So far, he realized all he really trusted was what Philly had told him, but not necessarily Philly, himself. That would have to do for now.

"Let's go then."

Philly didn't say anything this time. He just fell in behind Paul as they turned around and pedaled onto the Boulevard.

They only went a few more blocks. He heard the skull sounding to his right from a place he recognized from one of his childhood field trips of all things.

"That's the Fine Arts museum."

Philly laughed. "Yeah, and I think we can safely say your skull is here." He pointed to a banner hanging on a pole next to the building. A shiver that had nothing to do with winter worked through his back as he looked into the empty sockets of the skull he'd envisioned, its crystal red as blood.

"The Crystal Skull Exhibit." Philly read the banner. "Here through March tenth."

"Guess it's leaving sooner than expected." Paul climbed off his bike and walked it up to one of the many bike racks positioned on the right side of the building. He placed his bike next to a red bike that looked much nicer than his. He considered trading up, but it had one of those u-shaped bike locks on it.

"You got a lighter?" Paul didn't look forward to walking into a dark building, and this place was plenty big. They could have that skull displayed anywhere.

Philly looked disgusted by the question. "Sorry, kid. I don't smoke."

Just his luck...a health conscious vampire. What were the odds of that? He'd just have to make do with the lighter he had left, assuming it would even last. He suspected the fuel was burning up faster than it normally would, another byproduct of whatever had happened to this place.

"Let's go in and get it, kid."

"No." Paul glared at him. "I'm going in alone. You can wait here."

Philly parked his bike and sprawled on the grassy field as he slid on a pair of sunglasses. "Fine. I'll just work on my tan. Have fun."

"Vampire humor," Paul muttered. "Cute."

Philly just grinned, giving Paul a good look at his canines, pointed and deadly like a wild cat's. He didn't linger to admire them.

At least whatever had happened took place during the day. Meant all the doors to this place were unlocked.

Thankfully, he didn't need the lighter yet. The walls and ceiling to the museum had enough windows to illuminate the place by the moon. Just inside the entranceway, the floor was littered with bodies, all withered in the same manner as his doctor. At least two dozen small corpses formed a neat row along the right wall. They must have been a school group.

"Just don't think about it," he whispered to himself, a little less thankful now for all the moonlight.

The entranceway opened into the atrium. The ceiling must have reached three stories high. The front and back walls were all glass, making it much easier to see. He could hear the skull better. The note came from above him, but not directly. Was it on the second or third floor? He must have been close, because he could hear those staccato notes more clearly, too.

He wasn't sure which way to go. Two sets of stairs led up from the atrium and to the rest of the museum. He stepped over a body, moving deeper into the atrium. Orange chairs were gathered in the middle of the floor. People's bodies were still sitting there. One body had its back to Paul and had long, white hair.

"Don't think about the bodies," he reminded himself. That was easier said than done with so many. He didn't want to think about how many were dead, how many he'd killed. He

21

closed his eyes for a moment to reorder his thoughts. The desire to make right all that he'd done wrong was noble. He knew that, but he also knew he wouldn't survive to do shit if he didn't focus and find that skull.

Which way? He opened his eyes again and looked at the far stairs and then to the set starting just to his left. Another crystal skull banner was hanging on the wall with an arrow that pointed up the near set of stairs.

"Oh." Made sense the museum would post signs directing people to their star exhibit. He climbed the stairs to the second floor, stepping through the shadows of an overhang and onto a walkway connecting both sides of the second floor. The crystal skull signs pointed left, straight over to a set of sliding glass doors. "Which don't work without electricity. Great." He tried to slip his fingers through the slit running down the middle of the doors, but he couldn't get a good grip. How the hell was he supposed to get through here? He could hear the skull's note ring clear from somewhere beyond these doors. Maybe he could shatter the glass with the sword Philly had given him. He pulled it out, the feel of the hilt in his hand too unnatural to give him any confidence.

His thoughts about the skull, the sword and those doors stopped. Goosebumps prickled along his arms as he heard those staccato clicks, but they weren't coming from the same direction as the skull anymore. They were behind him.

He turned around, but he didn't see any movement, nothing that might be a threat, not that he really had a damn clue what to look for.

Fördröj frånfälle. Paul mulled over the term in his head, and he found it odd how it seemed simple for him to use. Foreign languages weren't his thing, and usually something like that would have left him joking, "Frodo Baggins ran and fell?" But *"fördröj frånfälle"* felt simple for him to handle.

Those staccato notes sounded louder than ever, but this time, he heard something else: the sound of a footfall on the marble tile of the walkway.

A single booted foot appeared from the shadows of the overhang on the far end of the crosswalk. Most of the leg and the rest of the body disappeared into the shadows as if nothing else was there. Then another boot stepped out of the shadows, as if cutting through the darkness until the entire figure appeared. In every aspect, he looked like a normal man, save for the brilliant white of his long, straight hair and the green glow to those eyes. That smile, though...that smile offered nothing human.

He thought the man's appearance from nothingness was a trick of the shadows, but then two more appeared, one on each side of the first.

"*Fördröj frånfälle?*" Paul's body shivered as he said the name. Only after the fact would he realize what a fool he'd been, letting his fear freeze him to the spot.

The one with the long hair nodded in reply. His arm drew a handgun from his jacket in a motion almost too fast to see. Paul jumped as he heard the trigger click. Surprise flashed in the zombie's green eyes, and he looked none too pleased.

Paul laughed, a weak grunt of relief. The Deadlands, however the hell they worked, must have stopped the gunpowder from igniting. "Sorry, that must be my fault." His legs finally took over and he ran up the stairs for the third floor, the zombies blocking his way back down.

He reached the top steps and looked left, the direction he needed to go to reach the skull. More sliding glass doors, but a body had fallen in-between, just enough room for him to slip through. "Philly!" he shouted as he went through the opening. What were the odds the idiot would hear him?

He ran straight, blind to which way ensured safety or if he could get back downstairs to reach the skull. Was he cornered up here? As he passed a large statue of a bird battling a snake, he looked over his shoulder to see the zombies chasing him. They disappeared and reappeared as their bodies stepped in and out of the shadows.

The skull was on the second floor, and he was on the third. He needed down. Running straight brought him to a set of stairs, but those zombies were gaining. Damn they were fast!

Their boots shrieked along the marble floor as they dodged displays to pursue Paul.

He ran down the stairs jumping the last few steps. In his fear, he surrendered to instinct. The skull's note called him, and he raced for it.

"Philly!"

He ran into a room which seemed nothing but shadows. He could only hear, not see, the zombies pursuing him. He heard one of them trip, probably on one of the many bodies on the floor.

Thin moonlight came from a connecting room ahead. The silhouette of a horse blocked his path. He dodged the animal's statue and saw more light ahead. Even better, he spotted a sign for the crystal skull, pointing to the left.

Moonbeams cut through a window and filled the room with light. Then he saw it. The red skull rested within a glass display case, glowing in the natural light. That glorious note sang proud and stopped Paul cold. It was like walking in on an angel caught singing in the shower. He suffered for that mistake.

One of the zombies tackled into him. Pain shot through his back as he slid across the marble tiles. The sword in his hand clattered to the floor as he lost his grip on it. The zombie failed to keep hold of him, an angry growl ripping from its throat as it scrambled after him. It was "Long Hair."

Paul grabbed the sword, but the victory was short-lived. Another zombie grabbed him by the throat and lifted him off the ground. He gasped for breath. He thrust the sword into the zombie's chest. He expected an explosion of blood or something equally gross, but the blade just thrust a few inches into the chest and stopped. The zombie grabbed the base of the blade and pushed it out. Dude was strong as hell.

The zombie smirked up at him as he ripped the sword from Paul's hand. Paul shoved his knee up into the zombie's jaw. He heard a satisfying crack of bone, but the zombie didn't flinch, didn't seem to feel any pain. The zombie's face clenched. With an irritated grunt, the zombie tossed Paul down. He landed on his back, giving his spine a rude wake-up call. He saw the zombie reach into its mouth, working the jaw as he seemed to manually right his teeth.

"Oh, hell."

The first zombie, Long Hair, looked down at Paul. He was plenty pissed, too. Paul rolled aside just before the zombie could plant a boot on his face. Long Hair grabbed Paul by the arm and jerked him up off the ground. His shoulder felt like it would dislocate held up like this.

The zombie licked his lips.

"Philly!" Paul shouted.

One of the zombies flew past Paul and Long Hair and struck the wall. As it stood, Paul realized the zombie was missing its head.

Unsure what else to do, Paul stabbed his fingers at Long Hair's eyes. That got a reaction, the closest thing to panic he'd seen from one of these things. The zombie dropped him and wailed as it retreated, temporarily blinded. Thank God. His arm couldn't have taken being held like that much longer.

Paul looked towards the door and saw Philly fighting with the shortest of the three, the one he'd kneed in the jaw.

"Kid, heads up!" Philly kicked the head he'd sliced off to Paul like a soccer ball. "Toss it out the window!"

Paul caught the head in his hands. The face looked at him, the eyes still working and that mouth biting in the vain hope of getting a mouthful of human.

"Out the window!" Philly yelled just before "Shorty" tackled him into the shadows of an adjoining room. "Cack!"

Paul didn't see why he needed to do anything with the head other than drop it until he looked up at the headless body, charging straight for him.

"Crap!"

Paul dodged Deadhead's body as it tried to grab him. Long Hair also swung at him. Paul rolled with the hit to his head, landing just beneath the window. He got to his feet and flung the head at the window, but the glass didn't break. The head just bounced back into his hands.

"Oh, not good."

Paul looked up in time to see Long Hair come at him again and ducked. The jerk didn't get another shot at him. Deadhead's body, chasing after its head, tackled into Long Hair, and they both went through the window. Shards of glass spilled down onto Paul as he dropped the zombie's head and covered his own.

Before he stood, Paul shook off the glass like a wet dog after a bath. Careful not to cut himself on the window, Paul looked down to see the two zombies. Long Hair was already getting up and seemed to be straightening his arms in the same manner Shorty had fixed his teeth and jaw. Deadhead's body flailed on the ground next to Long Hair. "What does it take to kill these things?" Paul almost chucked the head out the window, but then he figured the body might just put it back on.

"Needs your eyes to see what it's doing, huh?" he said to the head on the floor. One of the connecting rooms had some stairs leading down. He flung the head over the railing. Let the bastard's body waste its time trying to find a way back inside the museum and to its head.

He heard Philly struggling with Shorty in the other room, but he didn't run to help. *Just get the skull and get out of here,* his instincts whispered to him.

The glass box holding the skull looked pretty solid. He tried to lift it, but it was sealed shut. How the hell did they put it in there? He didn't have time to figure out that puzzle. He looked around for the sword and found it along the wall near the window. He glanced out the window again. Only the headless one was out there, stumbling about. Deadhead's body was heading straight in the direction where its head had landed. Weird, but at least that would keep him out of play. Question was how long it would take Long Hair to get back here, probably not long enough.

Paul gripped the sword with both hands and took it to the glass case like a bat. The first strike didn't shatter the case. "Holy shit." What was this stuff? Bulletproof glass? He swung again and again. Cracks appeared in the glass. "Come on!" Another strike and the cracks spead. He heard footfalls drawing closer, someone running in his direction. Long Hair? Paul screamed as he threw all his strength into one last swing. The glass case failed to shatter. Long Hair appeared from around the corner and tackled him. Paul's head cracked against the floor as a cold hand wrapped around his throat, pinning him.

Paul tried to yell for Philly, but he couldn't do more than gasp, struggling for a breath. He saw the zombie's fist pull back, ready to strike.

He'd lost his sword in the fall. He reached for it, but it was too far away! Dammit, he needed the skull, but it was still trapped in glass.

He remembered what Philly had said. He'd used it before, touched it without actually holding it in his hands. He fixed the image of that skull in his thoughts, and it was as if someone poured ice-cold soda directly on his brain—one of those moments where everything but him just stopped. He heard what seemed a distant sound, glass shattering, and the skull leaped to his hand. The red crystal no longer seemed so solid, but more fluid as the eye sockets and shape of the skull vanished, replaced with something else. The new shape, circular and curved outwards, wrapped about his forearm as he swung at the zombie's head.

The edge of that glass circle smashed into Long Hair's head, knocking him off. The screech from Long Hair sounded beautiful to Paul's ears. He'd begun to think nothing could cause these monsters pain. Judging from its expression and the way the zombie was gingerly touching the place Paul had struck it, the monster was just as surprised. It stumbled back towards the door. Those green eyes narrowed on him, the brief fear passing. Paul felt his courage growing, though. The feel of that reshaped crystal resting on his arm felt better than anything he'd ever known.

Long Hair roared, but just as he charged on Paul, a sword slashed across the zombie's throat from behind. The head bounced along the floor. That didn't stop the body. It was still running straight at him. Paul struck the headless torso in its gut with the reshaped skull. The strike flung the body across the room. The body struggled back to its feet, but not before Philly shoved it out the window to join Deadhead.

Philly slid his sword back into its sheath, and he looked plenty satisfied as he looked out the window at his handiwork. "Nice. Now let's get the skull and run for it."

"Already have the skull." Paul held up his right forearm to display his trophy. He glanced past Philly as he heard thudding from the neighboring room. "Where's the one you were dealing with?"

Philly pointed at Long Hair's head. "Same as that one, only I pitched the head back upstairs." The vampire's eyes stared at the red crystal on Paul's arm. "That's a shield, kid. Where's the skull?"

Philly glanced at the empty display case, obviously not satisfied with Paul's word.

"This is the skull," Paul said. "It changed."

"All right then, kid, let's go before these freaks get themselves back together."

That sounded like a good idea to Paul. He recovered his sword and shoved it back into its sheath. "Shouldn't we finish them off before they can put themselves back together?"

"Only way to do that is to cremate the damn things. Sadly, I'm fresh out of crematoriums."

"Oh."

Paul followed Philly out of the museum. He navigated through the place with a lot more ease than Paul, but then those glittering eyes probably worked better in the dark. The sliding glass doors where the zombies had confronted Paul were now open. Philly must have forced them open.

"Pedal hard, kid. We need one hell of a head start on these guys, and if they catch up before we can get out of the Deadlands, we're screwed."

Paul took him at his word and they rolled for the interstate.

***

28

The night never seemed like it would end. Paul's leg muscles were burning worse than after a three mile race. He wanted a hot bath to soak his legs, but that wasn't going to happen. The temperature just kept getting colder. Thankfully, whoever had owned his new jacket had stuffed some gloves into the pockets. He wasn't sure how he would have survived those coldest hours, otherwise, as he held onto the handlebars.

The interstate turned out a lot easier to navigate than the city streets. Most of the wrecks had gone onto the right or left shoulders. Unfortunately, they'd run into a few jackknifed tractor trailers with a few other cars plowed into them that blocked every lane. One pileup was so bad that it forced them to climb over the cars. That would have been tough enough without trying to lift a bike over the mess. Paul's new shield wasn't helping matters either. It was just one more thing to carry, and it must have been at least two-and-a-half feet in diameter. Still, he was surprised at how light it felt, even shoved up his arm enough for his hand to get a grip on the handlebars.

The ride didn't offer a chance for him and Philly to talk, not as fast as they were trying to move. That left Paul plenty of time to worry about how quickly those zombies would put themselves back together and how long it would take them to catch up.

Thinking on his shield was only slightly less troubling. He wasn't sure why the skull had changed for him or why into this shape. The bowl of the shield was solid. The straps on the inside were made out of the same crystal material, but they could stretch and bend to whatever length he seemed to need. He didn't see how this was going to keep his powers from killing more people, but Philly acted as if he was satisfied. For now, that was good enough for Paul.

"Exit ramp!" Philly shouted as he turned his bike onto the 118 exit.

Paul stirred from his thoughts and wiped his brow before the sweat could fall into his eyes. He wasn't sure how far from Fredericksburg they were at this point, just that they were north of Ashland. According to Philly, they'd be out of the "Dead-lands" once they made it past Fredericksburg.

"Why are we getting off here?" Paul shouted to make sure he was heard. He was having to do that standing-pedal thing just to get up the exit ramp.

"We need to get indoors," Philly said. "It's almost sun-rise."

"So?"

Philly looked back at him like he was an idiot and then pointed at himself. "Hello! Vampire! Moon, good; sun, really really bad!"

Paul rolled his eyes. "Sue me! I was more worried about the zombies that are chasing us. It's not my fault you sunburn so easily."

Philly didn't bother with a clever comeback. Probably a good sign he wasn't exaggerating his fear of sunlight.

They took a right and went down a tree-lined road until they reached the opening to a long driveway on their left. Once they started down the driveway, a two-story house came into view.

"This'll have to do," Philly said.

Paul looked toward the eastern sky and could see the black cover lighten ever so slightly into a dark grey.

Philly ditched his bike and ran for the front door. He kicked it open and ran upstairs. Paul made it through the front door in time to see Philly dart into the bathroom carrying a comforter and pillow taken from one of the bedrooms.

"You okay in there?" Paul asked.

"Yeah, just try to keep it down," he shouted through the door. "I'd like to get some sleep."

Paul heard him moving around in there. He looked down to see the edge of a towel stick out from beneath the door. Philly wasn't taking any chances on sunlight getting in there.

"What about the zombies?" Paul asked.

"Nothing more to do, kid." Philly's voice was muffled. Sounded like he was using the bathtub for his bed. "Just make

30

the house as sun-proof as you can. Otherwise, you'll be on your own if those zombies get here before sunset."

"Great," Paul muttered.

He looked around the house before he did anything else. Place was decorated like some farmhouse, just without a farm. To his relief, he didn't find any dead bodies. Whoever lived here must have been at work when everyone died. "Just don't think about that," he told himself. Instead, he did what Philly had asked. He found a linen closet and pulled out as many sheets as he could find.

He got a hell of a scare when he got to the utility room. Soon as he opened the door, he spotted three roaches on the floor.

"Holy crap!" He jumped back, ready to stomp the life out of them, but they didn't move. None of them scattered for shadow. They just sat there. He finally mustered up the courage to nudge one of them with his foot. Still no scattering. Paul laughed. The roaches hadn't survived the end of the world, after all. That would disappoint all the scientists.

He kicked the insect carcasses out of the way and searched the utility room until he found a tool box. The best he'd hoped for were some nails and a hammer. He did better than that. He found a staple gun.

Before long, he'd stapled enough sheets over the windows to put the house back into darkness. He had to leave the back door open just so he could have some light. The fireplace looked useable, but he decided against that. The light and warmth would have been really nice, but the smoke from the chimney would lead the zombies straight here. Might as well put up a sign on the interstate that said "Exit Here."

Once that was done, he realized he was hungry. The sensation scared him at first, but then he decided that might be a good sign. If he was getting hungry—normal-type hungry—then maybe what his body wanted was regular food and he didn't need to kill anyone to survive. That meant his new shield was doing something to help him safely leave this place. He didn't want to think about that too much, but he'd take what hope he could get.

Paul looked through the kitchen. The best he found was some seriously stale cereal. He suspected the box might taste better but stopped short of taking a bite out of it...the box, not the cereal (which was gross). He glanced at the fridge, but he sure as hell wasn't going to open that. Probably smelled something pretty nasty in there after almost thirty days without power to keep everything from rotting. He remembered seeing a few convenience stores and gas stations on the other side of the interstate.

After leaving Philly a note, he got on his bike and headed back for the interstate. He stopped on the overpass and tried to sense those *fördröj frånfälle*, but didn't hear any of those staccato notes he'd noticed back in the museum.

Talk about a damn, dreary sight. From here, he could see a good ways down I-95 North and all the wrecks he still hadn't gotten past yet. He figured it was well into morning by now, but he couldn't see the sun. The sky was completely overcast. He'd thought the grey look to the world had just been a trick of the night, but now that it was daytime, he could see little had changed. Whatever his powers had done, it was almost as if he'd sucked all the color out of the world along with its life. The only thing that didn't look grey in the whole damn place was the red shield on his arm. Something that had been a skull just a few hours ago was now the most lively-looking thing here. The shield felt as natural on his arm as a shirt's sleeve. He'd used this thing to kill hundreds of thousands, and it felt so right on his arm that he could almost forget it was there. *Then just don't think about it and keep moving,* he kept telling himself. He didn't want to dwell on what he'd done, all those people, his parents... *Dammit, just stop it and move!*

The convenience store turned out to be a good call. He found a bunch of stuff in there. The place smelled something awful. Thank God it was winter. He must have been starving, because even standing in that horrid stench of rotted food and decaying bodies, a hot dog or a sandwich still sounded awesome. He made do with the fruit bars and energy bars he found on the shelves. For dessert, he went with two packs of his favorite candy bar, a peanut butter Twix, washed down with a bottle of "room temp" Mountain Dew which wasn't half bad, thanks again to the cold weather.

Wasn't the best meal, but at least he didn't feel hungry anymore. He hoped that meant he wouldn't need to kill to survive. That's all it was now, wasn't it? Surviving.

He walked past the counter. A man who'd probably stopped for gas was lying on the floor. He leaned over and saw the cashier's body behind the counter. Trying not to think about what he'd done wasn't going to work forever. The shield he carried would be a constant reminder.

Surviving wasn't enough either. He needed a way to make this right, a way to make up for what he'd done, but he didn't see a way to do that. They were heading towards DC, but for what? He didn't know anyone there. He didn't even have any money. At this point, the only reason he had anywhere to go at all was get away from these zombies.

As he walked outside, Paul heard what sounded like someone stepping on gravel. That was scary enough, but when he heard it a second time, he recognized what he'd really heard, the distant sound of that staccato note.

"Oh no."

Paul scrambled back onto his bike and headed back towards the interstate and pedaled as hard as he could for the house where he'd left Philly. Even with the food he'd just eaten, he wasn't moving as fast as he had been. He could feel exhaustion setting in. You'd think after sleeping for more than a month, he'd be able to go longer without sleep. As he went across the overpass, he looked south. All he saw were those cars piled up like some psychopath's lego-creations. No sign of the *fördröj fränfälle*, but he could hear them getting closer, those sharp notes that he was starting to equate with death.

He ditched the bike in the front yard. A thought to hide the bikes had passed through his mind, but he realized that was pointless. Same way he could sense these zombies approach, they must have been homing in on him.

"Philly!" Paul shouted as he rushed through the front door. He secured it as best he could. Philly had done a real number on the bolt when he'd kicked it open. "Philly! Dude, we got company almost here!"

He ran up the stairs and slammed his fist on the bathroom door several times. Philly didn't answer. Must have been one hell of a heavy sleeper. All Paul could think was how irritated he was that he'd bothered trying to be quiet before he'd left the house for some food.

"Crap!" Paul ran back downstairs.

He grabbed the doorknob, ready to pull it open, run for his bike and ride. What was the point in just staying here and letting those zombies catch up to him? He "heard" them getting closer, though, and he knew there was no way he'd ever outrun them. That was the point, wasn't it? He could run all he wanted to, but these guys were faster and never tired. The only choice was to stand and fight them.

After standing there for a moment, he opened the door and walked outside. He closed the door behind him, in case Philly might come out of the bathroom. If he was going to wait here, then he wasn't going to hide, dammit. The idea of sitting out on the front steps to face these bastards when they showed up scared the hell out of him, but hiding wouldn't save him. It just made his death more pathetic.

He sat on the top step as he waited. His shield, shining in the gloom, rested on his right arm. He supposed he should shift it to his left. He needed his right hand for his sword, but the shield seemed to hurt these things more. "Guess I just need two right hands."

No, he needed to make a choice. It wasn't an insignificant one either, and not just because his life was on the line. He ran his fingers along the curve of his shield. The surface didn't move or change, but something to the feel of it assured him it was alive. The crystal warmed his hand, and he knew that wasn't natural. Nothing about this shield made sense, not that it hurt those zombies; that it felt connected to him...that it existed at all. As that last thought set itself into his mind, he knew that was the real choice. If he decided to face these monsters with this shield, then he was choosing to take a path that made no sense. It reminded him of the "Wizard of Oz" when Dorothy starts down the yellow brick road. There'd been a red road, too...red like his shield. "Not much of a choice is it?" he whispered, because he knew he couldn't go back to "Kansas" again. Not now. Never.

When he looked up, he saw the three figures at the end of the long driveway walking towards him. Paul set down his shield and stood. He started undoing that ridiculously long belt Philly had given him. He'd made his choice. When he'd gotten it off, he tossed the belt, sword and scabbard to the side.

"We gonna finish this?" Paul glared at the zombie in the middle, Long Hair.

The zombie nodded and continued walking closer. "Where's your twilight friend?"

That the zombie could speak startled Paul. They hadn't said anything at the museum. He didn't have time to consider it more. He slipped off his jacket and dropped it to the side. "Philly's getting some rest," he said.

The one on the right, Shorty, snapped his teeth in a rapid-fire manner, as if anticipating the taste of Paul's flesh. Paul knew the jerk was just trying to intimidate him. It was working.

He reached out his hand, instinctively calling his shield to him as he had in the museum. The red crystal leaped off the front porch, sliding into its proper place on his forearm. Long Hair and his pals hesitated a step when they saw that. Nice to know he could intimidate them, too, even if another part of his mind had just freaked at what he'd just done.

"You plan to lie down and die like a proper meal?" Long Hair asked. They'd gotten close, just ten yards away.

"No."

Paul charged at the zombies and threw his shield. The red crystal shot forward, curving to the right to strike Shorty's forehead. Paul cursed. He'd been aiming for the throat, but the short zombie had ducked. Damn, these things were fast. He'd directed the shield's path, though. Somehow, he'd known he could do it, just as he'd called it to his hand from the porch.

35

Before the shield could hit the ground, it bounced off the short zombie's head and back onto Paul's arm as he swung at Long Hair. The edge of the red shield slit across Long Hair's stomach. Long Hair howled as the cut left a wide, bloodless gash.

The third one, Deadhead, tackled Paul from the left. He'd gotten in under the shield, his shoulder jamming into Paul's side. Paul had played his share of football as a kid, gotten tackled by people twice his size. This zombie hit him a whole lot harder than any of those guys ever had.

Paul scrambled out of the tackle. He retreated on all fours, a graceless and panic-filled skittering that his shield did nothing to assist...but it worked. He made it to his feet before Deadhead could bite him.

Long Hair and Shorty surrounded Paul. Shorty pounced first, coming at him from behind. Paul spun to face him and planted his shield in that ugly, snapping mouth. Shorty wouldn't get all those teeth back into place anytime soon. Fingers brushed against the top of Paul's head as Long Hair failed to grab him. Paul struck Shorty again and ran past him.

"You can't outrun me, boy!" Long Hair chased Paul into the trees surrounding the backyard.

Paul realized he'd managed to separate them and decided to take advantage of it. He stopped in front of a tree, turned and sent his shield flying for Long Hair's throat. Long Hair dodged it. Paul saw his shield slide across the ground, sending a small wave of dead leaves into the air.

The zombie reached for him. Paul screamed as he tried what might have been the most insane thing he'd ever considered. Just as Long Hair reached him, Paul grabbed him by the jacket, ducked and jerked him forward, using the tall zombie's momentum against him. Long Hair's head slammed into the tree. Paul's shield, summoned the instant Long Hair had reached him, shot straight through the zombie's throat. The trap worked better than Paul had expected. The shock of the beheading forced the zombie to release his grip and jump back. The shield didn't stop with the zombie's head. It sliced through the tree trunk, too. Paul scrambled out of the way as the toppled tree landed on Long Hair's flailing torso.

"Holy hell!" Paul stared in disbelief at his handiwork as his shield returned to his right arm. "Couldn't have planned that if I tried." He glanced down at his shield. What else could it do that he hadn't thought of yet?

Shorty leaped over the fallen tree. He might have looked comical with half of his teeth missing, but the rage on his face more than made up for that.

Paul ran for the back of the house. Shorty chased him like some blasted Olympic sprinter. That probably made the back door the finish line. Paul's body slammed against the door. The door flung open just as Shorty collided with him. They smashed into the cabinets. Shorty took the brunt of the crash, the pantry door splitting at its equator, knocking down the boxes of cereal and biscuit mix. Paul struggled to free himself from the zombie's grip. Just as he thought he might, the iron-grip of those dead hands latched onto the waist of his jeans and the back of his shirt. His feet lifted off the ground as Shorty flung Paul into the den. Pain ripped through his left shoulder as his body shattered the drywall.

He dropped to the floor, on his knees. Paul just saw the blur of Shorty running towards him to finish the job. In his mind, Paul yelled at himself to move, to do anything. Brain and body just wouldn't connect. He forced all his will into his shield arm. He thrust his arm up. The edge of the shield connected with the underside of Shorty's jaw. The zombie lost more teeth. One of them bounced off Paul's head. Shorty's body was knocked onto his back, landing on the kitchen floor.

"Philly!" Now would be a freaking fabulous time for the vampire to wake up.

Paul staggered to his feet and scrambled for the front door. Shorty jumped to his feet and launched across the den. Paul tried to knock him aside with his shield, but Shorty outmaneuvered him. They struggled, bodies slamming against the front door and the stairs until Shorty had him pinned to the floor of the foyer. Shorty had learned his lesson, too. He grabbed Paul by both wrists, the placement of his hand trapping Paul's shield on his arm. The zombie also had Paul's legs pinned like a vice.

Paul felt Shorty's body shiver with his fury. His face just inches from Paul's, Shorty bared what teeth he had left in a cruel smile. "You're going to wish I still had all my teeth, because it's only going to make this take a lot longer." Shorty's jaw widened to what seemed inhuman proportions, ready to bite down.

A roar, a cross between a tiger and a wolf, startled both Paul and Shorty. They looked up to see a shadow fly down the stairs. Before Paul could recognize Philly, Shorty's head dropped from his body, severed by a sword strike, and bounced off of Paul's chest to the floor.

That didn't release him from the rest of the zombie's grip. Philly grabbed the zombie under its arm and flung it into the den.

"Jesus, kid, I can't leave you alone for a minute."

Then the front door burst open. Sunlight blinded Paul. He smelled a putrid burning smell, could taste it in the back of his throat, and felt something hot. His eyes adjusted to see Philly, all ablaze like a human torch, struggling with the third zombie, Deadhead. Paul rolled out of the way and into the dining room. Flames leaped up to the ceiling. Just like everything else in these Deadlands that seemed to require fuel, the fire was consuming the house far too quickly, giving him just minutes to get out of there. The front door was blocked by Philly and Deadhead, both on fire now. They seemed determined to keep each other there so the flames would destroy them both. Paul could already see through the ceiling of the foyer into the upstairs. He considered throwing his shield to behead Deadhead, but they were strug-gling too much, dancing in circles. He was just as likely to take Philly's head.

"Get out of here, kid!" Philly shouted.

Smoke filled the downstairs. A memory of a firefighter who visited his elementary school flashed through Paul's head, the warning that it was usually the smoke and not the flames that killed a person.

He ripped down the bed sheets he'd stapled over the dining room windows. The edge of the sheet was burning and spread the flames to the table on which it landed. Paul coughed. Crap, he had to get that window open. "No!" The window wouldn't move. Someone had placed screws there to keep the damn thing shut.

Paul stepped back and threw his shield at the window. The crystal shield burst through the glass. He climbed out, doing his best not to cut his hands. The fire hadn't made it to the front porch, but it was working on it. Flames were already escaping out the door and into the open air, seeking more oxygen to support itself. Paul dodged the flashes of yellow-orange tendrils as he grabbed his leather jacket.

Not that he'd ever seen a house burn, but the way that house caved in on itself so quickly just couldn't be natural. As he watched from a safe distance, Paul wiped the soot and tears from his face with the front of his shirt. To his relief, none of the *fördröj frånfälle* climbed out of the dead house.

"Thank you, Philly." He lowered his head and took a deep breath to settle his nerves. His entire body was shaking. Even the feel of his shield on his forearm, nor the warmth of his jacket, seemed to calm his body's jitters.

He lingered long enough to see that the fire was doing its job before he climbed onto his bike. As he got back onto the interstate, Paul saw the smoke curling thick and high, black against the overcast sky to the east.

Killing those zombies didn't grant him any comfort or calm. Instead, he was riding north and feeling more panicked than ever. His shield had helped save him from those monsters, but he still didn't know if he could truly reach the borders of the Deadlands. If what Philly had told him was true, then he had been the center of all this grey.

***

The grass turned out greener on the other side. Shortly after passing through Fredericksburg, Paul emerged from the

Deadlands. He knew it by the median strip on I-95. The portion of grass within the Deadlands had withered to a drab, lifeless brownish-grey while the portion without remained a healthy, dark green.

Everything about his exit from the Deadlands reminded him of some really bad anime film, complete with his head of shaggy hair which felt like it was going in all directions. At least his bike wasn't making that squeaky sound that anime bikes always made when the young hero was pedaling into the sunset.

Just past the overpass at Exit 136, he spotted a pair of headlights coming towards him. The black limosine turned to park perpendicular to the traffic lanes. Paul stopped just short of it, the first sign of human life he'd seen.

The back door opened and a man with long, white hair, just like the zombies, climbed out. Paul didn't hear the staccato notes or anything, so he felt safe in saying this guy wasn't one of them. He wore an embroidered, white shirt with long, wide sleeves. He reminded Paul of some desert priest.

"Who are you?" Paul asked.

"My name is Organal." Damn, this guy had a super deep voice. "You must be Paul. Although, I expected you to have company."

"Philly didn't make it."

The news was met with a pained look from Organal. "I imagine you have many questions." He stepped aside and gestured for Paul to get into the limo.

Paul considered the offer. Could he really be sure this was Organal? Even if it was, could he trust him? In the end, he knew he didn't have anyone left in this world he knew he could trust without any doubts. He'd have to take the risk. It was that or spend the rest of his life running from monsters.

He sat across from Organal, which had him facing the back of the limo. The inside turned out more luxurious than he'd expected. There was even a mounted laptop.

"A limo?" Paul asked.

"I own a company that builds naval vessels."

"Aircraft carriers?" He'd always wanted to go on one of those.

"Among others, but I would guess your questions have less to do with my 'day job' than how I knew where to find you, just what you are and the origins of the skull you now wear as a shield."

The air around Organal was relaxed, but that didn't completely put Paul at ease. After his time in the Deadlands, he wasn't sure he'd ever be calm again.

"You're not human, are you?"

Organal smiled. "No, but I am not an avatar like you."

Paul thought about the second heartbeat he carried. "You're one of those," he had to hunt for the word, "parasites?"

"Yes, my kind lives on the life of others. It's what sustains our worlds." He held up a hand to stave off Paul's next question. "The Avatar Light weakens the barriers between our dimensions and the worlds it touches."

"This has happened before?"

"Several times, but it was only in the pass prior to this one that we found your species on this world. Not all of us approved of slaughtering your kind. I was chosen to stay behind and prepare your world for the next pass."

The implication of Organal's last statement took a moment to register. "You mean you're thousands of years old?"

He nodded. Judging by the way his smile widened, he was rather proud of the fact.

"Let it suffice I've walked this world for quite some time. I and my followers, such as Phillip, have spent that time searching for certain bloodlines."

"Such as mine?"

He nodded. "My kind's passage into this world is eased by mixing our bloodlines with those of your race."

"So somewhere in my family tree, there's a parasite like you?"

"I think it safe to assume there's more than one. It's why your mind remains in control of your body. The second bloodline protects you against the parasite's control." Organal pointed

41

at his Paul's chest as he said that. "Tell me, how well do you know your Norse Mythology?"

The sudden turn in topic caught Paul off guard, but recovered enough to shrug. "Suppose I know a little. 'Thor' was one of the comic books I used to collect."

"Most of the mythological figures in this world and many of its religions were inspired by previous avatars. The shield you now carry was made from one of their skulls."

Paul felt something stir within the shield. The idea that this had once been part of a living person sent a shiver through his body, even if he had already come to think of it as having life to it.

"I presume there was a hole in the back of the skull," Organal said.

"Yes, how did you know that?"

"Don't look so surprised." Organal's smile widened. "There are not so many of those skulls to be found within this world, and even fewer that are true skulls. Most of the ones that have found their way into museums are poor imitations created by mortal priests and charlatans. But what makes me so certain I know which skull you found is that you changed it into a shield. This skull belonged to the 'god' named Thor.

"He carried a weapon called Mjolnir. The old mythtellers believed a hammer sounded more impressive, so the fact his favored weapon was a shield crafted from a crystal skull was lost. His shield looked just as that one does, although his was blue. It always returned to his hand and none could destroy it until he was killed from his wounds in battle with Jörmungandr, the Midgard Serpent. That hole in the back of his skull was from that battle."

"Thor's skull?" Paul looked down at his shield. His hand shook as it ran along its outer curve.

"When an avatar dies, the skull is all that ultimately survives, turning to crystal. They can be powerful weapons for other avatars to use and can also be a danger to others." Paul noticed Organal kept his distance from the shield. Probably explained why he hadn't gotten his hands on it before Paul used it. Organal didn't bother confirming it before he changed the topic. "I take it you were not awake for some time?" Paul nodded, uncomfortable with where the conversation was going.

"Some avatars need more time to change. They hibernate," Organal said, then quietly added, "and feast. The Deadlands...you might think of them as a chrysalis."

"Is there a way to undo it?" He wanted his parents back, a way to bring back all of those lives, but he feared he already knew the answer.

"The land will eventually heal itself, but it will take centuries. There are those who would use their powers to wipe out your race and leave this world barren. What happened to your home measures as little more than a blemish in comparison."

"Cheery thought," Paul muttered as he traced the edge of his shield with his fingertips.

"Your gifts are reason to celebrate, Paul. Thor's name remains one of a great warrior. You have that potential within you now. Hela, the goddess of the dead, knows this. That is why she sent her servants into the Deadlands to kill you." He leaned closer. "You have taken many lives, but you can save many more. The question is whether you are willing to do it."

He looked down at his shield and thought back to the steps of the library. Philly had given him the choice of suicide by zombie or fight to survive. Organal was giving him that same kind of choice.

He'd always been a good runner, but was there really any running from the end of the world? The Avatar Light had left him without a family or a home. Going into hiding now would be little better than killing himself. He couldn't bring back those who were lost, but he could do something to make things right.

It was time to get off his ass and deal with it.

FOUR IN THE HOLE

STAGNANT WATERS

BY BENNIE L. NEWSOME

Prelude

The full moon hung in the warm night air surrounded by millions of twinkling stars. One particular town beneath that swollen moon was very quiet. Everyone was secure in their homes. Doors were triple locked—some quadruple locked—and windows were blocked with planks of wood. Every citizen was safe and sound except for one small child who was unlucky enough to find himself outside after nightfall.

Scott Weber glanced about nervously as if he was a meerkat on the lookout for possible danger. A gust of wind swept across the fields creating a stir and causing the frightened boy to flinch. When he realized that the noise and movement was being caused by nature, he took a deep breath and continued on his way.

"I don't like this," Mitch said to his companion as they shadowed the child. "It seems too easy."

Taylor nodded his head, but the gesture could not be seen in the darkness. A small boy walking all alone at night was an iffy sight indeed. "I don't like this any more than you do," Taylor replied, "but we need to feed. The humans have been on guard for months and if we don't find food soon, we won't live much longer. There isn't even any wildlife left around in these parts."

Mitch groaned. He agreed with his friend's statement, but he still disliked the situation.

The two starving individuals hid in a field of corn while watching the kid hurry down a wide, gravel path. Taylor placed a hand over his painfully dry throat. Just seeing the tasty morsel made the fiery-like sensation in his throat burn fiercer. Once more, the pair scanned the surrounding area, but their supernatural sight was unable to see anything out of the ordinary. The only thing they could see was the small child.

Why is he outside alone without any gear, Taylor wondered. *It's not like them to be so careless.*

SMACK! The loud noise caused Taylor to turn toward his friend. "What are you doing?"

"I can't help it!" Dozens of mosquitoes flew around Mitch's head. "These bugs are getting on my nerves! I don't know how long I can take it!"

"Get it under control!" Taylor said angrily. "If you wanna eat, you have to stay quiet!"

The warning came a little too late. On the gravel path, Scott heard the slapping sound, causing him to panic and dash down the road. His feet slipped on rolling pebbles, but he never fell and he never slowed down.

"See what you've done now!" Taylor yelled. There was no longer a need for secrecy. Their presence was known. Realizing that their food was about to get away, Taylor burst from the corn stalks and pursued the child. With his unbelievable speed, he was able to catch up with the boy lickety-split.

"VAMPIRES!" Scott screamed. "HELP! VAMPIRES!"

Taylor snatched the child up and quickly lowered his mouth to bite the child's neck, but a metal collar blocked his attack. "Damn! He has a collar!" the vampire said as he turned to his partner only to discover that Mitch had never left the corn field.

"Coward!" Taylor hissed in the general direction of their hiding spot. He returned his attention to the squirming boy in his arms. "No matter. A vampire who doesn't work, doesn't drink."

As soon as the words left the vampire's mouth, huge bright lights filled the area. Taylor let out a painful howl and dropped the boy reflexively. He turned to flee, but the agony caused by the brilliant, solar lights kept him stationary.

Meanwhile, Scott fell awkwardly on his ankle after being dropped. He cried out from the sharp pain, but he couldn't afford to let a little discomfort stop him. He had a job to do. While holding his eyes closed against the intense lights, Scott reached into his pants pocket and removed a pair of sunglasses. Once the shades were placed on his face, he pushed himself up to stand on his good leg and lifted his shirt. A wooden stake was removed from the waistband of his pants.

"Adios muchacho!" Scott said as he put the wooden stake through Taylor's heart. The unholy creature released an unearthly scream and writhed in pain before disappearing in a puff of ash, leaving nothing behind but a heap of clothing.

The vampire's screaming ceased and the evening was quiet again—briefly. It was soon disturbed by loud whispering. Wary people slunk from their homes. Some emerged from hiding places among the field with much fear. "Weren't there supposed to be two vampires?" the people asked as they approached the smoking pile of clothes that lay on the road.

There was a large man that stood out among the group. He ran over and picked up the child. "Are you okay?" Mr. Weber asked his son. "Did he hurt you?"

"My ankle hurts a bit, but I'm fine." Scott hurriedly dismissed his pain and brought up a more important topic. "Dad, only one vampire showed up, but there were two like you said. The vampire that grabbed me was mad I think, because the other vampire never came out of the corn."

"I know." Mr. Weber stared at the whispering field of corn. He placed his little boy down and said, "I'll be right back."

Events had not unfolded as he had expected and a lot of people were going to be very disappointed. Mr. Weber had gotten everyone's hopes up with his little plan, which meant he would be the one to receive the blame if their goal—total vampire eradication—was not accomplished.

He slowly made his way across the gravel road. Rocks crunched beneath his feet, mercifully drowning out the doubtful whispers behind him, but Mr. Weber could still feel the judgmental eyes of the other townspeople focused on him. *It's all or nothing,* the big man told himself in order to ignite his anger and burn away his fear. *All of the vampires must expire tonight.*

FOUR IN THE HOLE

Mr. Weber clenched the muscles in his strong jaw and removed a wooden stake from the utility belt that was strapped around his waist before proceeding through the barrier of corn. He took a deep breath to calm his nerves, but he never faltered. The eyes of his peers were watching him, so into the corn he went. After a few paces, the man came to a spot where the vegetation had been trampled more than anywhere else.

There were two vampires hunkered down right here, he thought as he gave his surroundings a bit more inspection.

Pushed onward by unrelenting resolve, Mr. Weber retraced the vampires' footprints through the rows of corn. Eventually, he arrived at a wall that was made of dirt and tree roots. The cliff stood higher than Mr. Weber, who happened to be six feet and five inches tall.

I'm positive that the last vampire returned this way, he thought.

Determined to go on, Mr. Weber placed his wooden stake back into his utility belt so his hands would be free. He took hold of a protruding tree root and started climbing the nature-made obstacle. In a matter of seconds, he was at the top of the cliff.

His left hand came up to swat away a group of annoying mosquitoes that gathered about his head and buzzed in his ears. *I wish they'd go away. They're too much of a distraction,* Mr. Weber thought as he removed his wooden stake from his belt again and slowly trekked throughout the tall trees. He had been careful to avoid stepping on sticks and twigs, so he would not alert the vampire to his presence; therefore, Mr. Weber knew that he was not alone when he heard wood splintering behind him. The big man spun around and came face to face with Mitch.

"WRAAGGGH!" Mr. Weber let out a cry that was a combination of fear and fury.

The man quickly raised his stake, but the vampire was quicker and the weapon was easily knocked away—it fell out of sight among the underbrush. Mr. Weber reached toward his utility belt to retrieve another wooden stake, but both of Mitch's hands shot forward. One hand seized Mr. Weber's belt from around his waist, and the other hand went around the metal collar that protected the man's throat. The belt was tossed into a tree and Mr. Weber was lifted into the air like he was a toddler, not a two hundred and fifty-three pound man.

"You pathetic humans think you're so smart. Starving us, then launching an attack when we're weak and desperate. But you all forgot one important factor. I would still be stronger than you even if I was on my deathbed," Mitch growled.

Mr. Weber made a vain attempt to loosen the vampire's exceptional grip. It was of no use.

A gloating Mitch stared into the big man's frantic eyes. The amused look in the vampire's red eyes matched the sinister smile on his face. "As soon as I'm finished with you, I'm going to help myself to that delicious little boy of yours for dessert."

Just the thought of never seeing his son again caused tears to spill from the corner of Mr. Weber's eyes. One moment Mitch was laughing at the fact that he had hit a soft spot in the big man's hard exterior, the next moment the vampire was screaming in agony. The sudden change in mood startled Mr. Weber.

The vampire's clutch loosened. The man fell to his knees, too surprised to land on his feet, and Mitch turned into dust, leaving nothing behind but a pile of clothes.

His joy was short lived, because Mr. Weber looked up and he understood what had happened. Standing where Mitch had stood just a second ago was another vampire. The new arrival held a wooden stake in his hand and he stared down at Mr. Weber with those evil, red eyes.

This isn't possible, Mr. Weber screamed internally. *There's another vampire, but we counted and recounted! There were only suppose to be two vampires left, yet here stands number three. Was I off by one, or many? What do I tell the others? Will I live to tell the others?*

Mr. Weber stared up at the vampire. He was prepared to face his demise and he wanted to see death when it came, but in the blink of an eye the vampire was gone. The man sat there for a long time wondering if the creature was only toying with him, but no other attempt was made on his life. Unwilling to remain in those woods any longer, Mr. Weber stood to his feet. After he grabbed the clothes Mitch had been wearing, which was proof of the vampire's demise, he ran from that accursed spot.

Through the woods he sprinted. The big man came to the edge of the cliff and leapt forward without slowing down. THUMP! He landed in the field of corn and kept going until he made it to the gravel road. His heart was beating a mile a minute and his breaths were labored, but he was thankful to be alive.

He looked up and saw that everyone's eyes were on him still. The others wanted to know the outcome.

Should I tell them? Should I alert them to the fact that there is another vampire out there and somehow we miscounted? The creature did save my life and let me be. Maybe that's all he wants, to be left alone. Mr. Weber stared at the anxious folks before him and silently prayed, *Please don't let me be making a huge mistake.*

Mr. Weber held up the second vampire's clothing. "THE LAST TWO VAMPIRES ARE DEAD!"

Shouts of joy erupted all around him. His words were immediately repeated by everyone else and his proclamation rang through the entire city. "THE LAST TWO VAMPIRES ARE DEAD! ALL THE VAMPIRES ARE GONE!"

Chapter 1

In the United States of America, there is a southern state called Alabama. Somewhere in Alabama is a county known as St. Clair, and nestled in St. Clair is a small city called Margret. The Fourth of July was a couple of months away, but in the town of Margret, the citizens were celebrating their own independence day. Everyone undid the multiple locks on their doors and ran out into the crisp, night air. The town was filled with shouts of joy and it went on for quite some time. It had been years since the people had anything to rejoice about.

STAGNANT WATERS

The settlement was enveloped by woods galore. There were no restaurants, no gas stations, nor were there any shopping outlets. Needless to say, there was nothing to get excited about, which is why they never had a reason to jump up and kick their heels together. The citizens of Margret had nothing to do on a Friday night, and on the weekends they had to drive for miles just to enjoy the simplest pleasures of life—like grabbing a cheeseburger from a fast food drive-thru.

The only thing Margret had were houses with half a mile between them. Oh! And thousands of trees—the small town had plenty of vegetation. It was probably that very isolation from the other cities that made Margret a perfect place for vampires to take refuge. For some reason unknown to the citizens, the blood-suckers chose that town and they came upon the unwary people of Margret, besetting them. For seven years the townspeople lived in fear of the vampires…but no more.

A somewhat unplanned festival began. Barbecue grills were lit and the meat that had been defrosted in hopes of their victory were brought out. The citizens removed the metal collars from their necks and undid their utility belts. The wooden stakes were thrown up into the air like hats on graduation day, and when the people realized their error they ran for cover lest they be impaled by the sharpened sticks.

***

The last of the vampires were defeated Tuesday night. When Wednesday morning came, twelve-year-old Jayden Wallace lay in his bed snoring peacefully. His bedroom door flew open and his mother bombarded him. "Wake up!" Mrs. Byrd yelled as she shook her child. "Wake up! The last of the vampires have been destroyed!"

"Ugh," Jayden said groggily as he turned over and threw his blanket over his head.

She climbed on top of the twin size bed and started jumping up and down. "Wake up! Wake up! The vampires are gone! They're all gone!"

The woman was small, but she was still an adult and the force from her weight bouncing on the bed caused enough commotion to send Jayden into the air and onto the hardwood floor. Mrs. Byrd leapt from the bed and landed feet first on the floor next to her son. BOOM! The whole house shook from the impact she made. She bent over and yelled, "Wake up! The vampires are gone!"

Jayden rubbed his aching hipbone with one hand, while trying to hoist himself off the floor with the other. "Is it time for school already?" Jayden asked. The fact that the vampires were no more had not registered in his mind.

"Is it time for school? Haven't you heard a word I've said? THE VAMPIRES ARE GONE! All of them! There's no school, or work today!" Mrs. Byrd said as she ran out the room and down the hall. "Today has been declared a holiday!"

The vampires are gone, Jayden thought as the words finally registered in his head. *I suppose I should be happy— shouldn't I?*

Jayden quickly dismissed his thoughts as he climbed to his feet. After stretching his limbs and letting out a loud yawn, the child stumbled out of his room and strolled down the hall in his mother's wake. He stumbled blindly through the living room, because of the sleep that was still in his eyes, but he eventually made his way into the kitchen with no incidents. Jayden was disappointed when he saw that there was no breakfast in sight.

What did you wake me up for then, Jayden thought grumpily.

A bit of a ruckus caught his attention and he followed the loud noise to the kitchen window. His mother and father were out in the backyard hobnobbing with their next door neighbors, the Wilkersons. A hundred yards lie between their two homes, but the Wilkersons were still the closest which made them neighbors.

Jayden opened the window and stuck his head out the opening. "Momma! I'm hungry!"

"Hey, sweetheart! Come outside and have some of this barbeque," Mrs. Byrd said.

Mr. Byrd smiled and said, "Yeah, son, come on out!"

Jayden moaned loudly. "Y'all know I don't eat barbeque," he replied. "And I don't wanna come outside. It's hot and sticky and…there's bugs out there! And I'll just start sweating and itching, then I'll start stanking. If I start stanking, I'll have to take a bath and you know how much I hate unscheduled baths."

"Stop making excuses," Mr. Byrd said. "Come on out and breathe some of this fresh air. Plus, we have stuff other than barbeque on the grill. We have hotdogs and hamburgers out here, too."

Jayden smashed a mosquito that flew in through the window. As he stared down at the splotch of blood on his hands, he heard his mother's words replay in his thoughts, *THE VAMPIRES ARE GONE!* His attitude abruptly went from unconcerned to resentful. Jayden proceeded to wiped the blood onto his pajama pants as he returned his attention to the window and yelled, "No thanks! I don't eat what the bugs couldn't finish!"

The child slammed the window shut, washed his hands at the kitchen sink, and strode to the fridge. *They know I hate going outdoors so why are they trying to force me to go out?* Jayden fumed. *What's so great about the outdoors anyway?*

Jayden raided the refrigerator and found ingredients to make himself a ham and cheese sandwich. An ideal meal would have consisted of bacon, eggs, and grits, but he was not allowed to use the stove. After the sandwich was made, he grabbed a bag of chips and a can of soda before heading back to his room.

Chapter 2

Jayden was not the only child who stayed indoors that day; however, he was the only one who *chose* not go out. The kid that had served as vampire bait the night before sat in his living room with a sprained ankle. Instead of going outside and having fun with the other kids, he was in the house playing videogames. The only good thing about his condition was that he got to hook up his game console to the big television and he was allowed to eat anything he wanted.

Scott Weber, who was the same age as Jayden, reclined on the living room couch. He was furiously working the buttons on his controller, and in his lap was an empty bowl that had once held ice cream. "You finished?" Mr. Weber asked when he entered the room.

Scott craned his neck in the direction of his father's voice. "Yes, sir, I'm finished."

"Want anything else?" the man asked as he picked up the bowl.

"Sure. Since you're asking, how 'bout you go outside and have fun with the others."

Mr. Weber ruffled his son's blond hair before heading to the kitchen. "It's because of you that we all have something to celebrate about," the big hairy man called from the kitchen. Everyone in Margret claimed that the man was more akin to a bear than a human being. "I'm going to wait on you hand and foot until your leg is better. If you can't go out, then neither will I."

"Dad," Scott moaned, "that vampire was nothing next to the hundreds of vampires you've slain. If I hadn't lured the vampire out into the open, you would've gotten him just like you took care of that other vampire in the woods all by yourself."

Yes, the other vampire in the woods, Mr. Weber mused as he returned to the living room and took a seat next to his son. He was careful not to sit on Scott's propped ankle. "That may be true," Mr. Weber said, "but you did this town a tremendous service. We all owe you. I'm not going out when my son is cooped up in the house with a bum leg."

The sounds associated with a mighty good time seeped into the Weber's home and reached the father and son's ears. Scott paused his game then looked over at his father. "Daddy, I know you're here because you want me to be happy, but I would be a lot happier if you were out there with the others. You've been working for this very moment since I was five. Go and enjoy the fruits of your labor! My ankle will feel better before long and then we'll go hang out together."

Mr. Weber stared into his son's eyes. *There is wisdom in those bright, blue orbs,* the big man thought. The vampires not only fed upon the people of Margret, they also stole the children's innocence. The kids didn't know what it was like to play outside. They missed out on games that the adults had played in their youth. The little ones were trained to fight against the bloodsuckers at a young age; thereby, forced to grow up long before they should have. Mr. Weber hated that about the war most of all. Nevertheless, he was happy to see that his son was growing into a fine young man.

"Okay," the man said, finally relenting. "If you're honestly okay with staying here by yourself, then I'll go out."

"I'll be okay. Honestly," Scott said with a smile. "I have my video games, there's no school today, and the refrigerator is full of food. I'll be fine."

Mr. Weber tousled his son's hair once again and stood. "Alright, I'll be getting out of here. But I'll make sure to come home and check on you regularly."

"Cool," Scott said as he returned his attention to the television. "Bring me some barbeque back on one of your visits."

Chapter 3

Not too far away, there was one more child who could not go out and enjoy the festivities. Eleven-year-old, Tunisha Pugh was in the bed suffering from a cold. Her cute, little nose was stuffed with snot and red from constant blowing. The girl's eyes were puffy, her throat hurt, and her head ached something awful. But that did not stop her from wanting to go outside with everyone else.

"Why can't I go outside and play?" Tunisha asked her mother. Because of her cold, she sounded funny and was hard to understand.

Mrs. Pugh was in the middle of rubbing medicinal cream on her daughter's chest. "You need to rest if you're going to get better. The vampires are gone now, so you'll be able to go outside when your cold is gone."

FOUR IN THE HOLE

Tunisha looked through her bedroom doorway and saw her five-year-old sister run down the hall in a bathing suit. The pitter-patter of the little girl's bare feet and her shrill laughter made Tunisha feel worse than the effects of the cold. She turned back to her mother and insisted, "But I already feel better!" As soon as the words left her mouth, Tunisha coughed violently.

"I see," Mrs. Pugh said. "Well, stay in the bed anyway. I'll be back in a little bit to make sure you're okay. I'm taking Tasha to the swimming pool so she can splash around."

Tunisha moaned disappointedly as her mother left her room. "I wanna go to the pool," she mumbled when her mother disappeared.

The girl closed her weary eyes and tried to remember how it felt to go outside and play. Tunisha was at the age of seven the last time she had been out of the house without having to look over her shoulder. Of course the vampires owned the night, but when the monsters became desperate for blood they also braved the day. They wore long overcoats to protect their bodies, leather gloves to hide their hands, bandanas wrapped around the lower parts of their faces, and wide brimmed hats kept the Sun from touching their heads. They reminded her of the outlaws from the old western shows her father liked to watch.

It's finally over, Tunisha thought happily and a smile appeared on her face.

The last memory she had of herself going outside to play was brief and not very detailed. However, there was one thing that she would never forget. She remembered being happy while sitting on her little pink bicycle; the one with the training wheels. Of course, Tunisha had gotten too old for the bike and it would soon be passed down to her little sister, Latasha. But her father promised to teach her how to ride a two-wheeler without the training wheels.

"I can't wait until this cold is gone and I can go outside," Tunisha mumbled blissfully. "I can't wait to ride my new bike." Her simple statement caused her to cough. When she was done, she closed her eyes again and fell asleep with a smile on her face.

Chapter 4

Scott and Tunisha were confined to the house against their wills, and Jayden just flat out refused to attend the festivities. No matter their reasons, those three missed the party of a lifetime. That outdoor bash would go down in Margret's history books. Well, since the small city has no history books, that's highly unlikely, but the day would most definitely be recorded in every journal or diary that existed in Margret. The point of the matter is that the day of celebration would not be forgotten by anyone that had taken part.

The children played games that they had never been able to participate in while being cooped up in the house. For example, several hopscotch games were held in the middle of Margret's main road. A lot of kids learned how to use the swing set at the playground, while others played on the long, metal slide. There were children who laughed uncontrollably as they went up and down on the seesaw. Even the teenagers were having a good time. The big kids had fun spinning the merry-go-round at frightening speeds in an attempt to send the smaller children flying. The teenagers awarded each other ten points for every kid that lost their grip and went sprawling into the dirt.

"Hide-and-go-seek" was a typical game that the children of Margret had played indoors, along with "red light-green light" and "mother may I", but it was a lot more fun to play in wide open spaces. Some kids bounced on trampolines and went higher than their beds could have ever sent them. "Marco…Polo," was heard in a couple of swimming pools, while "cannon ball" was heard in more. Frisbees spun through the air, kites hovered as high as the tallest trees, and frisky dogs chased behind their owners.

Not every child participated in the normal and more fun activities. There were about twenty naïve kids who were conned into taking part in old man Henry's unofficial Olympics, which was held on his large estate. The place was overgrown with grass and weeds, because no one dared go outside with the vampires lurking about; therefore, the citizens were unable to maintain their yards.

Mr. Henry's unkempt yard inspired him to come up with his own Olympics, which consisted of three events. The first event was the weedeater competition, followed by the riding lawnmower race, and the final challenge was raking and bagging. An excited Marcus Hutchinson took home the first prize which was five dollars. Second place was four dollars, third was three dollars, fourth place earned two dollars, and the rest just received a bad case of the itches.

While the children enjoyed themselves, the adults sat on their porches and patios, or established temporary setups beneath tree canopies. Extension cords were found and radios were brought outside, adding music to the happy occasion. The grown folk engaged themselves in barbequing and card games—two activities that seemed to include a lot of loud talking and rambunctious laughter. The only time the adults paused their merrymaking would be to yell infamous phrases like: "don't do that" or "stay where I can see you" and the dreaded "don't make me come over there".

Ultimately, the sun disappeared along the western horizon, but that did nothing to dampen the partying mood. Porch lights were turned on, tiki torches were placed in yards and lit, candles were placed on tables, and electric lanterns were strung up. The kids played until they staggered home and dropped from exhaustion. Adults carried on into the wee hours of the morning before they decided that they too had had enough.

Chapter 5

While everyone else enjoyed a night with no curfew, Jayden lay in bed tossing and turning because of a reoccurring nightmare. It was the frightening dream where he was walking through the woods at night with no one to keep him company, but the full moon. The heavenly body shone brightly from its place upon its dark throne.

You can stop following me, Jayden thought at the moon.

When he received no reply from the celestial orb, Jayden decided to ignore the moon. Instead he focused on forging a path through the painful, thorny vines. Dry leaves, brittle straw, and pinecones crunched under his feet as he zigzagged through the tall, deciduous and evergreen trees.

Eventually he came to a muddy bank next to a trickling stream. It happened to be the same stream that Jayden traveled to when he wanted to catch crawdads and tadpoles; however, Jayden never came with a bucket or fishnet in hand when he dreamt of the brook. Instead of fishing, he would search for the source of the stream.

Ribbit ... ribbit.... The deafening sound of frogs croaking surrounded him. An owl hooted somewhere off in the distance, and mosquitoes buzzed all about.

Jayden traveled along the muddy border, going against the flow of the stream. His journey was slowed considerably because the tan colored muck kept sucking the shoes off his feet. A few minutes passed and Jayden noticed that a thick fog had appeared out of nowhere, covering the entire woodland floor. The substance was so thick that the silvery light of the moon, who still kept a watchful eye on the boy, was unable to pierce it. The fog was a clear indication that he was going the correct way.

Before long, Jayden came to the place he sought. In front of him lay a large pool of black water, surrounded by the thick mist. There were no ripples to break its smooth surface. All of a sudden, a swarm of mosquitoes attacked the boy. Jayden tried to escape by hurrying along the edge of the pond, but he couldn't shake the bugs. SMACK! He would slap himself when he felt a stinging bite. *Only the females drink blood,* he remembered hearing his dad tell him. Little good the knowledge did him at that moment.

As Jayden fled from the mosquitoes, he did not pay attention to the fact that he was getting dangerously close to the water. While fanning the creatures away, he stepped on a weak part of the bank and the dirt gave way beneath his weight. The child's right leg fell into the water and the rest of his body was quick to follow.

SPLASH! Not knowing how to swim, Jayden could only scream for assistance and thrash around in the water. No one but the mosquitoes knew of his plight and they only came to him out of a desire to feast. The moon was also aware of Jayden's predicament, but for some reason it refused to step down from the heavens and lift the boy from the water. It just watched with that same uncaring expression on its face.

While Jayden screamed and waved his hands in the air, he hit the root of a large tree. It was as if Mother Nature was reaching out for the drowning boy. Without delay, the exhausted child took hold of that root and began to pull himself up. Jayden let out a grunt with each strenuous tug. He was halfway out when he heard a tremendous splash behind him. The terrified child looked over his left shoulder and saw a pale hand come up out of the water—the hand of a vampire!

"HELP ME!" Jayden screamed. He tried to pull himself out of the water faster, but the pale hand gripped his ankle.

With unbelievable strength, the appendage starting pulling the boy back down into the dark abyss that was the pond. Jayden kicked and screamed, but nothing would deter the vampire. The frightened child lost his grip on the root of the tree and he clawed at the bank to no avail. The vampire continued to drag Jayden deeper into the water. Like a black maw, the pond swallowed him up to his waist, then moved up to his shoulders, his neck, and finally the water was over his head. The last sight the boy saw through the wavering surface of the water was the luminous full moon looking down on him.

Why did you follow me out here if you weren't going to save me? Jayden thought at the moon.

Chapter 6

The bedside alarm clock began buzzing annoyingly.

The morning after the day of celebration started with Mrs. Byrd rolling over quickly to hit the off button. When the noise ceased, she returned to her previous position. There was a moment of silence before Mrs. Byrd sleepily turned to her husband and mumbled, "I woke him up yesterday...your turn."

Mr. Byrd acknowledged his wife's comment with a groan and somehow found the energy to sit up a few seconds later. They had been two of the late partiers. Mr. Byrd's bare feet searched the cool, wooden floor near the bed until he found his slippers. Once his feet were covered, Mr. Byrd stood up and left the bedroom. With his eyes halfway closed, the man staggered through the hallway like a newly awakened mummy. And since he hadn't visited the bathroom to wash up yet, his breath smelled like one, too.

Mr. Byrd entered his son's room and yelled forcefully, "Jayden! It's time for school!" With the day of celebration gone, the adults had to return to work and the kids had school to attend.

When Jayden didn't answer, Mr. Byrd moved closer to the bed. At home, Jayden's nickname was Sleeping Beauty, because there was almost nothing that could wake the boy up. Nothing but the kiss of the floor. Mr. Byrd bent down to his son's ear and yelled, "GET UP!"

The boy's hand went to the side of his face like he was swatting away a fly, but he never woke.

"I don't have time for this," Mr. Byrd muttered to himself. The man took a firm hold of his son's bed sheet and yanked with all the strength he could muster. Jayden was pulled off the bed and he fell to the floor with a loud bang.

"Time to get up for school," Mr. Byrd said as he walked away.

"Yes, sir," Jayden mumbled as he rubbed his aching shoulder.

He sat up, but remained on the wooden floor for a moment trying to overcome the frightening experience of being drowned in the pond. The boy knew it was just a dream, but the fear was hard to dismiss.

After a minute or two, the sluggish child climbed to his feet and headed for the bathroom to get ready. Margret's unauthorized holiday had ended, and it was back to the usual hustle and bustle. Well…not quite the usual. Since the vampires were all vanquished, no one was required to wear their vampire battle gear. The equipment consisted of a metal neck band, body armor over the torso, a utility belt (which held wooden stakes, a canteen full of holy water, and pouches of garlic cloves), and metal wrist bands.

No more looking like a head case in front of the other people, Jayden thought happily as he brushed his teeth.

Since the people of Margret had no place that sold modern day commodities (other than Mr. Ripley's General Store), they had to venture outside of the small town in order to take care of their needs and wants. Grocery shopping, clothes shopping, and any other shopping had to be done in the neighboring town — Argo. The people of Argo thought their neighbors in Margret were insane with all of their talk about mythical vampires. The strange battle gear didn't make them look any saner. None of the other towns had problems with bloodsuckers. They all laughed at the rumors that came out of Margret.

Jayden spit the toothpaste into the sink and rinsed his mouth out. "Don't have to worry about that anymore," the boy said as he checked himself out in the mirror. Teeth brushed… check. Hair brushed…check. The corner of his brown eyes clear of crust…double check. He smiled at his reflection. The boy was quite handsome, even if he was very lanky and small for his age.

"Looking good and feeling fresh," Jayden told himself before leaving the restroom.

Chapter 7

After devouring a cold bowl of cereal, Jayden grabbed his book bag and stepped out onto the front porch. A warm breeze quickly embraced him as if he was a long lost friend. Once he had the door locked and was ready to depart, Jayden took a deep breath to calm his nerves. Everyone claimed that the vampires had been defeated and there had been no reported incidents during the day of celebration. Nevertheless, Jayden still felt uneasy about going outside alone. It was going to take some getting use to.

Maybe I should've came outside yesterday with everyone else, Jayden thought as he walked across the groaning planks that made up the porch. He quickly surveyed his surroundings out of pure habit. Everything seemed to be fine. *Being outside probably wasn't as frightening when everyone else was out, too.*

The boy ambled down the dusty flight of steps. He looked over the wood railing and stared at the overgrown yard. The awful sight brought a moan to Jayden's lips. He would probably be forced to go outside and cut the grass. The child could already imagine being drenched in sweat from the intense heat, while trying to fend off mosquitoes. It was not a pleasant sight.

"I wish Mr. Henry would let us host the next neighborhood Olympics in our yard," Jayden muttered to himself.

He overheard his mother and father complaining about the old man's antics. Even though Jayden wasn't one of the boys conned into landscaping Mr. Henry's large estate, they were still outraged by his actions. "I can't believe he tricked those kids into cutting his grass," Mrs. Byrd had said irately.

"I think his little Olympic scheme was ingenious," Mr. Byrd replied with a chuckle, "but he has more than enough money. He could have given them boys more than a couple of dollars. Kathy said that her boy only received five dollars for coming in first!"

"If you ask me, no one was a winner but that old fart," Mrs. Byrd said.

When Jayden came to a stop at the bottom of the stairs, he reluctantly turned to his left. He told himself that he wouldn't, but it was as if an unseen force was pulling his attention. That was how he came to be staring at the tree line where their yard ended and the woods began. Fear suddenly clutched at his heart and his pulse quickened. Without seeing it, the boy knew that a stream lay not too far from where the trees began. Jayden was also aware of the fact that if he was to travel upstream he would come to a murky pond of standing water; a pond which happened to be the largest of the breeding grounds for the mosqui-toes of Margret.

One of the biting insects buzzed in his ear, breaking Jay-den from his trance. He shooed the mosquito and quickly turned away from those woods. As if fleeing would put the memories behind him, he continued down the dirt path that made up his family's driveway. *All of the vampires are gone,* he tried to reas-sure himself. *There's no longer any need to fear the woods.* He wanted to believe in what he was telling himself, but he could not shake the feeling of dread that sat heavily upon him. And why were the dreams still plaguing him if the vampires were de-feated? The dreams had to mean something. Right?

Jayden stepped out of his yard and made a left hand turn onto an asphalt road that rose steeply, creating a sharp incline. As he climbed the hill, he passed a ramshackle trailer home that sat on his right. The place once belonged to the Wright family, but now tall weeds owned the house. A tear ran down Jayden's face as he remembered the folks who once lived there. He had been very young, but he still remembered how Mr. and Mrs. Wright were found drained of their blood along with their youngest daughter. The other two kids had disappeared only to show up later as vampires.

The child wiped away his tears after he passed the aban-doned home. Soon enough, he arrived at the bus stop which was located at the top of the hill. Dozens of children were standing around. Elementary students, middle school kids, and high-schoolers were all mingled together. They were talking excitedly about how free they felt without battle gear, and the fact that a platoon of parents were not needed to escort them to the bus stop.

Not a moment too soon, Jayden thought as the yellow school bus pulled up to the curb.

Chapter 8

Jayden was in a relatively good mood once he got on the bus. He even chatted along with the other kids, but he would have been better if he saw a certain person—Tunisha Pugh. Jayden had developed a huge crush on Tunisha when she and her family moved to town. He initially met Tunisha when their second grade teacher, Ms. McFarland, introduced her to the class. Jayden had fallen head over heels for her immediately, but he knew that she would not remain in town for long. There was no way.

As soon as her parents find out about the vampires, they'll leave, he thought sadly.

Now they were in the seventh grade, Tunisha had not moved away, and his secret admiration had grown with time. Jayden had never been so happy to be wrong about something in his life. Although they were not boyfriend and girlfriend, Jayden felt that there was a special bond between the two of them. No matter how bad things got, Jayden always had a good day when he was able to see Tunisha. Her beautiful caramel complexion, brown colored eyes, and long black hair was enough to brighten anyone's mood.

The fact that Tunisha was at home recovering from a cold was unknown to Jayden. Apparently, the bond he felt with her was not as special as he thought.

***

Actually, Tunisha tried her best to get out the door that morning. She had been in the middle of putting her jeans on, when Mrs. Pugh entered the girl's room. "Where do you think you're going?" her mother asked.

"I feel fine now," Tunisha replied. "I'm going to school."

"You do seem to be doing better, but we're going to keep you home one more day to make sure you're fully recovered."

"Aw, come on, Ma!" Tunisha whined.

"Don't 'come on Ma' me," Mrs. Pugh said. "Take off your clothes and get back into bed."

Tunisha put up a valiant fight, but seeing that the girl was not on the bus obviously meant Mrs. Pugh won in the end. Poor Tunisha wasn't the only child missing from the school bus. Scott

Weber's ankle still bothered him, but that was not what kept him at home. The boy had stayed up extremely late Wednesday night playing video games while his father was out celebrating with the others. Instead of waking up at his usual time, Scott over-slept.

"What difference will it make if he misses one more day?" Mr. Weber asked himself as he stared down at the angelic face of his sleeping son.

**

Back on the rumbling bus, the myriad of conversations began to lag and the ride became relatively quiet. In order to pass the time, Jayden turned his head toward the dust covered window. He watched as the extremely tall pine trees and mud caked houses blurred past. Some of the houses were similar to his. They sat on wooden stilts and a flight of stairs were needed to get to the porch. Then there were the beautiful, two-story homes where Jayden would have loved to live, and of course the town also had its share of hovels.

Eventually, the houses dwindled before disappearing completely and gave way to more woodland that consisted of sparsely scattered trees. For miles, Jayden stared at nothing but trees. After a few minutes, a familiar sight broke the monotonous scene. A wooden sign that read, "You are now leaving Margret. Come again soon." Some vandal had painted a big, black X across the word Margret. Below the X was the town's nickname…Stagnant Waters.

Margret earned its nickname because it was home to billions of mosquitoes—biting insects that were known to breed around foul, stale water. Therefore, the other towns of St. Clair dubbed Margret as Stagnant Waters. To the people of Margret, the name Stagnant Waters held an entirely different meaning, because of another type of bloodsucker that had once bred in that town.

Just our luck, Jayden thought. *The vampires are gone, but we still have to deal with mosquitoes.*

It was because of those blood stealing bugs that Jayden made sure to coat any exposed skin on his person with foul smelling insect repellant. It kept him from getting ashy better than any lotion could, and the chemical repelled the creatures instead of attracting them. Wearing scented lotions was just asking to be eaten alive. Even without lotion, the pestering bugs swarmed any warm blooded creature within five seconds of them coming out of their home.

Before long, the school bus arrived to its destination. They were a mile beyond Margret's town limits and two miles away from Argo. The bus turned off the highway and made its way down a bumpy, dirt road before coming to a stop behind two other school buses. The kids stepped off the public transportation and hurried to either of the two school buildings that sat side by side. The elementary and middle school was contained within one structure. The high school had a building of its own.

For Jayden, the day was uneventful and went by rather slowly. The children had been allowed to go outside for recess, but Jayden refused to go. They were out in the middle of the woods for goodness sakes, surrounded by thousands of insects! Jayden didn't need that. Instead of going outside, the boy stayed in the gym and played solitary basketball. After recess, he continued to count the minutes until it was time for him to get back on the long, yellow bus and return home. When Jayden did enter the confines of his own house, he ate his usual afternoon snack and refused to go outside and play with the others.

"No thanks," the boy replied when his friends came knocking on his door.

Jayden spent quality time with his parents when they came home from work like he always did. That night the boy went to bed at his normal bedtime and drifted into a slumber full of more nightmares. Thursday passed away and Friday arrived so the child could perform his entire routine all over again. Or so he thought....

Chapter 9

Jayden sat up in bed gasping. It took a few moments before he realized that he was in his bed and not drowning in a mosquito infested pond. *It was just another dream,* the child told himself. Once he calmed down, he glanced to his right and happened to notice unusually bright sunlight peeking through a gap in his boarded up window. Jayden's head quickly turned to his left. He looked at his bedside table where his clock sat. The red, illuminated numbers said that the time was twenty-four minutes after seven.

"Nooooooooo!" Jayden yelled as he hopped out of bed. "I'm late!"

He searched his floor and quickly found clothing that did not make him dizzy when he smelled the fabric. The boy threw on an outfit and rushed into the bathroom. Jayden quickly brushed his teeth and put deodorant under his funky armpits. He was just going to have to hope that the pleasant scent masked the other. Once he was done in the bathroom, the boy ran back into his room and stuffed his school supplies into his book bag. After he did a quick check to make sure he was not missing anything, he grabbed his can of insect repellant off his dresser and sprinted down the hallway.

"You forgot to wake me up!" Jayden yelled as he blasted past his parents' room on his way to the front door.

BOOM! He slammed the heavy door shut behind him. After securing the locks, he dashed across the porch and down the flight of wooden steps. In his rush to get to the bus stop, Jayden missed a step near the bottom and tumbled the rest of the way. "DANGIT!" he yelled as he climbed to his feet. Jayden quickly dusted himself off and rubbed his aching limbs before running full speed down the driveway. "Please don't let the bus be gone already!" he chanted. "Please don't let the bus be gone already!"

By the time Jayden made it to the top of the steep hill, he was huffing and puffing. His heart felt like it was going to explode in his chest. The boy slowed his run down to a brisk walk.

As he made his way over to the bus stop, he was surprised to see only two other children waiting on the bus. He had been expecting to see a whole group of kids, not two lone figures.

Intent on getting some answers, Jayden quickly strolled over to the other two. One person he recognized right away—the lovely Tunisha Pugh. His mind and heart cheered at the sight. The other person's name came to mind after much thought. It was a kid by the name of Scott Weber.

"Did we miss the bus?" Jayden asked after he came to a stop and began applying insect repellant to his arms, neck, and face.

"No, I've been out here over fifteen minutes," Tunisha said as she fought off a swarm of mosquitoes. "I don't know where everyone is. Nobody said anything about another holiday."

"You want some insect repellant?"

"Thanks," Scott said as he reached out and took the can. "You just happen to carry 'round a can of bug repellant with you?"

I wasn't offering it to you, Jayden thought, but he replied, "And you've lived in Stagnant Waters your whole life and you don't?"

"You got a point there," Scott said as he handed the can to Tunisha.

Tunisha applied the spray to her body and sent a couple of mists into the air before handing it back to Jayden. "Thanks," she said.

"No problem," Jayden responded as he looked off into the horizon.

After a minute of awkward silence, Tunisha said, "I just realized that I didn't see my folks before leaving the house. At the time, I was rushing to get outta the house so I didn't pay attention, but now I'm beginning to worry."

"I didn't see my momma or daddy either," Jayden said thoughtfully. "They usually wake me up in the morning, but for some reason they forgot to wake me up today. I was in a rush too, so I didn't have time to ask them about it."

Scott looked just as alarmed as the others when he admitted, "I haven't seen my daddy either."

Chapter 10

Out of concern for their families, the children raced away from the bus stop, but not before they agreed to return to that very spot within half an hour if anything was amiss. Jayden raced down the hill, which was a lot easier than running up. Back across the driveway he went and up the flight of steps. The boy came to a much needed stop on his front porch, struggling to catch his breathe.

Those video games are no substitutes for real exercise, he thought to himself as he leaned against the front door. Sharp pain stabbed him in his sides, his tiny heart was working overtime. "Too much…fresh…air at one…one time," he muttered as he pulled out his set of house keys and unlock the door.

"Momma! Daddy!" Jayden yelled when he entered the dimly lit house. The people of Margret had been so busy celebrating that no one got around to removing the wooden planks from their windows. The child's sneakers clunked on the wooden floor as he hurried through the living room and down the hallway. He arrived at his parents' bedroom and knocked on the flimsy door. "Hey, Momma! Are y'all in there?"

After a few seconds and no reply, Jayden pushed the door open slightly. *Urrrrrrrk!* The rusty hinges cried out for a can of oil.

The boy called through the small opening, "Hey, I'm coming in. Y'all better be decent."

He pushed the door open further so he could better scan the dark room. There was nothing to be seen, but two sets of glowing red eyes. *Glowing red eyes?* Jayden thought. *Vampires! Gotta go! Gotta go!* It was too late.

Before he could move from the doorway, those red eyes were right before his brown ones and he was instantly pinned against the hallway wall. His feet dangled above the floor.

70

"Good morning, son," Mr. Byrd said. His chocolate skin had an ashen tint, and his usually brown eyes were blood red.

Jayden desperately wanted to reason with his father, but he knew from experience that any attempt would be futile. The boy was well aware of the fact that although his dad's mind and personality had not been altered, the man was now filled with a lust for blood that overpowered all logic.

Sniff...sniff...sniff...! Mr. Byrd smelled the air and his face wrinkled in disgust. "What is that horrible aroma?" the vampire asked.

Jayden shrugged and replied nervously, "I don't smell anything."

Mr. Byrd leaned in toward his son quickly, then his head snapped back. "Ugh! The smell is coming from you!"

"Oh...uh, I didn't have time to take a bath this morning because I woke up late and I've been running," Jayden explained. He tried to catch a whiff of himself, but he obviously didn't smell what his father did.

Mr. Byrd pinched his nose close with one hand while holding Jayden effortlessly with the other. "Peeeww! You're going to have to take a bath before I bite you!" he said in a nasally voice.

"I'm not taking a bath then."

"Oh! Yes you are going to take a bath! I'm your father and you're going to do as I say!"

"I don't think...I shouldn't have to obey you under these circumstances," Jayden replied hesitantly.

A strong gust of wind filled the hallway. "Don't talk back to your father!" Mrs. Byrd said. She appeared out of nowhere, possessing the same ashen skin and red eyes.

Mr. Byrd pushed his wife away to spare her from their son's stench. "You don't want to bite him. I think he's spoiled or something," he told her.

"Did you check his expiration date?" Mrs. Byrd asked jokingly as she leaned in to sniff Jayden. Almost instantly, she jumped back as if she was repulsed by him. "Ugh! What is that?"

"I may be a little tart, but I can't smell that bad," Jayden said with a sigh. He should have been happy that they did not want to eat him, but the child was tired of being offended.

"Should we wash him off? You know, like a piece of raw chicken. You have to wash it off first."

"That's what I said, but he won't go take a bath." Mr. Byrd said. "You go wash him."

Mrs. Byrd quickly shook her head. "I can't wash him. I'm already fighting off the desire to throw up."

"Are you serious?" Jayden asked angrily. "Stop talking about me like I'm not hanging right here."

Mr. Byrd dropped his son to the floor—thud!—and turned to Mrs. Byrd. "How about we play paper, scissors, rock to see who has to bath him? Whoever gets two out of three wins and the loser does the washing."

"Maybe it was your stank breath bouncing off of me and hitting you in your face. You ever think of that?" Jayden asked from his spot on the floor.

"Hush your mouth when grown folks are talking," Mrs. Byrd told the boy. The two vamparents balled their hands into fists. "Paper...scissor...rock..." Mr. Byrd wrapped his opened hand around his wife's fist. The first point went to him.

"Paper...scissor...rock..." The second point also went to Mr. Byrd who hit his wife's scissor with his rock. "You're too predictable," he told his wife with a wide grin on his face. "Now you go bath our stinky, little piggy and I get the first bite." The vampire turned to his son, but Jayden was not there.

"See what you've done with your stupid, unfair game?" Mrs. Byrd asked.

Chapter 11

What is going on around here? Jayden wondered from his hiding place. *I was thinking that Momma and Daddy might've been sick from bad barbeque, but somehow they've been turned into vampires. How could this have happened and who could have done this?*

"Jaaaaaaay," his father called from somewhere in the living room. "This is pointless. You know that there is no use in hiding. That horrid smell of yours is masking the delicious aroma of your blood, but we can smell your stench a mile away. It's so strong that it might as well be visible, like a thick vapor cloud."

Jayden silently scolded himself for being so stupid. *Should never play hide-and-go-seek with vampires.*

"Come to your mother my little Jayden-Wayden," Mrs. Byrd called from in the kitchen. They were too close for the child's comfort and getting nearer every second. The vamparents knew where he was, which meant they were purposefully torturing him by delaying their attack. "We're not going to hurt you. We just want to give you a bath."

I have to do something...anything, Jayden thought. He frantically felt around in the dark until his hand came across a cold, metal can. He gripped the tall cylinder in his hand and removed the plastic lid. With his finger on the nozzle, he waited for his vamparents to come for him.

The door to the cabinet, beneath the kitchen sink, was snatched open. What little bit of light that was in the kitchen flooded the small compartment. "Gotcha!" Mr. Byrd said as he looked upon his child.

"No, I got you!" Jayden responded. He held the can of spray up and shot a stream of liquid into his father's red eyes. To the child's surprise, the vampire howled as if he was in intense pain. Mr. Byrd fell back and crashed into the refrigerator. Boxes of cereal and a large bag of chips fell onto the vampire's head.

"It burns!" Mr. Byrd yelled as he rubbed his eyes. "It burns!"

Mrs. Byrd suddenly appeared next to her husband. "What happened?"

Jayden looked down at the can of spray in his hands. It was simple household bug spray. He turned back to his father, who was closing and opening his eyes trying to relieve the irritation. Mr. Byrd's eyes were brown again. The whites of his eyes

73

were red from the bug spray…but the orbs in the center were brown.

He's human again, Jayden realized.

The child leapt out of the cabinet just as his mother lowered her mouth to her husband's neck. Jayden pressed down on the nozzle and sprayed his mother in her face. Mrs. Byrd fell to the floor and starting convulsing. Mr. Byrd, who got a little more in his eyes, balled up into a fetal position and cried out, "Stop spraying me in the eyes with that pesticide, boy!" The man's voice lacked that homicidal tone.

"I don't believe it," Jayden said as he looked down at the can one more time. He turned to his parents who flopped around on the kitchen floor like two fish out of water. "Who did this to you?"

"Is that your way of bragging? You did this to us," Mr. Byrd managed to say in the midst of his howling.

"Somebody help me flush my eyes out quick! I'm blind!" Mrs. Byrd screamed.

That was not what I meant when I asked who did this to you, Jayden thought. He decided to save his questions for later. There was someplace he had to be. He went back to the cabinet where he had been hiding and removed another can of bug spray and a box of bug foggers.

"Where do you think you're going?" Mr. Byrd asked when he heard his son's footsteps hurry by. The only reply he received was the sound of the front door slamming.

Chapter 12

Tunisha made her way to the Pugh's residence, ignorant of the fact that Jayden was racing to her rescue. Jayden's house was closer to the bus stop, which gave him enough time to discover the problem and rectify the situation before Tunisha could even get home. It was fortunate for her that Jayden was on his way, because she was not much of a vampire hunter. She had rarely encountered vampires during her five years in Margret.

And the times she did come across a vampire, her parents were always there to protect her.

She unlocked her front door and pushed it open slightly. Tunisha had no idea what awaited her inside, but a part of her insistently screamed that something was wrong. The hairs on the back of her neck were standing up and goosebumps rose on her skin. She moved hesitantly.

The living room was dark and silent inside. Like everyone else, her family didn't take the time to remove the boards from the windows. "Hello?" Tunisha called out. She dare not enter the dark house without receiving an okay from her folks.

"Tunisha, is that you?"

"Tasha!" Tunisha called out, happy to hear a familiar voice. "Where are you?"

"I'm right here," her little sister said from somewhere in front of the doorway.

Tunisha opened the front door wider to let more sunlight into the dark room. She caught a glimpse of her sister's legs as the little girl took a step back into the shadows. Latasha's legs look like she had been playing in talcum powder.

"Tasha, are you okay? What's going on?"

"I'm hungry Nisha," her sister replied.

Something about the whole situation just didn't feel right. "Momma! Daddy!" Tunisha yelled. "Tasha, where's Momma and Daddy?"

The voice from the shadows replied, "They're in their room sleeping. Come feed me Nisha."

"Step into the light," Tunisha insisted. "Come where I can see you."

"TUNISHA! DON'T GO...IN THERE!" a voice yelled from down the street.

The young girl stepped back out onto the porch and turned toward the source of the warning. That's when she saw Jayden running down the dusty road. "What's going on?" she asked after he came to a stop at the bottom of the stairs that led to the porch.

"Vampires…!" Jayden managed to say while trying to catch his breath. "Vampires…everybody…. That's why they're …they're not outside!"

Tunisha did not want to believe what she was hearing. They had just defeated the last of the vampires and now *everybody* was a vampire? How could that have happened, and who had the power to turn everyone in town?

"Are you sure?" she asked.

Jayden put his hands on his hips and lifted his head in an attempt to alleviate the aching in his chest. "I'm sure…just fought my folks…. Whipped their butts with a can of bug spray."

Bug spray? Tunisha wondered if she heard correctly.

"I don't know…what's going on, but they can be cured."

"Are you sure?" Tunisha asked again. This time she asked out of hopefulness and not disbelief.

Jayden nodded his head. "Side effects…blindness, hopefully temporary." When he started breathing normally, he continued without pause, "We can cure your folks, but we'll have to do it later. You're safe and that's all that matters for right now. We have to go and make sure Scott is okay." Jayden held a hand way above his head and said, "That boy's father is huge! We need to stop him from going into his house if we can. Do you know where he lives?"

Tunisha turned back to her house and looked inside. In the darkness was a pair of glowing red eyes. "Catch you later Nisha," her little sister said and then there was a wicked giggle that followed. Tunisha did not need to be a mind reader to know the implications behind those words. A shudder went down her spine.

Tunisha turned away from the doorway and hurried down the rickety steps to meet Jayden. "Yeah, I know where he stays," she said and they ran off down the road.

Chapter 13

Down the asphalt road they ran. The sound of their sneakers slapping against the pavement echoed in the morning air. *There is something seriously wrong here,* Jayden thought as he struggled to keep up with Tunisha. What struck the boy as odd was the fact that the only sound he heard was the noise they made while running. He did not hear the nonstop croaking of frogs, nor the irritating cricket's siren. There were no birds flying through the air and their beautiful songs were missing as well. What happened to the constant scurrying of squirrels?

Jayden slowly came to a stop as he stared at the surrounding woods.

When she no longer heard his footsteps, Tunisha turned around. She sighed when she saw that Jayden was no longer lagging behind, but had stopped altogether. "Come on, we have to get to Scott's!" she shouted after coming to a complete stop.

"Be quiet and listen," Jayden said harshly. "What do you hear?"

Tunisha looked around for a moment. "I don't hear anything."

"Exactly! And I can't remember the last time I've ever heard anything besides the buzzing of mosquitoes. It's the middle of spring and there is no wildlife whatsoever."

"Whoa! You're right," Tunisha said. "I guess we've been so busy creeping from one place to another and worried about vampires that we never took the time to stop and think about the silence. What do you think it is?"

Jayden slowly shook his head and replied, "I don't know. I know frog legs are a delicacy, but there's no way that vampires ate all the frogs and there's nothing they can get from crickets. Still I get this feeling that this has something to do with the vampires. I don't think we ever defeated all of them."

"Do you think we miscounted?"

For some reason, that question filled Jayden with both hope and fear, but he kept either from showing on his face. "We had to have miscounted, because only vampires can create other vampires."

Tunisha looked around the woods fearfully. "How many vampires does it take to turn a whole town in one night?"

Jayden could only shiver at the thought. He decided to ignore that question and focus on the task at hand. "Alright, let's get going," the boy said. "We need to reach Scott before it's too late."

Chapter 14

BOOM! The entire house rumbled when Mr. Weber punched a huge hole into a wall of the living room. The supernatural strength given to vampires, added with the powerful human might Mr. Weber already possessed, equaled a force to be reckoned with.

An angry Mr. Weber turned to face his son and glared at the boy with those blood red eyes. "Don't you run from you father, boy!" the vamparent growled.

Scott huffed and puffed as he kept a wary eye on his dad. "Don't you make me have to call child services on you," he replied smartly.

The child swore as he dived to his left. Just as Scott rolled to his feet, his vampire father had stomped a hole in the floor where he had been standing. The boy dived and rolled to his feet again and the vampire was where the boy had been standing a second ago. Scott came to a halt and glared at his father. The kid's breathing was becoming more labored. He did not know how much longer he could keep dodging.

Vampires are extremely fast and strong, making them *seem* invincible. But there are countermeasures to everything. Scott's father had taught him a long time ago that when dealing with a vampire, a person had to constantly be on the move. Vampires are so quick that they look like they're teleporting instead of running. In order to assail a vampire, a human has to move quickly and attack where they (the human) had originally been standing, because that's where the vampire would be next.

Scott was dodging well, but he didn't have a weapon in hand to attack with. His utility belt was too far out of reach.

Mr. Weber disappeared and Scott dived a millisecond too late. The vamparent clipped the boy on his recovering ankle and Scott was spun into the wall. Before the boy could regain his senses, Mr. Weber pounced on his son. The giant man placed one of those mitts he called a hand on Scott's head and lifted the boy into the air. The house shook as Mr. Weber slammed the boy into a wall.

"Now I gotcha, little rabbit!"

Scott stared into his father's red eyes and tears emerged from his blue ones. He was not weeping because he was about to be feasted upon by a vampire. No. The boy cried because he was going to have to kill his father.

When Dad was forced to kill Mom after she turned into a vampire, I blamed him for her death, Scott thought. *I told myself I would never do what he did to her. But now I see what it took for him to do it, because I'm forced to do the same thing. I forgive you Dad and I hope you can forgive me for what I'm about to do.*

Scott bumped the heel of his right shoe against the wall, and a flat wooden stake extended from the front of his sneakers.

"Ugh! What is that awful smell?" Mr. Weber asked in between gagging.

Just as Scott was about to jab the weapon into his vamparent's heart, the living room door flung open and two figures burst through the entrance. The fight paused so both Scott and Mr. Weber could turn to the source of the interference.

"I'm a little...musty...but there was no way you could smell me through that door," Jayden struggled to say. The child held two bug foggers in his hands and quickly activated them. Into the room the smoking canisters went and they slid to a stop beneath Mr. Weber.

Thinking that they were garlic bombs, the giant vampire dropped his son, pinched his nose closed, and was suddenly gone. Scott fell to the floor and rolled out of the enlarging fog.

"Tunisha! Help Scott get to the porch!" Jayden yelled as he removed two more bug bombs from his pockets.

While Tunisha did as she was instructed, Jayden kicked one of the smoking canisters that was already on the living room floor into the hallway. The other bomb he left it where it lay. The boy then proceeded to activate another bug bomb and that one he threw into the kitchen. *Alright, just one more,* Jayden thought. He slowly made his way into the hallway, which was quickly being filled with the foul smelling chemical. Afraid to go any further, Jayden set off the last fogger and tossed it down the hall.

When Jayden finally came out of the house and shut the door behind him, Scott looked at the boy like he had lost his mind. "I'm sorry; did you happen to spot a roach in there? Because I know you didn't set those foggers for the vampire."

"Just give it a few minutes and you'll see," Jayden said.

For fifteen long minutes, the kids stared at the house waiting on some sort of sign that the bug bombs had worked. The only sound they heard was the hissing noise of the canisters as they released their contents, and nothing more. Just when Jayden was beginning to doubt himself, a bone chilling bellow was heard from within the house and then a sound like something big falling to the floor soon followed.

Jayden looked at Tunisha and Scott with an 'I told you so' smile on his face. "Vampires check in, but they don't check out."

Neither Scott nor Tunisha could believe what they had just witnessed with their ears. The bug spray was actually hurting the big vampire. "You just happen to carry around a box of bug spray with you wherever you go?" Scott asked.

Jayden shrugged his shoulders. "You live in Stagnant Waters and you don't?"

Chapter 15

The three children ventured into that smoked out house to retrieved Mr. Weber, but they soon discovered that the task was beyond their combined strength. Tunisha, Jayden, and Scott took a hold of the big man and they tugged and they grunted, but the unconscious Mr. Weber would not budge. When they couldn't tolerate breathing in the bug spray fumes anymore, the kids hurried back out onto the porch.

Scott looked over at Jayden and asked, "Think you might've overdid it, Mr. Orkin Man?"

"Maybe just a little."

"Well, what are we suppose to do now? We can't just leave him in there breathing that stuff," Tunisha said.

The kids sat on the porch deliberating, but in the end, Mr. Weber came crawling out the front door on his own, hacking and spitting up on himself. "Dad!" Scott exclaimed as they hurried over to help him.

"I can't see!" Mr. Weber cried.

"Every miracle cure has its side effects," Jayden said meekly. "Hopefully it wears off."

As they helped the big man to a sitting position, Scott asked in an alarmed tone, "Hopefully?"

"Hey! Don't get cross with me. You were about to kick a stake into his heart and the side effects of that is death. A death that does not wear off with time. I would choose my side effects over yours any day."

An exorcised Mr. Weber called out, "Aye, boys! I'm just fine. You all did a remarkable job, especially you, little boy with the bug bombs."

"My name is Jayden, sir."

"Yeah, well good job, Jayden. Who would've known that bug spray cures the vampire disease? So many people could have been saved if we had only known earlier." The man thought of his wife and he muttered to himself, "So many peo-ple."

Scott, who stood next to his sitting father, patted the big man on his back sympathetically.

Instead of compassion, Mr. Weber's statement dredged up feelings of fear for Jayden. Memories of a vampire's hand came unbidden. The boy would never forget how the hand emerged from the stagnant pond near his home. He could still feel the limb's tight grip around his ankle, dragging him into the water. If it hadn't been for the sun causing wisps of smoke to rise from the hand, the appendage would have never receded into the dark water, and Jayden would have never been able to flee the woods.

"Yeah, good people could have been saved," Jayden replied solemnly after dismissing the fear-provoking vision of the past.

"Daddy, the whole town has been turned into vampires," Scott said, bringing everyone's attention to the more important matter at hand.

"It's all my fault," the big man muttered. "I knew what I did would come back to haunt me."

"Dad, what are you talking about?"

"I didn't kill the last vampire," Mr. Weber confessed. He was ashamed to have his child know of his weakness and deceit, but the truth had to be told. "In the woods…that thing…it nearly had me, but another vampire showed up and destroyed him. For some reason, the new, uncounted for vampire left me alive, and I took credit for the kill. I couldn't disappoint everyone so I announced that all the vampires were gone."

Jayden's heart started picking up speed as fear and excitement assailed him. *All of the vampires weren't destroyed after all!*

Scott gave his father a reassuring pat on the shoulder.

"Since the vampire spared my life, I thought it would be safe to ignore him and continue with our celebrations. I thought it would be safe for us to come out again, but I was wrong. The vampire probably saved me just so we would come out of hiding."

"Mr. Weber, one vampire couldn't have turned an entire town into vampires," Jayden said. "It's impossible. Were you bitten by a vampire?"

"No…I wasn't."

Jayden brought his point home. "The barbeque could have been bad, the vampires could have poisoned our waters, or the virus could be airborne, but this is not the work of one vampire."

"That makes a lot of sense, kid."

"Well, at least we have a way of saving everyone," Scott pointed out. "Instead of killing them with a stake or repelling them with garlic, we can cure the vampires. They're no more than these mosquitoes flying about."

Jayden's head jerked up at Scott's last statement. "That's it!"

"What are you talking about?" Scott asked.

"Mosquitoes! Tunisha asked me a question when we were running over here. How many vampires would it take to turn the whole town in one day? It would take hundreds of vampires! Hundreds of vampires that can sneak up on their victims without causing suspicion. Vampires that can bite and disappear without anyone being the wiser. Somehow the *mosquitoes* turned everyone in town into vampires."

Scott looked down at his father. "Dad, is that possible?"

"It's very possible," Mr. Weber answered in a bewildered tone. "I can tell you for a fact that no vampire laid fangs on me...ever. And mosquitoes have been known to spread viruses like malaria and yellow fever. As a matter of fact, they caused panic all across the country with the West Nile virus a few years back. It's very possible that they're spreading the vampire virus."

"It all makes perfect sense! Tunisha was at home sick so she missed the celebration. Scott was in the house with a sprained ankle, and I don't do outdoors. That's why we're the only ones who were not affected. Everyone else must've been bitten at some point when they were outside. We never ran into this problem before because we didn't go outside. And if there was a need to go outside, we would move from one cover to the next so quickly that the mosquitoes never had a chance to get us."

Everyone on the porch went quiet as they mulled over the new development. Tunisha was the one who broke the silence. "So not only do we have to cure everyone in town, but we have to find some way to destroy thousands of mosquitoes. How do we go about doing that?"

"And it's not like we'll be getting help anytime soon, because everyone we spray ends up blind," Scott pointed out.

"Alright, let's not get distracted by things that we can't control at the moment," Mr. Weber said. "Right now our main priority is to make sure everyone who is not affected gets somewhere safe for tonight. I have an underground shelter behind the house where we can hide. First, I need you kids to go to Mr. Ripley's General Store and obtained all the supplies we can get to fight these vampires. Explain the situation to him and he should be willing to help free of charge. The second task is to bring your parents to our shelter."

"My folks are still vampires," Tunisha said.

Mr. Weber asked, "Jayden, what about yours?"

"They're cured."

"Okay," the big man said. "After the general store, I want you three to go and cure Tunisha's family. Be extremely careful about it. Fighting vampires is no walk in the park. Once that's done, then y'all escort the two families over here. All of that needs to be done well in advance to the setting of the Sun. Is everyone clear on the instructions?"

"Understood," the three kids said in unison.

Scott left his father's side and went to enter the house. "Where are you going?" Jayden asked.

"If we're going to get all this done before this evening then we're going to need some wheels."

Chapter 16

Jayden relished the feel of the warm air blowing against his face. He dropped his right foot and kicked against the pavement, propelling the skateboard faster. The sound from the wheels against the asphalt was like music to his ears. Jayden was not fond of being outdoors, but he had to admit that he was quite enjoying himself. The child placed his foot back onto the board and shifted his weight, guiding the skateboard over toward Tunisha who was in the middle of getting used to rollerblading.

"You okay?' Jayden asked.

"I'm good," Tunisha replied. Her shoes, which were tied together at the shoestrings and draped around her neck, was making it hard for her to balance, and her ankles were bent at an awkward angle, but she seemed to be doing okay for a beginner. "This is awesome!"

Too much talking threw Tunisha off balance and she started wobbling. Afraid that she was about to fall again, Jayden reached out and took hold of Tunisha's hand to steady her. She laughed at herself for almost falling and said, "Thanks!"

"No problem," Jayden said as he savored the way her soft hand felt in his. He suddenly realized that he was still holding her hand and he let it drop. Without saying another word, Jayden kicked out his right foot again and gave himself a couple of pushes. He heard the wheels of Tunisha's rollerblades clap against the pavement as she tried to keep up. Before long, the both of them caught up with Scott who was coasting down the road on his new bicycle.

"These are awesome!" Jayden said as he came up to Scott's left side. He was referring to the rollerblades, the skateboard, and the bike.

"Thanks," Scott said. "My dad bought me this stuff as a reward for helping catch the last two vampires. Daddy has a pair of rollerblades, too, and we were going to go skating together during the celebration, but I couldn't."

"When did you learn how to ride a bike?"

Scott dropped his hands from the handlebars and kept the bicycle steady with his legs. Jayden was aware that the boy was showboating, but he couldn't help being impressed. "My dad taught me how to ride a bike when I was five," Scott replied. "I guess it's true what they say. Once you learn you never forget."

Tunisha gripped the back of Scott's bicycle seat and allowed him to pull her along. "My dad was supposed to teach me how to ride a bike on the day of celebration, but I was sick.

Hopefully I'll get the chance again. They already bought me a new pink bicycle, now I just gotta get my folks back."

"Don't worry," Jayden assured her. He didn't like the fact that her hand was so close to Scott's bottom, but he showed maturity by focusing on the more important issue. "We'll free your parents and the blindness won't last long."

"So what about you?" Scott asked. "Tunisha got a brand new bike, and I got all this. Did your folks buy you anything for the celebration?"

Jayden shook his head. "Naw, they didn't buy me anything. I don't go outside."

"You won't even go outside even now that the vampires are gone—were gone?" Tunisha asked

"Nope. I wouldn't even be out now if it wasn't so important. But it's good that I don't come outside, because I would be a vampire like the rest of the town and you two wouldn't have the pleasure of my company."

Tunisha and Scott laughed at Jayden's little joke.

"If only we had known about the mosquitoes," Jayden said with a sigh. "We could have put off the celebration for two more months."

"Why two months?" Tunisha asked.

"The life span of an adult mosquito is anywhere from four to eight weeks. With the last two vampires gone, they wouldn't have had anything to take blood from since the animals have disappeared. They wouldn't have been able to nourish their eggs and the adults would have eventually died out."

"Someone's been reading the M encyclopedia," Scott said mockingly.

"Naw," Jayden said as pain wrenched at his chest. "My dad was an entomologist. He taught me all about mosquitoes and a lot of other insects."

"I thought Mr. Byrd worked at the plant in Argo. My dad has ridden to work with your dad plenty of times," Tunisha said.

"Oh, he does, but he's my stepfather. My real dad was an entomologist."

"That's why your last name is Wallace and your momma and daddy's last name is Byrd. I just thought you were adopted," Scott said.

"My dad's name was Anthony Wallace. When he...died ...my mom remarried sometime after, but she let me keep my father's last name," Jayden said sadly. "He would probably still be alive if we never moved out here so he could study mosquitoes. I was four when we came. Margret has the largest mosquito infestation in the United States so Daddy decided to settle here and do his research. 'They even call the place Stagnant Waters,' he told us when we arrived. Dad would take me with him when he went hiking through the woods by our house, and that's how I learned so much about mosquitoes."

"What happened to him?" Tunisha asked softly.

"Hey look, there's Mr. Ripley's General Store," Jayden called out before kicking off on the skateboard. The other two just followed in silence.

Chapter 17

There were no distinguishing marks to separate Mr. Ripley's General Store from any of the other houses located in Margret. The so-called store was a one story building with green paint peeling from the splintering exterior. There was a large, dust covered porch attached to the front of the house and the only thing that sat on the porch was an old, rickety rocking chair. The windows were boarded up like every other house and the entrance to the place was a regular doorway. In other words, the store was basically a home.

"Well, it doesn't look like a store, but the number that Dad gave us is on the front of it," Scott said as they made their way up the weed choked sidewalk. "One hundred and forty-five."

"Can't hurt to check it out," Jayden said as they climbed onto the warped boards that made up the porch. "Mr. Ripley is most likely a vampire like all the others so let's be careful."

"Right," Scott and Tunisha said.

They parked their modes of transportation against the house before slowly making their way to the front door. Jayden was the one who arrived at the door first so it was him who rapped his knuckles on the wooden barrier.

There was a long moment of silence before a crackly voice responded. "Come on in."

The kids removed the spray cans from their pockets immediately and held them in the ready position before opening the door to the house. A stale, musty aroma invaded the children's nostrils as they slowly made their way through the doorway and entered what was obviously the living room. The only source of light came from the sunlight that entered through the opened door. There was a very old couch sitting against the right hand wall and a matching recliner sat on the wall across from them. In the middle of the room was an antique coffee table buried under a clutter of various items. Dingy dollies were all over the furniture and several old photos were haphazardly hung on the wall.

"Mr. Ripley, where are you?" Jayden called out before walking any further.

"Just keep a going straight, I'm in tha kitchen," the old man replied. His voice was coming from the doorway next to the recliner.

"Mr. Ripley, there's something going on in town and we're going to have to ask you to come into the living room," Jayden explained.

"Get 'em King!"

Instead of seeing an old man emerge from the kitchen, a gigantic rottweiler came bounding toward them. Jayden's heart leapt into his throat when he saw the red, glowing eyes of Mr. Ripley's guard dog. His bug spray was ready to fire, but the boy was paralyzed with fear and could only watch as the giant beast jumped for his throat.

Sssssssssssssssssh! Tunisha quickly sprayed the animal and Jayden moved out of the way, allowing it to crash to the floor. The huge dog howled in pain and scratched at its eyes with its paws.

"Thanks," Jayden muttered. He was embarrassed by his lack of action.

"No problem."

An old man quickly hobbled out of the kitchen and entered the living room. "You don't have any more dogs do you?" Scott asked over the rottweiler's howling.

"No mo dogs," Mr. Ripley said nonchalantly. "I sent ole King after ya, but ya can't blame an old vampire for trying now can ya? What cha do to 'em anyhow?"

"We cured him," Jayden said as he slowly made his way toward the old man. The boy was not too happy about having a giant dog sicced on him. "Now it's your turn."

The old man held up his hands defensively and backed away. "Don't be too hasty, young buck! I invited chu in here, but I ain't give ya permission to go spraying me in the face with that elixir of yours. What cha 'bout ta do is considered assault and I'll press charges. 'Fore Lord, I swear I will!"

"I'll claim self defense," Jayden countered.

"Mr. Ripley, you know we don't show vampires mercy," Scott said sternly.

"And who are you ta judge me? Huh?" the old vampire asked. "I have every right ta say how I wanna be and becoming a vampire is tha best thing that's ever happened ta me. I'm eighty-two for crying out loud! You're too young ta know how it feels ta pray every night, 'Take my soul if I should die' and know that ya might just get what cha askin' for. Child, I'm a vampire now and I'll live forever. I ain't going back."

"Mr. Ripley, leaving you as a vampire is too big of a risk," Jayden explained.

"A risk to whom? My old bones had me walking 'round so slow that the increase in speed only brings me up ta a normal gait." The old man strutted around as fast as he could in an attempt to demonstrate what he meant.

"You're just speed walking," Jayden said unconvinced.

"No child, that was me running at mach speed. You should've seen me before I got super quick." Mr. Ripley could look at their expression and tell that his walking around was not proof enough for them. "Okay, so y'all still don't believe me. Well, looka here!" He leaned forward and opened his mouth.

"You don't have any fangs," Tunisha stated after a brief glance.

"No fangs! False teeth don't grow fangs. How can I be a danger ta anyone? What Imma do, gum 'em ta death?"

"Well, if we leave you as a vampire you'll starve to death. How will you eat? What will you eat?" Scott asked.

Mr. Ripley shrugged and said, "I guess I'll just drink animal blood through a straw. Something like that."

The blind rottweiler near the opened front door let out a yelp and bolted through the entrance.

"Now see whatcha done did. Ya left my front door wide open and let my dinner get away. But I'll be willing to forgive ya if ya let me be and don't spray me wit that miracle spray of yours. I ain't gon be no trouble to anybody. These cataracts dull my vampire vision down to less than twenty-twenty."

Jayden looked at his friends.

"Well, Daddy let a vampire go. I guess we can show a bit of mercy, too," Scott said.

The old man did a little bow. "That's all I'm askin for, a little mercy. Now what brings ya three ta my humble abode?"

Chapter 18

"Well, now I've done heard it all. Mosquitoes turning a whole city into vampires and three chil'ren coming ta tha rescue with cans of bug spray," Mr. Ripley said as he led the kids into the kitchen. He flipped the light switch on and a dim bulb filled the room with a yellow tint. "Ya couldn't make this stuff up if ya tried."

The kitchen walls were lined with many shelves and groceries sat on those shelves. There were can goods and other nonperishable items in boxed or plastic packaging. The food sat on the window sills and was strewn all over the stove and dining table in no semblance of order. Food that needed chilling was kept in the refrigerator, the freezer, and the deep freezer. All the children could do was stare in horrified amazement.

"I only keep groceries in here. People don't like it when ya put pesticide and cleaning products near their food, so I keeps it outside in the shed," Mr. Ripley explained. "If ya don't mind me askin', how ya plan on restoring the town? You can't bust down every door and spray everybody in tha face. Eventually, they'll figure ya out and they'll either hide, or fight back like cornered animals."

"We haven't figured all that out yet," Scott replied. He was feeling quite uncomfortable under the scrutinizing gaze of Mr. Ripley's red eyes.

"Well, when ya do figure it out, stay away from my house." The old man came to a stop and started sniffing the air. His face abruptly turned into a scowl. "Did y'all step into some dog shit?"

The children checked their feet. Scott and Tunisha shook their heads, but Jayden just sighed. "Nobody stepped in any dog crap. I didn't have a chance to take a bath this morning and we've been ripping and running all over the place. I wish everyone would just let it go."

Mr. Ripley shook his head. "No, it ain't that, but ya might wanna take care of that as soon as possible. No, the smell is coming from the three of you and it's repulsive."

Jayden, Scott, and Tunisha began sniffing themselves. "Oh!" Jayden exclaimed with a laugh. "It's bug repellant, or in this case I guess it can be used as vampire repellant! And here I thought I was smelling so bad that I was offending the vampires."

"Well, that smell is worst than garlic," the old man said as he put a hand over his nose. "I can't take that stench much longer so listen up. I want ya three ta go out ta my shed and get what ya need. There'll be no charge in exchange for you not spraying me."

"Thanks," Jayden said.

The old man quickly nodded his head then pointed toward the backdoor. "Go! Wait...let me go into tha living room 'fore you open that door. Don't wanna avoid tha spray just ta get zapped by the light."

The kids did as Mr. Ripley requested and waited until he disappeared in the living room before they opened the back door and stepped out into the yard. "Let me get some more of that bug repellent," Scott whispered to Jayden after they shut the door behind them.

Jayden removed the spray from his pocket and applied it to his exposed skin before passing it Scott who in turn gave it to Tunisha. "This is a lot better than wearing all of that body armor," Tunisha said.

Scott quickly agreed. "I know, right!"

Mr. Ripley had a large pasture for a backyard with trees defining his borders. The first thing the children saw was a leaky faucet protruding from the base of the house. Beneath it was a tangled hose laying in mud. Not too far away stood a decrepit structure, which they assumed to be the shed, and a large barn, sat at the end of the field.

The trio waded through the waist high grass and eventually came to the dilapidated shed. Scott undid the wooden latch and Jayden helped him pulled the door open. It proved to be a difficult task, because the high grass would get wedged under the door making it hard to pull. After much effort, the boys opened the door and they entered warily.

"Is there a light switch in here?" Tunisha asked.

"I think I…wait a minute." Jayden fumbled on the wall and found the switch. He flipped the lever into the on position and a weak light came on overhead.

The room had the same cluttered look that Mr. Ripley's kitchen had. The walls were covered in shelves that started near the floor and went to the ceiling. All kinds of knick-knacks and bric-a-bracs lined the shelves while random items sat in corners or laid on the ground. "Here's some cans of bug spray," Tunisha announced as she checked the wall closest to her.

"Good," Jayden said. "Let's get a can to put into each pocket and let's see if we can find some more insect repellant."

"I found it," Scott called out.

On his way over to Scott, Jayden stumbled over a large water gun. "Hey look," he said to the others. "It's a supersoaker! I haven't seen one of these in—there're some more over here, too." He picked up one and looked it over.

"What are you going to do with that?" Scott asked as he handed Jayden some insect repellant.

Jayden placed the smaller can in his back pocket, because his front pockets each had a tall can of bug spray. He looked around the room until he saw what he was looking for. "Here's a big bottle of concentrated bug spray. You have to mix this with water before you use it. What if we mixed some of this in these water guns and used them to fight vampires with?"

"That's the coolest thing I've ever heard," Scott said.

"Yeah, I still surprise myself sometimes."

So the kids each grabbed one supersoaker and two small water pistols. They went to the leaky water faucet out in the backyard and filled their water guns with both pesticide and water. Jayden, Scott, and Tunisha were well armed by the time they made it around Mr. Ripley's house and returned to his front yard. Each child had insect repellent in their back pocket and a can of bug spray in both front pockets. The supersoakers were held in their hands and the water pistols were tucked into their socks. They felt invincible and pretty cool by that point.

Scott climbed onto his bike, Jayden stepped onto the skateboard, and Tunisha put her rollerblades back on. "Let's go get your folks," Jayden said as he pumped his supersoaker.

Chapter 19

By the time Jayden and his small entourage arrived at Tunisha's house, the Sun was directly overhead. If either of the children knew how to read the position of the Sun, they would have known that it was noon.

"Alright, since Scott has the most experience with hunting vampires, I think he should be in charge of this assault," Jayden whispered as they stood near the bottom of the house's steps.

Jayden and Tunisha looked at Scott to see if he would comply. Like father, like son, Scott couldn't bring himself to shatter the hope he saw in his friends' eyes. "I've never raided a vampire's nest, but I've heard my dad talk about doing them all the time." Scott took up a small stick and drew a plan of attack in the dirt, while explaining to the other two their positions and what they would be expected to do.

"Ya got it?"

Jayden and Tunisha nodded their heads as they continued to study the details in the dirt.

"Alright, well let's go."

The bicycle, skateboard, and the rollerblades were left at the bottom of the small set of steps. The children crept up onto the porch as silent as could be, not wanting to wake the vampires if they were sleeping. The element of surprise would be their best ally.

Scott led the procession alongside the house and came to a stop next to the door. He looked behind him, made eye contact with Tunisha, and motioned for her to move.

With butterflies in her belly, the girl moved from the back of the line and went to stand before the door. Trying to be as stealthy as possible, Tunisha unlocked the door (which she was positive she had left open) and pushed it open like they had discussed. Scott instantly pointed his supersoaker at the doorway and so did Tunisha, ready to provide cover fire for Jayden who entered the house.

The light in the living room was extremely faint, but Jayden was able to tell that the room was empty. Without looking back, Jayden gave Tunisha the hand signal which meant everything was clear. She hurried in and pointed her water gun toward the left hand side of the room, while Scott followed quickly and pointed his to the right. Another silent signal was given by Scott and the children made their way across the empty living room and down the hallway to where Tunisha's sister was said to sleep. The kids figured Latasha would be the easiest vampire to defeat, so they chose to eliminate the weakest link first. One less vampire to deal with.

Jayden came to an abrupt stop at the girl's bedroom door, with Scott behind him and Tunisha guarding the rear. He gave the signal that said he was preparing to open the door and everyone braced themselves for what awaited them.

Eeeeeeeeeeeek! The door was shoved open and Scott moved from behind Jayden and entered the room. Jayden hurriedly followed Scott while Tunisha stayed outside the room to guard the hallway. By the slivers of light that came in through the boarded up window, the boys were able to see that Latasha was in bed asleep. Scott approached the little girl, slowly pumping his super soaking, building up pressure. Jayden's job at that moment was to provide cover if Scott should need it.

Don't fire until you see the reds of her eyes, Scott instructed himself as he aimed the water gun at Latasha's angelic face. "Wake up!"

Latasha's eyes popped open. Scott saw what he was looking for and he pulled the trigger on his water gun. Direct hit! The little vampire was hosed in the face. The mixture of pesticide and water got into her eyes and burned fiercely. Scott was quite pleased with himself, but then Latasha let out a terrible shriek, causing the three human children to cover their ears.

Vampire screams never came up during the planning process. Another factor not discuss was how parents reacted when their children were being attack. Especially vampire parents who were even more protective, and a lot more aggressive.

Mr. and Mrs. Pugh sat up in their bed suddenly and rushed from their room. Their speed generated a strong gust of wind, which filled the hallway. "THEY'RE COMING!" Tunisha yelled. Before she could even flex her index finger on the trigger of her supersoaker, the girl was thrown against a wall. Her back impacted with the unrelenting obstacle, forcing air from her lungs. Tunisha's water gun fell to the floor a few seconds before she did.

The frightened boys turned toward the bedroom door, unprepared for the ferocity of the vamparents attack.

Chapter 20

Jayden held his supersoaker up, ready to fire, but Mr. Pugh knocked the water gun out of his hand and sent it clattering to the floor. Before Jayden could reach into either of his pockets, the vampire jerked him into the air. Intent on a fast kill, Mr. Pugh's face darted for the child's neck, but the smell of the bug repellant brought the monster to a halt. The vamparent pulled his head back.

"You like my new cologne?" Jayden asked with more bravery than he felt. "It's called *Get Back.*"

Mr. Pugh growled and tossed the flippant boy across the room. Jayden bounced off a wall that held one of Latasha's many cartoon posters and fell to the floor. "Ow!" he cried out when he felt his small can of insect repellant digging into his left butt cheek.

Latasha's vampire screams had become fearful human whimpering. "Momma!" the little girl called out, not understanding why she could not see. "Daddy!"

Jayden heard the girl in the background, but he never found the time to answer her. Mr. Pugh went on the attack again. Right away, Jayden went for one of the cans of spray in his pockets, but still he was too slow. The vamparent picked him and pinned him against the wall. "Breaking and entering is a crime," Mr. Pugh growled. "Breaking and entering a vampire's home is beyond foolish. An offense punishable by death."

"How about you turn the other way and pretend like I was never here?"

Mr. Pugh looked over at his five-year-old daughter who was crying and then returned his glare to Jayden. "If only that were possible."

"WHOA!" Jayden cried out as he was thrown across the room again. The second time he collided with the little girl's dresser. *I am going to be sore in the morning,* he thought after he hit the floor. Desperate to escape Mr. Pugh's barrage, Jayden pretended to ball up into a fetal position. Secretly, he was reaching for the small water pistol that was tucked away in his sock.

He had the weapon removed by the time Mr. Pugh hurried over and stepped down on his leg.

Jayden let out a painful cry and struggled to lift the vamparent's powerful foot, but it was no use. Even if he had been able to use two hands it would not have helped. When Mr. Pugh thought the child had had enough, he lifted the boy up into the air so he could taunt him some more. "Any last words?" the vampire asked.

"Yeah, I hope this burns a lot!"

He lifted his hand that held the water pistol and fired into the vampire's red eyes. *Squirt, squirt, squirt, squirt.* Mr. Pugh dropped Jayden and fell to his knees howling in pain. His inhuman cries mingled with Latasha's frightened screams, forcing Jayden to cover his ears. When the racket died down a bit, the boy sprawled out on the floor next to a writhing, human Mr. Pugh.

"How you like them eye drops? It sure 'nough gets the red out don't it?"

Chapter 21

When the vamparents burst into the room, Jayden was thrown against one of the bedroom walls, but Scott sailed clear out into the hallway. He landed on the floor and slid into a solid wall. "Dammit!" Scott cried. Events were seriously going awry. The boy pushed himself up onto his elbows and happened to look over at Tunisha who lay on the floor not too far away. Scott only had a moment to stare into her frightened eyes before he was yanked up and tossed again.

Down the hallway he went. The fact that he was flying and had no clear indication of where he was going to land, frightened him immensely. Fortunately, his flight came to a stop on the living room couch. He bounced off the cushion of the back support and fell onto the floor with a bang.

"My daughter isn't allowed to bring boys into the house!" Mrs. Pugh yelled as she launched at Scott again.

The boy quickly rolled under the coffee table and crawled away from the menacing vamparent. "I need reinforcements!" Scott screamed at the top of his lungs. Before he could get anywhere, Mrs. Pugh grabbed him by his ankles and pulled him into the air, holding the boy upside down. The female vampire looked like a fisherman taking a picture with a squirming whopper of a catch.

"Now where do you think you're going?"

"I can cure you." It was hard for him to talk while the blood was rushing to his head.

"Cure me? Child, there's nothing to cure! I've never felt better!" With an impressive show of feat, Mrs. Pugh lifted him farther into the air by his leg until he was face to face with her. Mrs. Pugh stared at his neck and smacked her lips hungrily. "Now I'm going to cure you."

She promptly leaned in for the kill, and like every other vampire, she came across a scent that sent her retreating. "What is that horrid smell?"

"Well that depends on whether you're referring to the smell that's coming from me, or the stank that's coming from you."

"Your mother should have taught you some manners."

The vamparent was about to hurl the child across the room for his insolence, but a heart wrenching sound changed her plans. Mrs. Pugh heard her husband's horrible howl mingle with her youngest daughter's terrified scream and she instantly wanted to go to them. She immediately dropped Scott, who had to roll so he did not land on his head, and she dashed back down the hallway with supernatural speed.

SPLAT!

Before she could reached Latasha's bedroom door, she was blasted in the face with a strong, steady stream of pesticide. Tunisha had just made it to her feet when she saw her mother streaking through the hall like a bolt of lightening. Afraid that her mother was coming for her, Tunisha held her water gun up, closed her eyes and fired. With one lucky shot, Mrs. Pugh was down on the floor emitting a screech that rivaled her husband's.

"That wasn't so hard," Tunisha said when she opened her eyes.

Chapter 22

The rooster clock that hung on the kitchen wall said it was thirty-five minutes after twelve o'clock. Scott, Tunisha, and Jayden were at the table having a lunch of chips and sandwiches. None of the children had eaten breakfast, and they were not about to forgo another meal—Armageddon or not. Mr. and Mrs. Pugh were in the living room trying to cope with their loss of eyesight while consoling their youngest child.

"I'm starting to think Mr. Ripley might've had a point," Jayden said. He picked up his soda can and took a long gulp without elaborating on his statement.

"What's that?" Scott asked.

"There's no way we can cure every person in Margret. It's impossible. There are some families that have more than three members. This time there was an even amount on each side. We had three humans, they had three vampires, and we still had to struggle. My body hurts so bad that there is no way I can fight again today; maybe not for the next two days. Taking on one nest every three days isn't going to cut it. And what'll happen when we come upon a family of four? Heck! Forget four; the Johnson's have six family members!"

"And it's not like we're getting any help," Tunisha added. "Everybody we save is blinded so that still just leaves the three of us to fight this thing."

Scott shrugged his shoulders. "You're both right, but that's a matter for the adults to figure out. We carried out the mission we were given. We went to Mr. Ripley's General Store, got the supplies, rescued Tunisha's folks, and now we just have to get everyone to the rendezvous spot. I say good job for today and worry about tomorrow when it gets here."

Jayden lifted up his can soda. "Here, here!"

Tunisha and Scott picked up their drinks and banged them against Jayden's.

After that conversation, the kitchen was filled with the awkward sound of sipping and chewing as everyone retreated into their private thoughts. Although Scott suggested that they should be satisfied with what they had accomplished, they still worried about what would become of the town.

Eventually, the plates were void of food and the soda cans were empty. "So when do we move?" Tunisha asked.

"I suppose it should be right away," Jayden replied. "It's still early in the afternoon, but the sooner we get to safety, the better. Plus we've done enough for today."

"You're right," agreed Scott. "Alright, I suppose this is how it should be. Tunisha and I will escort her family to my house. We shouldn't run into any problems, but I think Tunisha should have a partner in the event that something does happen. Jayden, you're pretty capable of handling yourself in tight situations. You've defeated four vampires by yourself today."

Tunisha started clapping and Scott joined. Jayden looked down at the table and smiled bashfully.

"You can bring in your folks without any assistance, right?" Scott asked.

Tunisha defeated two vampires and while you only caught a kid while she was sleeping, Jayden thought sullenly. *It sounds like you're the one who needs an escort.* He was not angry with Scott. As a matter of fact Jayden had become quite fond of the boy during their short time together. Scott was like the brother he never had; however, Jayden would have liked to been partnered with Tunisha.

"Yeah, I can get my parents. No problem," Jayden answered. Before they left the table, the boy decided to make an announcement to lighten his own mood. "And since the issue of how many vampires I've reformed came up, I would like to thank Tunisha for saving my life twice with her two defeats."

It was Tunisha's turn to smile timidly as the other two clapped while hooting and hollering. "Alright, that's enough," Tunisha said. There was a big smile on her face as she pushed away from the table.

The children went to gather their supplies. Supersoakers, cans of bug spray, and water pistols had been knocked all over the house. Jayden departed after saying his goodbyes. Scott and Tunisha rounded up the Pugh's and guided them down the dusty road.

Chapter 23

The journey to the rendezvous spot was uneventful. Before leaving either house, everyone was bathed in bug repellant and the children made sure to steer clear of mosquitoes, which was hard to do because swarms of the biting insects were all over the place. About an hour after they left the Pugh's residence, all three families were safely tucked away in Mr. Weber's underground shelter.

The safe place was a large, square room with concrete making up the fours walls, the ceiling, and the floor. A soft humming could be heard from a generator that sat out of sight. The proof of its existence came from the artificial light given off by a bare bulb hanging from the ceiling. Three cots sat on one side of the room. The makeshift beds were originally brought in for Mr. and Mrs. Weber and their son. For the time being, two cots were assigned to Scott and Jayden while Tunisha and Latasha shared the third one. The only other furniture in the shelter was a large refrigerator and a wooden wardrobe.

At the moment, the children were on their cots while the parents sat on pallets made of blankets. There was a debate going on between the parents, and the kids watched intently to see what their fates would be.

"We didn't have the money to move away five years ago and we don't have the money now," Mrs. Pugh said to the other blind parents who were gathered nearby.

"Money is not the issue with us," Mr. Byrd said, "but we call this place home. I know it's a stubborn attitude, but we refuse to be run out by a bunch a bloodsuckers. Not only that, but how can we leave our friends and kinfolk to this cruel fate? Just two days ago, we were celebrating the fact that we were finally free of the nightmare and now we're in a worst predicament then we were last week."

Mr. Weber let out a sigh. "I understand where y'all are coming from. I don't desire to leave this town anymore than any of you, but we have to think reasonably. The only ones we have to fight this war are the kids. The rest of us are either blind, or overcome with vampirism. And let's not forget the thousands of mosquitoes that are flying around carrying the vampire virus. I don't know about y'all, but I've lost one family member in this war, I'm not willing to lose another. Especially not my son."

Mr. Weber's last statement hit home with the rest of the parents.

"There are more than three hundred vampires in this town now," Mr. Weber continued. "In addition to the vampires, there are thousands of mosquitoes throughout these woods. It is impossible for these children to defeat every single vampire while avoiding the mosquitoes. You already heard them tell you how difficult it was to take down a nest of three vampires. Come sunrise tomorrow, the vampires will have relocated and fortified a nest with larger numbers. There is only one option. We must flee this city."

"But what about the neighboring towns?" Mrs. Byrd asked.

"What about the neighboring towns?" Mr. Pugh answered. "We've gone to them for assistance before and they laughed at us, called us crazy. No one came to our aid. No government officials came to investigate when people started to go missing. They wouldn't have found anything, but they would have at least discovered the vampires. If you ask me, I think they know and they're just ignoring it because the danger hasn't hit home. Well it nigh time that they defend their own borders instead of us doing their dirty work."

It sounded like a selfish attitude, but everyone in the room was in consensus with Mr. Pugh.

"When do we leave?" Mrs. Pugh asked sadly.

"I was thinking first thing in the morning," Mr. Weber replied. "Any hesitation on our part can cost us lives."

In one fashion, or another, everyone agreed to leave in the morning. Everyone except for Jayden. "Um, I don't mean to throw a wrench into your plans, but uh, how are we going to leave when all of you are blind? No one in this room can drive," Jayden pointed out.

Mr. Weber groaned. "That fact never occurred to me."

Chapter 24

Outside, the Sun was going about its slow descent. The Moon had shown up a couple of hours early for work, only to find that there was a dreadful pall over the city. No animals frolicked about. Not a soul was seen out in the streets. The town that had been brimming with life two days ago was ghastly still. The card tables were empty, jump ropes went unused and lay tangled on the lawns, while bikes sat on their sides. The merry-go-round turned slowly from the blowing wind, and the empty swings rocked back and forth. The only sign of life came from the mosquitoes that zipped about the town as if they owned the place.

Meanwhile, no answers had been found for the surviving humans' current dilemma. How to escape town? The children grew bored from watching their parents think. They distracted themselves with idle talk, but they were beginning to get restless. "I wish I had my video game," Scott muttered.

Jayden nodded his head. "Me, too."

"Nonsense," Mr. Pugh said. "You don't need all those fancy gadgets to have a good time. Back in my day, the popular thing to play was marbles."

"What's that?" Tunisha asked. She lay on her cot stroking her snoozing sibling's hair.

"What's *that*!" Mr. Weber exclaimed. "You kids nowadays. I'll tell you what that is. Marbles was a game where you draw a circle on the ground and the players placed their marbles inside the circle—"

"Yeah, I remember walking around with my pouch full of prized marbles," interrupted Mrs. Byrd. "I was something else with that shooter."

"What's a shooter?" Scott asked.

"The shooter was a large marble that you shot into the circle in an attempt to hit the smaller marbles. Any marbles you knocked out of the circle was yours to keep."

Jayden let out a loud sarcastic yawn and the other two children laughed.

"You don't know what a good time is," said Mrs. Byrd. Her following question was directed at the adults. "Do y'all remember jacks?"

"What's that, a card game?" Scott asked.

"Naw it ain't a card game," Mr. Weber said. "There were these silver pieces that we placed on the ground. They had little legs to stand on, and there was a small rubber ball that was also needed to play the game. We would bounce the ball on the ground and swipe up as many jacks as we could before the ball came down again. After you got the jacks, you had to catch the ball before it hit the ground."

"And you used to get a fallen tree branch and push around a bicycle tire," Tunisha said with a laugh.

Jayden added, "Oh, don't forget how the only thing they got for Christmas was fruit."

"How can we forget?" Scott said with a chuckle. "They tell us all the time. Did y'all have to hear the story about how they use to go and get their own switches for their whippings?"

Tunisha and Jayden groaned together.

"Ya think you're funny don'tcha," Mr. Weber said when he heard the children rolling around on their cots in a fit of laughter. "I'll give y'all something to laugh about."

Blind Mr. Weber playfully lunged at the spot where he heard the children. Tunisha was the closest one so she happened to be the child grabbed by the big man. Mr. Weber found her armpits and started tickling, causing her to squirm and laugh uncontrollably.

"What's going on?" Latasha asked. All the hubbub had brought her from her nap. Mr. Weber started tickling her and she started laughing as well.

Jayden and Scott hopped up to their feet. The two boys ran to Tunisha's aid by jumping on Mr. Weber's back and tickling his sides. "Two against one is no fair," Mr. Weber called out. The other parents heard the merriment and decided to follow the sounds. In no time, help had arrived and a tickling match ensued. Parents against kids, kids against parents, even parents against parents. Before long, they were all laughing and having a good time.

Chapter 25

Inevitably, darkness fell about the town. The vampires awoke from their slumber. Starving for blood, the monsters ventured beyond their doors only to find that there was nothing to drink. Everyone was vampires! "We can't survive long in a dry city," one vampire said.

"We can go to Argo," another suggested. "Anybody got any gas money?"

"Alright, let's think before we do something stupid. If we all ride over to Argo and start feeding, how long do you think it'll take before we're discovered? We'll bring the wrath of the townfolk down on our heads."

"Hey, Momma! Lookit how many push-ups I can do!"

"I see you!" the mother gushed. "My baby's strong!"

"Well, what do you suppose we do about food?"

"The best solution would be to leave the town in shifts. Some will have to go further out. We can't have too many feeding in one area."

"Argo!" several vampires shouted at once. "No, I called it first!"

"Momma look! I can pick up this car!"

"Put that down before you hurt yourself!"

"There are like three hundred of us. We're going to have to relocate all over the United States. Like two per state."

"Alabama!" several vampires shouted at once.

"Nope, I called it first!"

"Hey! Is that Mr. Ripley's rottweiler?" The poor dog let out a loud yelp as the multitude of thirsty vampires went in pursuit.

***

Back in Mr. Weber's underground shelter, everyone was fast asleep. The place sounded like a log sawing contest. It was as if all the adults were trying to out snore the other. Poor Jayden was trapped in one of his nightmares again. Instead of walking alone through the woods, Jayden was with his father—Anthony Wallace. It was daytime, but in the boy's dreams, his nighttime and daytime look a lot alike. The sky was dark, but the Sun was a blood red, making the landscape red as well.

Anthony was observing the behaviors of giant, brown mosquitoes. The flying insects were the size of his hand. Jayden was not interested in the mosquitoes that flew about. He had a bucket in one hand and a fish net in the other. Jayden's eyes were focused on the stream.

"Come on, Jay, let's go down the stream a little bit more," Mr. Wallace said.

"Okay, Daddy."

The two of them walked through the dark woods, following the trickling stream. Jayden continued to look for life in the shallow water. Mr. Wallace scribbled notes in his steno pad. Eventually, the pair came to a place where a thick fog sat. There was nothing alarming about the mist so they continued through. Jayden gave up on his tadpole hunt, unable to find anything through the substance.

"Hey, it's a pond!" came Mr. Wallace's excited voice.

The fog was too thick for Jayden to see his father. "Daddy! Where are you?"

A hand extended from the mist followed by Mr. Wallace's face. "I gotcha, son, I'm not going to leave you." Jayden smiled at his father. Mr. Wallace returned the kind expression.

Mr. Wallace led his son to the pond and they stared at the still, black surface. "The mosquitoes' breeding grounds," he told Jayden.

Suddenly, they were aware of danger. Jayden and Mr. Wallace turned around just in time to see a vampire emerge from the trees. The creature leapt onto Mr. Wallace's back, burying his fangs into the man's neck. Jayden could only stare in horror. Mr. Wallace tried to fight the vampire, but the creature was too strong, so the man mustered all his strength so he could face his son and gurgle, "Run."

Chapter 26

"AAAAAHHHHHHHHH!" Tunisha awoke suddenly, screaming at the top of her lungs. She thrashed about wildly. Her violent, uncontrolled actions knocked Latasha onto the floor and flipped over Jayden's cot. The five-year-old girl immediately started crying.

Jayden hit the hard, cement floor, but he had a different reaction. "I'm up," he mumbled. As he rubbed his eyes, he realized that there was a lot of screaming and crying going on. "What's wrong?"

Tunisha did not give him a reply. She was busy clawing at her skin, but the burning sensation would not go away.

Everyone else in the room was soon snatched from their sleep. "What's going on?" Mrs. Pugh asked panicky. She recognized her older daughter's screaming and her younger daughter's crying. Her blindness had never made her feel so helpless as it did then.

Scott crawled over to where Tunisha was rolling around on the floor. "What's the matter?" he asked. The boy had to scream to be heard over her shouting. He took a hold of her shoulders trying to keep her still, but he soon found out that she was surprisingly strong. During his tussle with her, Scott caught a glance of her eyes. He saw that they were glowing red and he immediately loosed her and backed away.

"Tunisha's a vampire!" Scott yelled.

Jayden groaned. "Oh no…!"

"Not my baby!" Mrs. Pugh screamed.

Mr. Weber tried to remain calm. "Scott! Are there any other vampires or mosquitoes hiding in this room that could have done this to her?"

"No, sir," Scott said after a quick scan.

"She must've been bitten at the bus stop this morning," Jayden said sadly. He hated seeing her in such pain. "She said she left the house extra early. She had been at the stop for a while before Scott or me. I offered my insect repellant, but I guess it was too late."

"Why is she screaming like that?" Mr. Pugh wanted to know.

"It has to be the insect repellant we put on before going to sleep," Mr. Weber said. "It must be burning her skin."

"Spray her quick!" Mr. Byrd yelled from his spot on the floor.

"Right!" Scott said as he dived for his can of bug spray. Just as he grabbed the tall cylinder, Tunisha hopped to her feet and ran for the exit.

"Tunisha! Noooooooooo!" Jayden yelled. He tried to get to her before it was too late, but she had unfastened the locks and ran out into the night.

Mr. Pugh embraced his hysterical wife.

"I'm going to get her!" Jayden declared without a moment's hesitation.

"You're not going out there!" Mrs. Byrd yelled just as quick.

"Your mom is right," Mr. Weber said. "If you go out there to save her, neither one of you will come back."

Jayden stared up at underground exit. He looked at the night sky, but all he could see in his mind was Tunisha's smiling face. He thought about how much fun she had throughout the day. Jayden thought about her plans to ride her new bicycle. The child thought about how sweet she was, how kind she was, and …how soft her hand felt in his hand.

He came back down the ladder. He walked back to his overturned cot and started gathering his bug spray cans and water guns. "I'm going to get Tunisha."

"Jayden! You listen to your mother!" Mr. Byrd screamed. "You're not going out there!"

"Before the vampires fully showed themselves, you two were always telling me that I need to go outside and play more. Just two days ago, you wanted me to go out and get some fresh air. Well, here's me going outside."

Scott watched his friend get ready to go outside alone. "Dad, I love you. We'll be back soon with Tunisha."

Mr. Weber could not find the strength to forbid his son, nor give his blessings.

Jayden looked over at Scott as the boy gathered his gear as well.

"Thanks," Jayden said. Scott just smiled.

After they had their stuff together, the boys climbed up the ladder. Their feet clanged on the metal rungs. "Y'all be careful!" Mr. Weber yelled finally. His voice wavered and tears came from his eyes. He knew he would never see his son again.

Chapter 27

A scream pierced the night air—Tunisha's scream.

"Come on, she went this way," Jayden said as he hurried toward a grouping of trees.

The two boys sped into the woods with the full moon following overhead. The giant orb gave off enough light for Scott and Jayden to navigate the woods without seriously hurting themselves. They jumped over fallen logs, and ducked under low hanging tree branches. The duo weaved throughout the trees while listening to Tunisha cries of pain. The vampire girl was getting farther away and the noise she made was becoming harder to follow.

"Is there anyway that this is going to end in our favor?" Scott asked.

"Sure there is. You just have to believe in the magic of friendship," Jayden replied with a laugh.

"If I knew that's all we had to rely on, then I could have stayed at the shelter and sent you some positive vibes."

"Well, thanks for coming with me."

"No problem," Scott said. "That's what buds are for. Plus, you already got four vampires to my one. This is a good time to catch up."

In time, they could no longer hear Tunisha's screams, but the boys continued their course. Every once in a while, Jayden and Scott would cry out from being scratched by thorny vines. The cruel plants dug into their clothing and cut their skin. Bloody whips were all over their bodies. Nevertheless, the boys gritted through the pain and kept running.

***

"Stupid dog! Where could he have gotten off to?" a vampire asked.

"Who knows! He'll have to come out sooner or later."

"Momma! Lookit how high I can jump!"

"Very nice," the mother vampire said without looking at her child. The boy was chipping away at her last nerves.

"Hey! Do you smell that?" another vampire asked. "Smells like fresh blood!"

"I think you're right! It's coming from that direction!"

All at once, the vampires abandoned what they were doing and hurried toward the scent. An aroma that happened to be coming from Scott and Jayden's multiple cuts and bruises. "Last three hundred or so there are thirsty vampires!"

Mr. Ripley was at home when he smelled the blood. "King, is that you?" he called hopefully. He hurried out onto his front porch just in time to see a mob of bloodthirsty vampires sprint past his residence. The old vampire sniffed the air. "Nope, it's not King. Smells too sweet to be dog. Children maybe. But what children could be…oh, no!"

Mr. Ripley stood on the porch and watched with growing sympathy as vampire after vampire ran past his house chasing the scent. There was no way that the kids would withstand such an attack. "Well, what is immortal life if you have to live with guilt for all eternity?" the old man asked himself. He quickly stepped off the porch and headed to his backyard. "After all, they did spare my life. I suppose the least I could do is try to save theirs."

Mr. Ripley went through the opening in his rusty, chain link fence. He bypassed the leaky faucet and overlooked the dilapidated shed. He sped walked through the waist high grass until he came to his long, unused barn. Using his superhuman strength, which was not much, Mr. Ripley slid the barn door open. A decaying smell hit the old vampire in his face, but he bore the wretched odor. He immediately saw what he had come for.

"It's been a long time since I've used this baby," Mr. Ripley said as he walked over to his small, red and white aircraft. He rubbed a hand across the grimy exterior. "It's been a very long time, but now we have some crops that need dusting and some pest that need getting rid of."

Chapter 28

Without warning, the boys burst from the woods and came upon a small clearing. A light mist covered the ground, and in the middle of the clearing was a large, stagnant pond that fed a thin stream. Hundreds of mosquitoes flew all over the clearing.

The boys both came to a halt. Jayden stopped out of fear, Scott came to a standstill out of indecision.

"Which way should we—Jayden, what's the matter with you?"

A horrified expression was etched in Jayden's facial features. After seven long years, the boy had finally returned to the place that had haunted both his memories and his dreams. "This is the place my daddy was taken from me."

"Vampires?"

Jayden nodded his head. "Remember when I told you about my dad? How he use to take me out into the woods when he was doing his bug research?"

"Yeah, I remember."

"One night, Daddy decided to go out and observe the mosquitoes. Back then I was always following him around. I was his little shadow. So, I went along with him that night." Jayden pointed down the brook and said, "We walked along that stream. He was jotting notes into his steno pad, I was looking in the water for critters. Before long, we came to this pond. It's a huge breeding ground for the mosquitoes. As Daddy gushed over the find, he was attacked by a vampire. They had just come to the town and Daddy was the first victim. It would be months before they finally made themselves known."

"I'm sorry to hear that," Scott said. "I can see why you don't like going outside."

Jayden shook his head. "No that's not it. I remember telling my mother what happened, but they never found a body. My mom was heartbroken. She thought Daddy had run off. One day, I was determined to find my daddy's body and prove that he didn't run away.

"I went out into the woods alone and followed the stream to this pond. That's when a swarm of mosquitoes attacked me. I was so busy fighting them off, that I failed to notice how close I was to the water. I fell in. I grabbed hold of this tree root…that one right over there…and I started pulling myself out. All of a sudden, a hand shot out of the water and grabbed my ankle. I looked down and recognized the wedding band on the hand. It was Daddy. Daddy started pulling me into that water, but before he could take me in too far, his hand started smoking from the light of the Sun. His hand went back under. I ran away and never went back outside unless it was when I was going to school or somewhere like that."

"Wow!" was the only thing Scott could say.

"Yeah, I know," Jayden replied. "You're the first person I've ever told. I haven't even told my parents what happened to my dad."

Without warning, the pond's water started bubbling as if it was boiling. Jayden and Scott took several steps back. There was a loud splashing noise, then two individuals shot into the air and landed on the bank. A soaking wet Tunisha quickly crouched as if in a defensive position. Her red eyes were focused on the individual in front of her—another vampire. The second vampire held two broken sticks in his hands. The jagged edges were pointed at Tunisha.

Scott looked from the second vampire to Jayden, from Jayden to the second vampire. The two looked as if they could have been twins. "Your father?"

Jayden stared in amazement at the man…the vampire he had not seen in seven years. "Yeah, that's my dad…."

Mr. Wallace let out a battle cry and charged at the girl vampire. His makeshift stakes led the way. Seeing that his father was intending to kill his secret crush, Jayden darted forward. "DADDY! NOOOOOO!"

Chapter 29

Jayden jumped in front of a frightened Tunisha. The boy lifted his supersoaker and pointed the plastic muzzle at his father. "Daddy! Don't slay her!"

"She's a vampire!" Mr. Wallace said.

"You're a vampire!" Scott screamed. He was aiming his supersoaker at the adult vampire as well.

Mr. Wallace quickly glanced at Scott then he returned his attention back to Jayden. "Why are you pointing water guns at me?"

"We found the cure for vampirism. Ready for your shot?'

"Okay! Why are you pointing your guns at me? Point 'em at her!"

"Are you saying we should trust you over her?" Jayden asked.

"That's exactly what I'm saying. I'm trying to protect you. I've always tried to protect you."

"Why did you try to drown me when I was five? I know that was you, I recognized your hand."

"I wasn't trying to drown you," Mr. Wallace said. "I saw you fall into the water and I couldn't help myself. I had to go to

113

you, to let you know that I was somewhat alive. I grabbed your ankle, but you started screaming, then the sun started burning me. That was when I realized that my old life was over and I could never return. I stopped trying to contact you after that."

Jayden stood there digesting his father's words. They sounded honest enough.

"Just turn around and spray your little friend there before I finish her myself."

"Don't do it, Jayden!" Tunisha pleaded. "If you cure me then he'll get all three of us. I can protect us while I'm a vampire."

"She makes a good point, Jay!" Scott said.

Mr. Wallace lowered his hands. "Jayden, remember what I taught you? Do you remember the black widow spider, the praying mantis, the mosquito, or the wasp? Take your pick. How did I teach you to apply those cases to your everyday life? What did I tell you over and over again?"

The praying mantis female eats the male. Only the female mosquito drinks blood. Jayden looked up at his father and said, "They may look beautiful and innocent, but you told me never to trust a female anything."

"Exactly."

Jayden spun around, but he was too late. Tunisha let out a beastly howl and launched at the boy. She was almost upon him, but a strong blast of water hit her in the face. She cried out in agony and dropped to the ground, rubbing her burning eyes.

"I'm glad I was able to teach you something," Mr. Wallace told his son.

Jayden smiled up at his father. More than anything, he wanted to go and embrace his dad, but a noise caused his expression to change. A lot of hooting and hollering was heard coming from the woods.

"I can smell them! There's three of them!"

"I'm going to get me one all to myself!"

Vampires! Mr. Wallace and the children were completely surrounded by hurried footsteps and crunching forest debris. "I think we have company!" Scott said.

The boys moved closer to a newly blind Tunisha who lay on the ground weeping. "You wouldn't happen to have any war games at home would you?" Jayden asked.

"Of course I do."

"Are you any good?"

"I guess we'll find out just how good both of us are in a few seconds," Scott said. The boys pumped their supersoakers and waited for the vampire assault to come from the woods.

Chapter 30

A great battle broke out near that stagnant pond: *The war for Stagnant Waters*. Over three hundred thirsty vampires descended on the Scott, Jayden, and a blind Tunisha. They came jumping out of the treetops and running across the ground on all sides. Jayden and Scott stood back to back and began firing their water guns. It did not matter where they shot. Nine times out of ten, they were going to hit a vampire in the face.

With an improvised wooden stake in each hand, Mr. Wallace moved around the boys with unbelievable speed. The good vampire floated like a butterfly, stung like bee. Any vampire that managed to elude the water guns disappeared in a puff of ash.

"Hey! There's Mrs. Wright! She failed me in her math class!" Jayden shouted. He turned his water gun toward her and blasted her in the face.

"Good thinking!" Scott yelled over the tumult. "I haven't had a chance to do my homework, so if you see Mr. Lyons let him through. I want your dad to take care of him."

The boys laughed despite the never ending onslaught. The poor vampires that Jayden and Scott shot would fall to the ground screaming only to be jumped on by the starving vampires that followed. The smell of blood was everywhere and it slowed the charge, but the vampires kept coming.

"I'm out of water!" Scott yelled.

"Me, too!"

The boys dropped their large water guns simultaneously and removed both cans of bug spray from their front pockets. "Daddy! You might want to move away!" Jayden called.

Not knowing what the boys had in mind, Mr. Wallace obediently moved away and started slaying vampires in other areas. "Follow my lead!" Jayden screamed at Scott. The child held both hands out to his sides and began to spin, creating a three hundred and sixty circumference of protection. As he spun he began to walk around Tunisha who continued to sit on the ground crying. The noises surrounding her were frightening and she knew it was only a matter of time before she was eaten. Scott began to do the same thing. They closed their eyes and held there breaths as they created a large cloud of bug spray.

Vampires were being slain by Mr. Wallace and others were being cured by Jayden and Scott only to be feasted on by more vampires. The population of Margret was steadily dwindling like a microwave timer. The boys' spray cans were spent in no time. When they came to a stop, Scott and Jayden fell to the ground dizzy. The world spun around like a carousel that had a Hemi motor and the boys felt extremely nauseous.

Vampires saw that the bug spray cloud was gone and they began to move in on the dizzy boys and the terrified, blind girl. Mr. Wallace tried to slay more, but even he was growing tired and getting slower.

I suppose this is it, Jayden thought as he stared up at the sky. The large moon was circling him, laughing at his predicament. Just when he was prepared to face his demise, another object appeared in the sky. *Is it a bird...a plane? I think it's a plane!*

Mr. Wallace heard a sound coming from the sky which caused him to look up. Approaching the clearing was a red and white crop duster, and following the small aircraft was a large cloud of pesticide that was steadily being released.

Mr. Wallace quickly abandoned the fight he was currently in and ran for the pond. SPLASH! Just as the plane flew overhead and the whole area was dusted, the vampire disappeared into the murky water. The other vampires were too distracted with feasting to be concerned with anything else. Mr. Ripley and his small plane made a U-turn and the old vampire continued to spray the entire area.

Epilogue

Once again, all the vampires were no more. The blood-suckers had either been cured, or vanquished. However, there was no celebrating the event. The people of Margret would not have been able to party even if they wanted to mark the occasion. The remaining townsfolk that had not been destroyed while being vampires, or eaten by vampires after being cured, were inside their homes coping with their blindness. It took the rest of the night and half the next morning for Mr. Ripley and Mr. Wallace to get everyone to their homes, or someplace safe.

The only two people who were not vampires and not blind—Jayden and Scott—were carried home and placed in bed. The boys had become very sick after breathing in so much pesticide that had been dropped from the plane. And that is how the seven year war against vampires ended. The conclusion was quite gruesome.

In the end, what seemed like a hopeless situation began to brighten a bit. Two days after the battle, Mr. and Mrs. Byrd received their eyesight back. The rest of the townspeople began to gain their sight seventy-two hours after being sprayed. Some of the people went outside to discover that Mr. Ripley and Mr. Wallace had not been idle. Every night, the two vampires took turns flying the crop duster over the entire town. The mosquito population was nearly decimated.

***

"This is awesome!" Tunisha yelled as she tilted her head back and let the warm air blow across her face. The girl was feeling mighty exhilarated as she sped down the road on her new bicycle.

Jayden was having just as much fun riding his new bike, but he was tired. The three of them had been bicycling for hours and the Sun was setting. "Tunisha!" the child called out. "I think it's time that we go inside." All of the vampires were gone, but the town still had a strict curfew.

"He's right," Scott said. He brought his bike alongside Jayden's. "It's almost dark."

"Alright," Tunisha reluctantly replied, "but y'all have to promise that we'll go riding right after school tomorrow."

The two boys laughed and promised that they would. After they said their goodbyes, the children went their separate ways. Jayden flew down the hill that led to his house and turned into his driveway. He jumped off his bicycle at the base of the stairs and was about to go inside, but his attention was drawn to the woods. After a moment of deliberation, Jayden propped his bicycle up with its kickstand and hurried across the muddy yard to enter the woods.

Jayden journeyed until he came to the stream associated with his childhood and he sat down on the mucky bank. He was not concerned with the seat of his pants getting soiled, nor was he worried about the wet sensation he was feeling on his buttocks.

Jayden sat there and stared at the slow moving water.

"Life will return to the stream in due time."

The startled child flinched, then turned to the familiar voice. The first thing he saw was his father's red eyes beneath a wide brimmed hat. "You scared me."

Mr. Wallace, looking like an old western outlaw, sat down on the bank next to his son. "I get that a lot."

"I suppose you would," Jayden said as he turned his attention back to the brook.

"So how are you feeling?"

"Good," Jayden replied.

Mr. Wallace smiled. "What brings you to my neck of the woods so close to nightfall?"

Jayden picked up a small rock and threw it into the water. There was a soft plunk, then the area was silent again. "Why haven't you been cured?" the boy asked. "Is the need for blood overpowering your desire to be human again?"

Mr. Wallace laughed. "Well, I would love to be human again, but I think the best thing for everybody would be for me to stay a vampire."

"How would that be best? I need you and I bet Mom would like to see you."

"And I would love to see your mom, but I still have feelings for her. Seeing each other again might rekindle our past love and that won't be good."

"Why not?" Jayden asked.

"Because your mom has remarried. If I was to come back on the scene, that would not be fair to either of them."

Jayden had never thought of it like that.

Mr. Wallace continued, "And you needn't worry about my bloodlust. I haven't drunk blood a day in my vampire life."

"How is that possible? You must drink something."

"Remember how I told you that only the female mosquito drinks blood and that's to nourish her eggs."

Jayden nodded his head.

"Well, the males drink plant nectar. When I became a vampire, I tried tree sap and plant juice and discovered that nectar quenches the burning in my throat just as well as blood would. I guess you can say I'm a vegetarian. I passed this little tidbit on to Mr. Ripley and he's doing just fine."

"I guess I'll just have to deal with everything as it is then," Jayden said sadly.

Mr. Wallace placed his arm around his son's shoulder. "Everything will be fine. And you know I'm not far away."

Jayden smiled up at his father.

All of a sudden, a spider crawled onto the child's leg ruining the sentimental moment. Jayden instantly froze, afraid that if he made any sudden movement the spider would bite him.

"Calm down," Mr. Wallace said with a laugh. "You don't have to be afraid of that little guy. It's called a wolf spider. Their bite is not harmful to humans so you have nothing to worry about."

Jayden heard his father, but the words did nothing to ease his apprehension. "You wanna get it off me?" he asked nervously.

Instead of going to his son's aid, the man just stared at the eight-legged creature. "There're a lot just like him running around these woods. My guess is that the large mosquito population attracted them here. Stagnant Waters was like an all you can eat buffet to them. I'm glad to see that they've survived the dusting. Probably because the wolf spiders dig tunnels. They're also known to hide under rocks and sticks."

Jayden looked at the spider. He noticed that it was shaped differently than any spider he knew, but there was nothing really unusual about the arachnid. It was a simple brown spider, wasn't even hairy. "Why is it called a wolf spider?"

Mr. Wallace shrugged his shoulders. "I'm not sure, but that'll be something good for you to research—"

"OUCH!" Jayden yell. He kicked his leg and knocked the spider onto the ground. "Your harmless wolf spider just bit me!" Father and son watched as the spider scuttled off and disappeared beneath a large leaf.

Without warning, Jayden began to feel woozy, his skin felt like it was on fire. "Are you sure…that the spider bite…that the bite isn't poisonous?" he asked as he stumbled to his feet.

Mr. Wallace quickly went to his son. "Are you—"

Hair started sprouting all over the child's body. Jayden began to scream as his whole structure began to mutate, causing him to shift into something altogether inhuman. "Daddy! I think you better get back!" the boy yelled. The last thing he remembered was looking up at the newly risen moon and releasing a bone chilling howl.

THE NIGHT
WE DIDN'T GO HOME

BY G.R. MOSCA

The yellow school bus creaked and clattered along country roads and rural highways with its precious cargo of children, some of whom yawned sleepily after a day of running and playing in the warm afternoon, others who looked curiously out of the windows at the slowly setting sun; catching the wind in their hands as they rested their small arms on the metal frame of the window glass.

A transistor radio nestled against the front windshield played tunes from an earlier decade; music that evoked drag races, dead man's curves and love lost and longed for. The driver leaned toward the radio, momentarily swerving the bus in the same direction, and turned the dial. Static issued from the tiny speaker followed by snatches of unrecognizable music and dialogue; a random word insistently shouting through the noise. Suddenly the moan of a pedal-steel guitar and Hank Williams' soothing voice filled the front of the bus.

"That's what I'm talkin' about; Hank can strum that g'itar for sure. Sum'bitch can sing."

"Mr. Fishell, *language, Please.*" Katie gave the driver an eyeful that said, *"Watch your mouth, buster, these kids are my responsibility. Shut up and just drive the damn bus."*

"Sorry, ma'am. Just sayin', that sum'bitch can sing."

Mr. Fishell smiled knowing he was treading on thin ice with Katie but not caring too much. He was a gristled older man with a complexion that came from spending too much time out in the sun. His family had farmed in the area for generations and he still planted a small parcel of land every spring. He had been driving a school bus for the Unified School District of Spring

121

Grove for thirty years and was close to retiring. He honestly didn't care what some sixteen-year-old camp counselor thought about his use of the English language.

Katie left her seat and walked very slowly to Mr. Fishell. She leaned closely to him to whisper softly in his ear, "Listen, you old bastard, I hear any one of these kids saying *sum'bitch* or anything that isn't taught in Sunday school, I will tear you a new one the next time I see you on this bus. Okay?" Katie stood and stared down at Mr. Fishell with a smile on her face that you will only find on beauty pageant contestants or game show hosts.

"Yes, ma'am. I was just sayin'..."

Katie pointed an index finger at him, "Enough."

Mr. Fishell spit out of his side window onto the road and mumbled under his breath something only he and God could hear. At that moment a newscaster's voice emitted from the small transistor radio speaker:

> *We interrupt this broadcast with late-breaking news from our affiliates in Philadelphia. We have received several reports of animal attacks involving residents in these areas. As of this broadcast these attacks are unconfirmed but several deaths are being reported. More on this story as information becomes available. We now return you to your regularly scheduled program.*

The sweet sounds of Hank Williams' band returned in time to wrap up their tune. As Katie walked back to her seat, she looked curiously at Roger, her fellow counselor, with raised eyebrows.

"What kind of animal attacks are they talking about?"

"Beats me, Katie, rabid dogs, crazed pigeons, maybe squirrels hopped-up on acorns?" Roger laughed. Katie glanced back at the children behind her. She smiled, too, "That's not funny, Roger."

"Yeah, but what kind of animals do they have in the city that we don't have here in Spring Grove? Seriously, Katie, the crap they put on the news when there are real problems in this country. It's just smoke and mirrors."

"Goddamn hippies if you ask me," Mr. Fishell mumbled under his breath. Katie gave him a withering glance that brought his full attention back to the road.

The sun slid further down on the horizon illuminating the sky with a pleasant pink glow. Mr. Fishell, Katie, Roger and the seven children on the yellow school bus watched the sky fade into a lavender velvet evening. A faint moon barely peeked out over a blanket of clouds as a stray light blazed across the sky.

Roger grasped Katie's hand in his and whispered to her, "Look at that, a falling star. Quick, make a wish, Katie." She squeezed his hand back and looked longingly into his eyes. She didn't have to tell him what her wish was. Every sixteen-year-old has the same wish when she is in love. Roger smiled at her and tenderly stroked her hand.

Penny, one of the twins sitting behind Roger and Katie started to make a gagging sound; her twin sister Jenny completed her thought. "Eeewwww. Roger and Katie sitting in a tree. K-I-S-S-I-N-G." Katie turned around and smiled. The other children on the bus picked up the song: "First comes love. Then comes marriage. Then comes Miss Katie with a baby carriage." Katie heard one of the children (probably James) say, "retard" instead of baby. She made a mental note to sort this out later with the boy.

Everyone, with the exception of Mr. Fishell, started laughing now as the darkening sky gradually passed into night.

"All right, kids, fun's over. Let's settle down. We'll be home soon and I'm sure your parents don't need you wound up more than you already are." Katie was still smiling as she admonished the children but Roger looked irritated.

She scanned the row of seats mentally checking to make sure all the children were present. Jenny and Penny, the twins, were directly behind where she and Roger were seated. Penny was dressed as Cinderella with flowing blue gown, tiara and scepter. Jenny wore a witch's costume complete with peaked black cap, and matching frock. In her small hand, Jenny held the ubiquitous Barbie doll that never left her side. It was often the cause of endless teasing from her sister, but also an odd source of comfort to her.

Seated across from the twins sat James. He was a tall and lanky boy with flaming red hair and a perpetual sour expression. He was a bully in the making, possessing ham-sized fists, a bad attitude and hair-trigger temper. Perhaps it was no coincidence that he wore a devil's costume complete with horns and a red-spiked pitchfork. Katie thought the costume was almost too fitting for James and smiled while at the same time feeling sorry for him. Next to James was his best friend Daniel (*Lord knows why*, Katie thought). Daniel was well liked by his classmates, a very personable boy who enjoyed roughhousing with friends and playing sports. Even at his age, he had a lean and powerful frame and excelled in any game in which he participated. In a few years, he would probably turn his full attention to sports and girls though not necessarily in that order. Daniel was wearing his little league baseball uniform. He set his cap jauntily over his brow and kept his Louisville Slugger close to his side.

Andrew and Brian sat in the row behind Daniel and James. They too were best of friends but unlike Daniel and James, they kept to themselves and were often the focus and brunt of James' bullying. Andrew was small-framed and shy. He had jet-black hair and for this Halloween party, wore a Super-man costume. Andrew loved Superman and digested Adventure Comics with an unabated voraciousness. He often daydreamed about flying around Spring Grove plucking kittens out of trees or saving friends in distress. Katie really liked Andrew for his quiet dignity and the respect he showed everyone around him. Brian, like Andrew seemed small for his age and was also a shy boy. Brian was particularly disliked for some reason by James and perhaps that brought him and Andrew closer as friends. Brian wore the costume of a gun fighter from the old west, complete with chaps, bandana kerchief and two holstered six-shooters.

Sarah sat quietly a few rows back. She was that rare youth who would be a great beauty when she finally matured into adulthood. Her long blonde hair cascaded down her back and sides framing a classic countenance which seemed to perpetually wear a bored and disinterested expression. She idly inspected the ends of her hair while balancing her cheerleader baton across her lap. At times she and Daniel would hang out together but at their tender age it was more platonic than romantic. Perhaps given a few more years the two of them might be crowned Homecoming King and Queen or something commensurate with their popularity and beauty.

Katie turned towards Roger who was dressed in an oversized pinstriped suit and bald-cap. "Who are you supposed to be again?"

Roger turned and smiled, "Inspector Clay."

"I don't think I know that one."

Roger stretched his arms out in front of him and made a growling noise as he pretended to lumber towards the twins. "Rrrrrrarghhhh!" Both girls laughed and shrank in mock terror. Roger turned back towards Katie, "Inspector Clay? *Plan 9 From Outer Space?*"

Katie still wore a blank expression as she turned towards him, suddenly feeling that something was watching her. Just over Roger's shoulder she spied the pale visage of a stranger looking at her through the window of the school bus, returning her stare. It floated in space beyond the edge of the road easily keeping pace with the bus' progress while it scowled at her with a mocking and judgmental expression. The appearance of this phantom startled her, sending a seismic shiver through her body. Roger's amused expression turned inquisitive then concerned. Katie focused her attention again at the face staring at her, while knitting her brow in confusion before realizing it was her own reflection in the window glass. She had forgotten the costume she was wearing: a ghost complete with whitened face, hands, flowing grey gown and cowl. She had not recognized the thing in the window, the sight of her reflection momentarily seeming foreign and frightening to her. Katie let out an uncomfortable laugh and rubbed her arm now dappled with tiny goose bumps. In counterpoint to her momentary shock, the horizon crackled with lightening as sheets of rain suddenly began pounding the roof of the bus and road. The twins let out a shriek as Katie involuntarily jumped again.

"Hang on, we're in for a bumpy ride," Mr. Fishell warned over the thunder.

Although it was just past six o'clock, the sun had disappeared behind a curtain of darkness. Mr. Fishell steered the clumsy bus around fishtail curves and switchbacks with skill and care, but the steadily driving rain hampered their progress towards home. To compound the problem, more than once the bus had to veer past their usual route because of a washed out road caused by flash flooding. Mr. Fishell's knowledge of the area was encyclopedic and Katie more than once thanked her stars that he was driving. She almost wished that she hadn't been so curt with him now that he was doing his best to get them all back home safe and sound. Throughout all of this the radio broadcast a steady stream of static punctuated every so often with snippets of music or the nightly news updates. As they turned a corner, the radio burst into life:

> *...confirm with our affiliates that earlier accounts of animal attacks in major cities have been updated. Reports are now coming in to our station that unknown assailants are attacking individuals, many of whom have sustained serious injuries resulting in death. Unconfirmed reports from other areas are even more unusual saying that individuals killed in these attacks are somehow coming back to life and attacking others. We will have more information as it comes in to our news-*

room.

In a related story, astrono-mers are speculating on the appear-ance of a meteor over North Ameri-ca earlier this evening...

Katie and Roger looked at one another as the radio broadcast blared back into incomprehensible static. Roger was the one who said it first; "This must be a joke, like the *War of the Worlds* broadcast. I mean it is Halloween, right?"

Meanwhile, the children grew restless. Katie could see that Jenny looked like she wanted to cry. James had grown excited (she was sure he muttered "cool" when the broadcast mentioned people coming back to life) and the rest of the children began a buzz of conversation amongst themselves. Only Sarah still maintained a bored expression and an attitude of disinterest regarding events unfolding around them.

Andrew pressed his hands to either side of his face and peered out of the bus window. He was fascinated with storms and loved the way they would light up the sky and the surrounding countryside. As the bus navigated the twists and turns of the narrow road, he was amazed at the way a cornfield would suddenly light up sending fingers of shadowy stalks across the neighboring fields and then all would be dark again until the next flash. Andrew waited impatiently for that next bolt of lightening when the meadow they were driving past was suddenly lit up and in the distance, he saw small figures running across it towards the road, then all was dark again. This odd scene piqued his curiosity as he held his breath and waited for the next flash. A crack of thunder sounded across the valley and he literally jumped in his seat. Brian gently pushed his friend away from him. "What's up, Andy?" he chided.

Andrew ignored him and pressed his face back on to the glass. A new flash illuminated the field once again, and Andrew spied the figures running towards the road, closer now and larger, however, added to this tableau were new figures in the foreground advancing towards the runners. These new figures moved in an odd way, a way Andrew couldn't quite make sense of yet. The sky darkened again. Andrew felt a nudge on his shoulder; he almost jumped out of his skin. This time it was James.

"What are you lookin' for, faggot? Is your boyfriend out there?"

"Leave it alone, James. He's just looking out the friggin' window," Brian came to his defense.

"I'm lookin' out the window," was all Andrew could say.

"Jealous he might find somebody better than you?" James directed this to Brian who started to redden in the face.

"Leave us alone or I'll tell Miss Katie you're bothering us."

"Tell her and you're dead." James' face began to redden, but he wore a mischievous grin.

Andrew felt the next crack of thunder and jumped again in his seat, accidentally pushing into James.

"Get off me, faggot!" James pushed back and Andrew found his face pressed against the window as a flash of lightening again lit up the sky. In that millisecond of light, he couldn't understand what he was seeing. The lumbering figures had joined with the running figures in the middle of the field. They were twisting and moving now as one. Were they dancing, playing, or fighting? He couldn't be sure. Darkness engulfed them again.

He distantly heard James muttering something and Brian whispering something back to him but Andrew was frozen at his place by the window. Another crack of thunder failed to move him from his spot. Then a final bolt of lightning lit up the field like a flashbulb going off in a dark room and he imagined he saw the bodies of those runners being torn limb from limb and flung about like straw in the wind. He could barely hear himself screaming over the final peal of thunder.

Andrew, eyes tightly shut, was now screaming at the top of his lungs while James slapped and punched him. Brian was trying to grab hold of James' arms and fists in an attempt to help his friend. It was only with great self-control that Brian did not burst into tears in response to the surprise and sudden ferocity of James' attack.

Katie flew over the bench seats and grabbed James by the collar of his costume pulling him off and away from the other boys. James turned and in the heat of the moment raised his fist at Katie but stopped himself in time. Instead, he lowered his hand and still breathing heavily mumbled, "bitch" under his breath. Katie's arm was a blur of motion as she slapped him hard; leaving a dark crimson mark on his cheek that remained there for several minutes. All sounds stopped on the bus with the crack of her slap and every eye was now on James to see what he would do next. James' face flushed red as he stared daggers at Katie. For seconds that seemed to go on forever they stared each other down but James could not hold her gaze. He shrugged her hand off his collar and stalked off to the back of the bus muttering an incomprehensible string of expletives and threats under his breath. James took the last seat with a heavy thud and violently kicked the bench in front of him.

"You do that again an' I'll show you some kickin', boy," Mr. Fishell yelled towards the back of the bus adding "sum'bitch" to the tail end of his pronouncement. This seemed to calm James down immediately. For all his bravado, most everyone respected Mr. Fishell and no one wanted to get on his bad side.

Brian put an arm around his friend who had now quieted down; Katie leaned over the boys with concern in her voice, "What happened, buddy?" Andrew looked up at her with big watery eyes and pointed with his finger towards the window.

"He was looking out the window during the storm," Brian started, "something spooked him."

Sporadic bursts of lightning flashed in the distance illuminating patches of grey clouds. The storm was moving away leaving behind a driving rain. Katie leaned toward the glass and looked out into the blackness. She couldn't see anything that might be unusual enough to upset anyone. "There's nothing out there, silly." She tousled his hair and touched his cheek with her hand. "Are you going to be okay?"

"Yes, Miss Katie. I'm sorry."

"Do you want to sit up there with me?"

"No, Miss Katie. I'll be good."

In the meantime, Roger had gotten out of his seat and walked back to where James was now pouting. Roger did not approach James; he simply sat in the opposite row across from him. The only sounds in the bus now were the crackle of the radio and the rain steadily tapping on the roof. All else was quiet for the moment. For this, Roger was glad.

>*...several theories are being discussed. One theory posits that the violent behavior in these incidents is the result of a chemical contamination of unknown origin in the water supplies of the affected areas. City officials are investigating the possibility of a communist plot of epic proportions while others are blaming the hippie or youth movement of dumping toxic levels of LSD in reservoirs and treatment plants. Tonight's guest is Staff Sergeant Dickerson of the Army Rangers, recently returned from a tour in Viet Nam. He will discuss Agent Orange and other chemical weapons and their effects on...*

Katie felt the bus round a curve and gradually slow down. Through the rain, she could make out a pair of car headlights pointing off towards the side of the road. As the bus drew closer, she could see a Rebel Rambler blocking the road, its front end wrapped around a tree trunk. The blare of its horn was unrelenting and unmistakable even with the sound of the rain. The bus crawled to a stop and she heard the ratcheting of the emergency brake as Mr. Fishell pulled the keys out of the ignition and fumbled for his coat. The engine died and every surface of the bus now seemed to echo the sound of the driving rain and the blare of the Rambler's horn.

"Katie, y'all stay here. I have to go see if anybody is hurt."

"Wait up, Mr. Fishell, I can go with you." Roger was already moving towards the front of the bus.

"Y'all can wait in here. No sense both of us gettin' drenched. Either someone is hurt, dead or long gone. If I need you, I'll come git you."

Roger momentarily stopped then moved towards Katie. "You definitely give a yell if you need me."

Mr. Fishell opened the folding doors, muttered a "sum'bitch" which everyone heard (Katie and even a few of the children couldn't help but chuckle at this pronouncement) and then he was outside heading towards the car in the road.

Not many things frightened Mr. Fishell but as he approached the vehicle, he felt a shiver run down his spine. The maroon body of the Rambler reminded him of a leviathan that had been beached and left for dead. The blare of the horn sounded like the wail of a dying beast, intensifying in volume as he drew closer. When he reached the vehicle, he noticed the windows facing him were fogged up preventing a clear view of the interior. He could not yet tell if there was anyone in the Rambler. He cautiously walked around the car noting a large radial crack in the front windshield; possibly caused by the driver's head smashing into it at a high rate of speed. The center of the crack bore a dark, crimson stain, not a good sign. The front end was crushed and wrapped around an old hickory tree, with smoke still emanating from under the hood. How long ago did this happen?

Mr. Fishell next tried the driver's door. Locked. He put his face up to the driver's window and could barely discern the outline of a figure slumped forward in the bucket seat, head lying against the steering wheel. Not a good sign at all. He walked over to the passenger side and tried the door. It was unlocked, its handle lifting easily and unlatching from the pillar. He swung the passenger door open wide and looked in. He saw a young man, in his early twenties, wearing a red plaid hunting jacket, denims and boots. The man's head was pressed against the center of the steering wheel. Mr. Fishell placed his knee on the passenger seat; the interior of the car felt hot and clammy; and from inside, the horn blared even more loudly. He tentatively put his hand on the man's shoulder and shook it. "Y'all right?" No answer. Then he felt the man's neck for a pulse and found none. "Sum'bitch." He mumbled. Falling heavily into the seat, he tried to think of how to proceed, but merely stared out at the cracked windshield not knowing what to do next.

Sitting next to a dead man is unsettling in itself and hardly something anyone would take lightly, but Mr. Fishell had been in the "Great War" and had seen his share of death. However, Halloween being what it is, he might have possessed the insight to exit that car as quickly as humanly possible, but not tonight. As Mr. Fishell sat contemplating the spider web of fractures in the glass, he failed to notice that the car horn had suddenly stopped blaring. He barely had time to take in the fact that a corpse he now saw reflected in the windshield was lifting its head and turning its ruined countenance towards him. When he turned towards it, he didn't have time to notice the flap of skin torn from its cheek to its chin nor its bloodstained teeth now fixed in a sardonic smile. He could not comprehend how it suddenly locked its teeth onto the front of his face to begin tearing at his flesh. He did not know the exact moment of his death or his reawakening as something else, but when he finally opened his eyes he was suddenly very, very hungry.

The sky cleared revealing a moon whose ghostly pale light cast eerie shadows along the sides of the road and across the hood and roof of the crashed vehicle. The inside of the school bus was pitch black as the children talked nervously amongst each other or stared out of the windows at the trees and the darkness beyond. Katie and Roger had watched intently as Mr. Fishell strode towards the car in the road. They had seen him check the doors and finally enter the vehicle. It was a little later when the car horn had stopped blaring. Katie remarked that perhaps it was a good thing. Maybe Mr. Fishell was helping whoever was in the car and everything would be all right. Maybe they would finally start back home and this night would be over. Roger suggested that the reason for the car horn no longer sounding might be because the car battery had died and he should go out and see what was happening. They exchanged worried glances as they looked out of the windshield of the school bus at the Rambler.

"What could be taking him so long?"

"I don't know, Katie, maybe whoever is in there is in pretty bad shape and Mr. Fishell is doing what he can."

"Then why doesn't he come out of the car and let us know what is happening? He went in there with nothing, Roger. No first aid kit, nothing. How can he help if he has nothing with him?"

"Maybe I should go out there and see if he needs help."

"Maybe you should. This is starting to seriously freak me out."

Jenny first noticed the driver's side door open slightly. She yelled for Katie. "Look, Miss Katie, someone's getting out of the car!"

Everyone on the bus became quiet as nine pairs of eyes keenly focused on the vehicle sitting in the road, its front end still tightly grasping the trunk of an old hickory tree. As the car door slowly opened, inch-by-inch, a figure in red plaid shifted its body from the driver's seat and swung its feet tentatively down on to the road to stand next to the vehicle, swaying uncertainly as if drunk. A shaft of moonlight fell on the figure illuminating its damaged face. All of the children seemed to commence screaming simultaneously as the figure in plaid began a plodding shamble towards the darkened bus. Katie turned to the children and tried to calm them down: "It's all right children. It's someone who needs our help. He's hurt and we need to get him to a doctor. Don't look at him; it's the accident, that's all. Roger started towards the front of the bus. Katie grabbed his arm and whispered: "Where's Mr. Fishell?"

Katie's words did not bring calm or comfort to the children who grew more agitated as the car's driver neared the bus. The moonlight only brought its ruined face into sharper focus causing Penny and Sarah to begin sobbing violently with fear. However, it was when the passenger side of the Rambler opened and Mr. Fishell got out of the car that panic really set in. Everyone on the bus could clearly see Mr. Fishell's face, now a pulpy mass of bloody tissue and bruised flesh, his nose attached only by a piece of cartilage and bouncing up and down on his chin as he stumbled towards them. But even with his features in ruins, they all recognized the blue eyes that peered out madly from amidst the gore. The children started screaming again and upon hearing the sound of their fear, the thing that had been Mr. Fishell opened its mouth and flashed a toothy smile. This is when Katie's world went black.

Consciousness came back quickly and she found herself in Roger's arms being carried towards the rear of the school bus. All of the children were crowded into the last two rows of benches crying and casting fearful glances towards the front of the bus. Katie could hear a combination of grunting and moaning from the front of the bus as something banged heavily on the glass of the folding doors trying to get inside.

"Roger, put me down. I'm all right."

"Thank God Katie, I was really afraid."

"Afraid? You are kidding me, right! We have god knows what trying to get in here and you're afraid because I fainted? We have to get these kids out of here and now."

Roger put Katie down in the aisle and she momentarily staggered before regaining her balance. The sound of breaking glass filled the bus and the wail of the children became louder.

"Roger, are both of those things at the front of the bus?"

"You mean Mr. Fishell and whatever that other thing is?"

"You really think that thing outside is still Mr. Fishell?"

Roger looked at her and felt stupid. "Yeah, they're both trying to break the door in,"

"Okay. Roger, go back up to the front and distract them but keep an eye on them for a minute. I need a head start to get these kids out the back of this bus and away from here. As soon as you see this emergency door open, run back here and we'll get these kids out."

Roger nodded his head but did not attempt to move.

Katie shouted, "Now!"

As if awakened from a slumber, he gave her a last look and turned towards the front of the bus.

She moved quickly now to where the children were and crouched down.

"We need to get out of here."

More whimpers, more glass shattering. Jenny and Sarah physically jumped as Andrew took hold of Katie's hand.

"What's happening," Andrew cried, tears streaming down his red cheeks. "Why is Mr. Fishell doing this?"

"Never mind that now. We need to leave, okay. I'm going to open the emergency exit and when I do, we have to stay together. Roger and I will help all of you down and then we are getting out of here. Okay?"

Seven heads anxiously bobbed up and down in agreement as Katie stood now and moved towards the emergency door. The door was bolted shut with a large steel lever that latched into the body of the bus. All she needed to do was lift the lever and open the back door.

Roger was standing next to the driver's seat of the bus staring with disbelief as the two things pounded at the glass of the bus door. Starbursts and spider webs were already visible and as the door took more punishment, shards of glass flew inward towards him. It seemed to Roger that his mere presence at the front of the bus was not a distraction but an incentive, spurring the two things to a frenzy of activity in their effort to breach the doors.

A door panel flew off and in an instant one of the things arms was reaching inside the bus trying to grasp Roger, who instinctively kicked at it. The thing almost grasped his leg, but Roger reflexively pulled back before it could gain a firm hold. For that brief moment, Roger felt the strength in that arm, sinews like steel trying to grasp at his soft flesh. It was what those arms might be capable of doing to him that frightened him. He looked back to see what progress Katie had made and saw that she was struggling with the emergency door lever. He heard the radio crackle and spit as an announcer's voice blared out into the void of the bus:

> *...the police have been called out to restore order in major cities reporting outbreaks. Curfews are now in effect. Law enforcement officials announced that police officers have been ordered to shoot on sight anyone on the street. I repeat. Reports from all across the country are coming in and they confirm that the dead are coming back to life and attacking and killing citizens. Reports confirm attacks where individuals are bitten and turned into the living dead or are torn apart and cannibalized...*

Roger could feel the blood draining from his face and he felt as if he might faint. Then he noticed that the pounding had ceased. He turned towards the door and found both the hunter and Mr. Fishell staring at him with keen eyes and almost imperceptible grins. He paled at the sight of those two things staring at him with oddly satisfied looks on their faces. It seemed to Roger that they too had heard the broadcast and understood it to mean that they would win. It was just a matter of time, but they would be triumphant and seeing the fear, and hearing the screams seemed to underscore their coming victory.

Without thinking, Roger grabbed the radio leaning against the dashboard and threw it at the door. It further cracked the glass and clanked noisily to the bottom step but for a moment Roger swore that he saw the things jump, saw fear; if even for a second; in the eyes of those undead creatures. He realized two things in that fleeting moment, the first epiphany was that they surely could win but his second thought was that they could still feel fear.

Katie pulled upwards with all of her might but could not feel the lever budge. She closed her eyes and thought only of moving that lever upward and how she had to do it and quickly. She emptied her mind of all thought and distraction except for the sounds of the children. She heard their quiet sobbing, their pleading, and she keenly felt the responsibility for their survival resting on her shoulders,

She pulled upward and this time felt the lever nudge ever so slightly. She tried once more and with a grunt, freed the lever from its bracket. She reached for the safety latch on the emergency door and pulled it open, allowing the door to swing out and away from the bus. She yelled for Roger and could hear his steps coming towards the rear of the bus. Katie jumped out and down onto the road and smelled the woods, the sweet air and the hint of sulfur from the rain.

The woods exploded with sound: trees creaking and swaying with the wind, night creatures singing their nocturnal arias to no one in particular, the wind howling and whispering through the branches. She turned quickly and raised her arms toward the rear opening. Katie could see Roger now at the back of the bus throwing the children to her. A princess jumped into her arms: Penny, next a cheerleader: Sarah and lastly a witch on her broomstick flew at Katie: Jenny. Soon a ballplayer came leaping out onto the ground, then a devil and finally a gunfighter.

Roger stuck his head out and looked nervously at Katie. She yelled: "Where's Andrew?"

Roger nervously replied, "They're right behind me." Before Katie could answer, Roger jumped out of the bus with Andrew in his arms and they landed clumsily but safely next to her.

"They're on the bus, Katie, we have to go now."

"You don't have to tell me twice. Where are we going?"

Roger scanned the road quickly then pointed towards the

woods. "Through there. It looks like there's a clearing on the other side."

Katie looked to where he was pointing then spoke to the children in a soft but clearly audible voice. "Girls come with me, boys with Roger, quickly. Listen to everything we say and stay together. We're going through the woods."

They moved quietly, Roger leading the boys followed by the four girls and lastly Katie making sure no one straggled or got left behind. Andrew kept looking over his shoulder and side-to-side at the darkened trees surrounding them. His friend Brian quickened his pace until they were next to one another.

"Andy, man, what did you see out there? At this question Andrew gave his friend a haunted look and shook his head back and forth in reply. "Come on, man. Tell me. What did you see in that field when we were driving here? What got you goin' so bad that you lost it?"

"Yeah," James piped in from behind while giving Andrew a push with the flat of his hand. Andrew stumbled in surprise but regained his footing. "What got Superman peein' in his trunks, huh?"

James laughed at his own joke as Daniel smiled in embarrassment. *Sometimes it wasn't easy being friends with James*, Daniel thought; the kid could really be an asshole. Brian turned his head back towards James and rolled his eyes.

"What are you lookin' at, you faggot," James spat out. Andrew turned towards James and said in a voice loud enough for the whole group to hear, "Why don't you go to hell, you're already dressed for the trip."

Everyone burst into spontaneous laughter as Andrew stared James in the eye. James dropped back from the two boys mouthing "I'll get you for that one, you little faggot."

They came to the edge of the woods as a bolt of lightning suddenly flashed in the sky illuminating the horizon and causing some of the children to suddenly jump. But Roger pointed excitedly when he saw that the lightening had silhouetted a house perched on a small hill located on the other side of the field.

Andrew gave Brian a look and said, "I have a bad feeling

about this." Brian turned towards his friend and felt a shiver run down his spine.

Katie and Roger stood at the edge of the clearing surrounded by the children. They faced a field that stretched before them before being enveloped in a thick fog. The fog obscured their view adding to the group's growing feelings of dread and fear; the only interruption of this darkness coming with the occasional bolt of lightning that highlighted the scene in a silver-gray flash. It reminded Katie of puppet silhouettes cut from stiff paper whose shapes would cast eerie shadows against the walls of her childhood bedroom.

Roger tentatively stepped into the field and walked for a few feet, then turned and waved for the boys to come forward. He whispered to them to step carefully and to beware of the vines spreading across the floor of the field. Roger realized their journey to the house would be a slow one, hampered by the gloom and thick undergrowth. Katie and the girls soon followed until the nine figures were all out of the woods and amidst the pumpkins.

From a distance it made a strange sight, nine figures: a well-dressed bald man, a demon, a superhero, a gunfighter, a ball player, a witch, her princess sister, the cheerleader and a ghostly wraith all seemingly floating through the fog of the night. When Katie asked that they pair up and hold hands as an additional precaution James announced that "holding hands" was for faggots and sissies. In the end Daniel and Sarah held hands as did Penny and Jenny while Brian and Andrew walked side-by-side. Roger stayed in the lead with James behind him, mostly because no one really wanted James' company. Katie stayed in the rear keeping an eye out for stragglers.

As they navigated through the field, bolts of lightning flashed above them highlighting dark patches of undergrowth between the pumpkins. Brian scanned the vine-covered floor to find his footing but began feeling uneasy about their surroundings. Out of the corner of his eye he thought he could spot things lying amidst the undergrowth that puzzled him; shapes that didn't quite fit with his notion of what one should find in a pumpkin patch. He wasn't the only one to notice. They had all either grown up on or near farms and it began to dawn on most of them that this field had something peculiar about it. It was not anything of immediate concern but as the lightening storm increased its intensity, the secret of their surroundings was about to be revealed.

Andrew turned to Brian and asked in a low voice: "Do you really want to know what I saw out the bus window?" Brian nodded. "Okay, I'll tell you, but whatever you do, don't freak out."

Brian gave his friend a puzzled look and gestured for him to get on with it. All the while they moved forward, further into the field and away from the woods.

Andrew started, "We were going past a field, maybe even this field. I don't know. It wasn't too long before we stopped on the road. The rain kinda made things hard to see but when the lightning flashed, it made everything clear. Just for a few seconds at a time, kinda like it's doing right now. I saw these people running, I don't know why they were running or where they were running to, but then these other people appeared. They walked slow but funny."

"Funny how?"

"Funny like they weren't sure how to use their legs right."

Brian flashed his friend another puzzled look.

Andrew continued: "They didn't walk fast, they didn't have to, 'cause there were a lot of them. They seemed to come from all over. Maybe not a lot, I'm not too sure about how many, but the people running, they were running away. I'm pretty sure of that.

Brian could hear the excitement and anxiety in his friend's voice. "Stop it, Josh, you don't have to tell me anymore. You sound like you're gonna lose it again."

"You asked."

"Okay, go on."

The other people finally caught up with the people running away and that's when I'm not sure what happened."

"What did you see?"

"The other people caught up with the running people and I think they had a fight. They were holding each other. But then, I don't know."

Brian put his hand on his friend's shoulder. "What do you think happened?"

As Brian finished his question, both boys saw Roger suddenly trip and fall over something in the undergrowth. Everyone stopped. Roger slowly got up as James, Andrew and Brian walked slowly over to him. Roger's face was pale and he was trying to wipe something off of his pants.

"Don't come over here boys, stay where you are."

The three boys stopped where they were but as the lightning flashed they all saw what Roger had tripped over. Tangled in the vines was an arm that once might have belonged to a young woman. Its hand was pale and delicate and the skin around the shoulder was still soft and supple. Roger turned away from the boys and vomited violently onto the ground. James turned pale and turned away.

Andrew faced his friend saying, 'I think I saw those people being torn apart by the funny ones." Andrew was quick enough to catch Brian as his friend suddenly fainted.

Everyone froze.

As bolts of lightning danced overhead, illuminating the field, they could clearly make out various body parts scattered about the field surrounding them. A dismembered leg was half-hidden under a vine, a torso poked out from behind a large pumpkin, and everywhere, scatted in a random, haphazard manner lay other pieces of what were once people. It was impossible to calculate how many victims were represented by the carnage surrounding them, but it was more than one or two.

Katie and Roger recognized immediately that they stood in the middle of a killing field. The best chance of protecting the children lay in seeking shelter as quickly as possible. Roger turned to face the group and began to speak but stopped before he could utter a single syllable. He stood frozen, looking past them at the clearing they had left behind. At its edge, he saw two small figures: one in a red plaid hunting jacket and the other flashing a bright smile from amidst its bloody and ruined face.

He looked nervously behind them to gauge the progress of their dead bus driver and his new companion. The fact that their bus driver was dead was upsetting, but that he was currently pursuing them was incomprehensible. The two walking corpses were actually keeping up a slow and steady pace. Andrew was right; Mr. Fishell and the hunter did have a peculiar way of walking—almost like they both wore invisible braces on their legs. But despite this wry observation, they were quickly closing the distance.

Roger was thinking that *"slow and steady wins the race"* was just about the damnedest thing right now. It was amidst these thoughts that Roger sensed other activity in the field. Moving his head from side to side, he could discern vague silhouettes moving through the fog and gloom towards them. It was difficult to judge how near or distant these figures might be, but Roger felt an urgency to engage them, to attempt to discover if they might be of help in escaping their current, dire situation.

He stopped and turned back to the group following behind him. The group hesitantly stopped as he motioned at the shadowy figures still moving towards them from either side. Some of the group welcomed the respite while a few others; notably Andrew and Brian seemed almost panic-stricken. But it did give them a moment to catch their breath and regain their strength. Roger moved cautiously towards the figures approaching from his left side.

"What's he doing?" Andrew turned to Brian.

"I think maybe help is here." Brian sounded hopeful and tired.

Andrew looked around with wide eyes, becoming more concerned and panicked as he observed Roger moving through the gloom towards the shadowy figures. He didn't understand at first what Roger was doing until he was able to see the figures in the fog. They were the funny people, more of the same kind that hunted them. They were the things that he had seen tear apart innocent people like rag dolls. Andrew screamed, "Roger. No.

142

Come back."

Roger was perhaps thirty feet from them when he turned. He lifted his hand to wave before turning around again to continue his march forward. They watched in anticipation as he waded deeper into the fog and undergrowth of the field, then watched helplessly as shadowy figures suddenly rose from the vines and fog to grab Roger with their pale hands and drag him down into the shadows. They barely heard a muffled grunt as Roger disappeared into the gloom.

Katie felt her world crumble as she began a long and uninterrupted scream. Flashes of Roger as she had known and loved him played through her mind, deepening the disbelief and sorrow that was quickly creeping over her. Her vision dimmed and narrowed into a pinpoint of blackness as she felt herself plunging into a well of despair. Roger had been her love and her life, her past and future and in one stunning moment, on one unreal Halloween night, her world had changed forever. She thought all of these things as the soundtrack of her life turned into an unrelenting cry of horror. So consumed by her grief that Katie did not feel the arms of Sarah embrace her and shepherd her forward and away from this tragedy.

Stunned and disbelieving of what they had just witnessed; all were screaming and running as fast as they could towards the house on the hill. Those who could not run were carried. Those who fell were quickly picked up and helped back on to their feet or pulled forward by those faster and more surefooted.

Tears marked their passing like breadcrumbs in a fairy tale.

The house grew in size as they neared it. Sarah now held hands with Katie, both of them taking great gulps of air to maintain their pace. Katie was pale and rivulets of tears ran down her cheeks washing away the greasepaint, carving gashes of crimson against the pale whiteness of her face.

Everyone wore an expression of shock on his or her faces except Andrew whose face was a mask of determination and solemnity. He thought sullenly that he did not wish to lose anyone else. He realized that Superman would never have allowed any of this to happen. It was about time he stopped acting like a child. His friend Brian looked at Andrew's stern expression and could only wonder and worry about what his friend might be contemplating.

The old brick farmhouse silently stood in front of them as they scurried onto its front porch. They could feel the warped boards of the porch beneath them, see the peeling paint, and its two front doors staring quietly back at them like pale grey eyes reflected in the gloom. They saw old toys left abandoned in a corner against the dirty porch railing and ragged lace curtains hanging in the windows. Daniel looked beyond the curtains into the gloom of the house and could see dusty furniture, mirrors and sconces askew on the walls, a staircase leading upwards, doors half-open with others that he sensed had been left closed. It felt like a sick house and their immediate feeling was to run away before it infected them. While their collective fear had driven them here, that same fear was now cautioning them to stay out.

Andrew turned to look towards the field of fog stretching endlessly like an opaque curtain and could barely discern figures in the mist slowly moving towards them. He squinted, *use your super-vision*" he thought, focusing harder. There it was, finally. He could see a red plaid hunter's coat, another's Cheshire Cat-like smile shining through the gloom and finally a smartly dressed bald man stumbling towards them. The three were lead-ing a horde of the "funny people" and their interminably slow progress just made Andrew madder than hell.

Katie seemed to be alternately babbling and crying, while holding onto Sarah's hand. The twins shared looks of con-cern as Daniel and James began pounding on the front doors. The reverberations died instantly within the house adding to the feeling that it had been abandoned long ago.

"Miss Katie, what should we do?"

Daniel voiced the question, but it was in the mind of eve-ry child as they stood on the porch waiting in the gloom for her to give them an answer. Katie was still crying, with wide eyes she stared as if looking for guidance from beyond. She whimpered and looked into the pleading faces of all of them in turn before nodding her head and covering her face with her hands.

"She's toast," James declared to no one in particular.

Daniel looked out at the field then turned to the door and suddenly heaved his shoulder into the heavy paneling. He felt it give ever so slightly.

"Help me, James."

The two boys put their shoulders to the door and heaved. With a crack, the door burst inwards sending Daniel and James stumbling onto the floor. A great cloud of dust flew up, momentarily enveloping them in its welcoming embrace. The rest of the children scurried inside followed lastly by Katie. Brian walked slowly towards her and gently moved her aside so that he could close the door behind them.

They now stood with their backs to the door taking in the great room. It was as gloomy within as it had been without. Jenny and Penny walked over to the window and pushed aside the dirty lace curtain. They stuttered in unison that there were more figures moving towards the house. Katie let out another whimper as the rest of them continued scanning the room. Sarah spotted an old wooden chair in a corner and walked over to it. She picked it up in her hands and walked back to the front door. Katie still stood as rigid as a statue on the spot where Brian had placed her. Sarah moved Katie aside by gently taking her hand and leading her to where Andrew and Brian now stood. She then walked back to the door and placed the chair firmly beneath the brass doorknob.

"I hope there's a back way out of here," Sarah said to Daniel.

He nodded as the group quietly began to make their way through the house. Each of them eyed the doorways with trepidation as they passed from the Great Room down the long, dim hallway to the kitchen. None had the curiosity or courage to open those doors that connected to the Great Room perhaps because no one was eager to find what lay on the other side. As they gathered in the kitchen, they saw a set of windows and a door that faced the back of the house. This side had been hidden from them as they crossed the field, but they could see through the windows to an abandoned garden behind the kitchen and just beyond the garden to a small family cemetery.

"Hell."

What is it, Daniel?"

Look at the graveyard."

"What?"

The children closest to the windows strained to see better in the gloom until they could clearly make out the graves, some of which had been recently disturbed. Two of the graves lay open to the sky. They could not tell if the graves were waiting to be filled or recently vacated.

Daniel looked back at the group. "We either leave this house right now or we check to make sure we're the only ones here."

Katie let out another moan. At this Sarah took Katie's hand and gently held it in hers.

"I think Miss Katie should stay here. She's too freaked out to go through this house. Sarah, I think you should come with us and Andrew can stay here."

Andrew looked at Daniel and nodded his head in assent.

"Good. Let's split up. I'll take Sarah and Brian and go through the upstairs. James, you take Jenny and Penny and make sure this floor is okay. Okay?"

James looked over at Andrew and mouthed something that Andrew couldn't quite decipher. The groups quickly formed and they soon headed out into the house leaving Andrew and Katie alone in the back kitchen.

Andrew led Katie to a lone chair by the kitchen table and carefully sat her down on it. He stood next to her keeping an eye on the back door. He could hear the two groups beginning to separate within the house; Daniel's group starting their climb up a creaky staircase and James opening doorways leading into rooms on the first floor. Katie stared at her hands and occasionally looked up at Andrew; smiling when she did. He returned her smile but felt uncomfortable. So much had changed in such a short time. He wanted to be home, he wanted everything to be back to the way it was, and he wanted Katie to be Miss Katie again. Andrew did not like this house and especially did not like being alone with Katie in this particular part of the house. He felt afraid that at any moment Mr. Fishell or the man in red, or for that matter Roger could come bursting through the door and Andrew would not know what to do.

"Miss Katie, why is all of this happening?"

Katie looked up at Andrew and saw the worry on his young face. Her eyes cleared for the first time since the field and she took his hand in hers.

"I don't know, Andrew, but everything will be fine. I promise."

For a moment Andrew felt the way his mother could make him feel. He felt comforted and safe from harm. Katie was holding his hand tighter now as he saw tears begin to cascade down her cheeks.

"Don't cry, Miss Katie, everything will be fine. I promise."

Katie let out a short, embarrassed laugh, "That's what I just said to you."

"Then please don't cry, okay?"

"I'll try not to, Andrew. I promise, I'll try not to."

Daniel, Sarah and Brian slowly moved up the main staircase of the old house. Their eyes had become accustomed to the gloom as an autumn moon glowered at them through the windows; bathing the interior in a dirty grey light. Daniel and Sarah unconsciously found each other's hands as they neared the top of the staircase.

"Dan, what if there is something up here?" Brian's eyes looked like saucers in the dark as he looked to Daniel for an answer. Daniel returned Brian's stare lifting the Louisville slugger with both hands and mimicking his best batter's stance.

"Batter up."

Brian smiled feeling a bit more confidant and brave. Daniel looked at Brian's cowboy outfit, complete with hat, vest, bandana and six-shooter in each holster.

"Just make sure those guns are loaded and ready."

Brian lightly touched the plastic grip of each pistol and slowly nodded his head up and down. He then tipped the brim of his brown felt "Stetson" with thumb and index finger at Daniel and Sarah in turn. "Pardner. Ma'am."

They reached the top of the staircase and stood on the landing. The landing divided the long hallway in half with each section containing three doors, two on the north side of the house and a lone door facing south. The three friends stood silently, listening to the quiet and trying to adjust to the change in darkness. In the hallway, the gloom had given way to pitch black.

"We can split up and do this faster or we can keep together and do it slow."

Sarah looked at Daniel, "Let's keep together."

"I thought you might say that." Daniel had a look of relief on his face though none of them could see one another in the dark.

Daniel started towards the end of the hallway with Brian and Sarah following closely behind. He was scared like he had never before been in his life. His heart was pounding like a loud drum inside his chest and his blood beat against his ears. He'd been afraid when he played ball, a sport he dearly loved. When it was a big game and bases were loaded, bottom of the ninth and he was up. It was the fear of maybe missing the ball and letting the team down and disappointing the crowd that had come to see him make that homerun.

He knew how his imagination could make him afraid, like when he had seen a scary movie in a theater and that night he would lie in his bed unable to sleep because everything in the room felt different. The creaking mattress would sound like the quiet footfalls of a monster creeping ever closer to the bed. The closet in his room would become a sanctuary for the loathsome and unnamable. But this immediate and deep feeling of fear was different. This fear struck at his very core because it was life and death. These monsters were real and they were not going to disappear when the credits rolled at the end of the movie. They would have to be dealt with and it would be bloody. Daniel knew in his heart of hearts that someone or perhaps everyone might die and it froze the blood in his veins. He turned and looked over his shoulder barely seeing the outlines of Brian and Sarah behind him.

They stopped in front of the door and Daniel reached for the doorknob.

"Wait!" Brian put a hand on Daniel's shoulder. For a second Daniel felt like jumping out of his skin, Brian's interruption had startled him and broken his concentration.

"What?" Daniel clearly sounded annoyed.

"Let Sarah open the door and you get your bat ready." Brian took out his six-shooters and held one in each hand. He thumbed the hammers back until they clicked and locked into place.

"Goddammit, Brian, you are a real asshole." Sarah rolled her eyes.

"No, Sarah, maybe Brain's right. If there is something in here, we can't just open the door and ask it if it'll leave. We have to be ready."

Daniel could see the white's of Sarah's eyes staring at him through the gloom.

"Right. Fine. I'll do it. Let's just get it over with." She changed places with Daniel in front of the door. Grasping the doorknob, she pulled the door towards her. It didn't budge.

"Sarah, did you pull the door?"

She rolled her eyes again, "Yes."

Daniel sounded exasperated, "Push, Sarah. Don't pull."

Sarah grasped the doorknob again and pushed the door inward. It creaked interminably before stopping against the inner wall of the bathroom. Moonlight shone off the yellowed tiles as Daniel and Brian stepped past Sarah into the room. It was small, but it was also unoccupied. Sarah followed them and the three friends looked quickly around the room. The tub had no shower curtain with which to hide a ghoul, and only a broken toilet sat near the window. Brian walked over to the window and glanced out.

"Hey, guys, take a look."

Daniel and Sarah walked over and joined him. They all looked down towards the back of the house and saw a ghost walking towards the kitchen garden. Brian had a puzzled expression as he turned to Sarah and Daniel.

"What's Katie doing outside?"

Andrew paced the floor of the kitchen as he heard sounds echoing through the house. He worried about his friends. He could hear James clumsily crashing through doorways, creating an unnecessary commotion and the footsteps above him that could only be Daniel, Brian and Sarah in the midst of their quieter and more deliberate search. Andrew hoped they were safe and that all of them would make it through this night and return home. He glanced towards Katie and wished he could do more for her. He thought about Superman and how nothing was ever difficult for the Man of Steel. Superman always knew what to do and always chose the right path. Andrew wished he was that confident.

A light fog hung over the fence line as a pale moon occasionally peaked out from behind the clouds, bathing the trees and backyard in a silver glow. Katie stood at the kitchen window looking out onto the abandoned garden. She thought about Roger, replaying in her mind the moment when the field had swallowed him up and dragged him under. She put a hand on the windowpane and felt an ache for her lost love. It was still difficult to believe that he was gone. She sighed as a single tear slowly formed in the corner of her eye and fell, gracefully tracing a line down her cheek.

As she continued staring out at the deserted garden, the fog thickened and rolled towards the house in an undulating wave. Lost in her thoughts, she did not realize that the fog had moved close enough to the back of the house to obscure a view of anything lying beyond the small garden. A lone figure began to shamble its way out of the fog, occasionally stopping for no apparent reason before continuing.

Katie suddenly saw a shadow beyond the garden. She could not tell who or what it was, but as the moonlight outlined a silhouette against the thick fog, its shape seemed familiar. She focused her gaze more intensely upon the figure as she struggled to discern what it was that slowly approached; then the shadow stopped, as if regarding her presence for the first time. Katie closed her eyes and thought again about the last time that she had seen Roger. As she slowly reopened them, her breathing all but stopped as she saw Roger standing by the garden fence. He was smiling at her and smoothing the creases in his absurdly large suit. His bald cap was slightly askew, but that was to be expected with all of the day's confusion and excitement. Katie felt excited and closed her eyes, hoping against hope that somehow Roger had survived his ordeal unscathed and was returning to her. Her heart skipped a beat as she opened her eyes once more.

Roger had advanced to the garden gate, only yards away from the back door of the house. He was still smiling as he beckoned her to come out and join him. She let out a soft moan and turned to look back at Andrew. She saw that he was still pacing and looking towards the interior of the house, trying to listen for any activity of his other friends. Katie turned back to the window.

She was startled when she found herself face-to-face with Roger. He was on the other side of the glass; an inch away from her; staring at her with strange, alien eyes, but his smile was as warm as she remembered. She closed her eyes once more and softly moaned. When she opened them again, Roger was once again at the garden gate beckoning her to come to him. As she watched, the fog slowly rolled around Roger; enveloping him and rendering him once more a silhouette backlit by the moon.

Without a moment's hesitation, Katie raced to the back door, fumbled with the latch, and flew into the night. Approaching the garden gate, she looked for Roger but saw no sign of him. A sound emanating from deep within the fog caught her ear and she glimpsed a shadow slowly walking through the family cemetery. She ran towards it calling Roger's name. Feeling hope and excitement, she implored him to stop, to let her join him, to show himself. Tears of joy ran down her cheeks. Then she spied him standing near a lone elm that grew at the edge of the property. Beyond this tree lay the field, still masked by a thick blanket of fog. As she approached, he lifted both of his arms towards her, inviting her to embrace him again. She flew towards him on wings of angels.

James made short work of going through the rooms on the first floor. He wanted to find something, ached to see some monster jump out at him and try to scare the pants of him. It would be in for a big surprise.

Jenny and her sister were shadowing James as he approached the doorways kicking them inwards and leaping into the rooms brandishing his devil's pitchfork. The girls were horrified at his bravado and total lack of caution as they each expected the next door he opened to be a gateway to hell. If not that, then surely the next one would be the one that would reveal a monster who would end their young lives. As James eliminated all but the last room on the first floor, Jenny and Penny felt certain that something foul would be awaiting all of them behind this remaining doorway.

James stood in front of the door, turned towards the twins and in his most charming voice asked, "Well, ladies, would you like to do the honors?"

Jenny and Penny responded simultaneously, "Go ahead James, we know you want to."

James laughed thinking how funny it was that they always said the same thing together at the same time. He raised his foot and prepared to kick in the door when the girls stopped him.

"James, wait."

He lowered his foot.

"What?"

"Only Jenny spoke this time, "Listen."

Penny interjected, "Do you hear that sound?"

They both continued, "It's coming from behind THIS door."

James wasn't sure what sound he was supposed to be

hearing. Stepping back, he raised his foot again to piston his leg into the door when he suddenly became aware of a buzzing sound. It was very subdued but now that the girls had made him aware of it, he could hear it. He put his leg down and moved closer to the door putting his ear to one of the door panels. The buzzing gained in volume and strangely, he could feel the vibrations through the panel. It was definitely coming from behind the door. He put a hand on the doorframe and felt the palm of his hand vibrating ever so slightly. He couldn't be sure what it meant or what it was but the door had to be opened.

"Do you hear it?" Jenny asked.

"Do you feel it?" Penny followed.

"Be very careful." They both stared at him with concern on their young faces.

James laughed.

"Careful? I promise I'll be careful."

With a sudden swift motion, he kicked the door inward. The smell of rotted meat burst from the room and cascaded over the three of them in an overpowering wave. The twins stepped away from the door and immediately pinched their noses closed with their thumbs and forefingers. James had been propelled into the room by the force of his kick and stood in what had been a sitting room. The wallpaper, once a vibrant flocked purple pattern was now faded and peeling off the wall and onto the floor. A tattered couch lay against another wall and a high-backed chair stood in the middle of the room facing a picture window. James realized that the chair was the source of the buzzing sound. He walked slowly towards it with his pitchfork held in front of him. Sweat stood out on his brow as he felt perspiration begin to run down his neck and pool at the base of his spine. With each step forward, the buzzing increased in volume, quickly becoming a cacophony of riotous sound. Its effect was unsettling. James felt his heart race and his nerves jangle with the effort of moving forward.

He was now close enough to touch the back of the chair; the buzzing reaching a fever pitch and its vibrations seeming to move through every nerve of his body. When he could stand it no longer, he jumped in front of the chair pointing his pitchfork in front of him.

The tattered chair held a pile of rotted flesh that was slowly falling off the seat and collecting in a heap on the floor with a sick, wet slapping sound. Thousands of flies twitched and buzzed around this sickening pile as white maggots as thick as his thumb undulated over and through the flesh in a ceaseless writhing motion.

James felt the blood leave his face and the bile rise from his stomach as he tried to let out a scream. He turned towards the door to leave but it was closed. Suddenly feeling dizzy and confused, he couldn't remember closing the door unless the twins were playing a joke on him by locking him in the room. If that were the case, he would get even with both of them. His sudden anger made him feel better and it helped clear his head until he noticed a dark figure facing him, its back against the closed door. Blood red eyes stared out at him and sharp teeth seemed to shine with an inner brilliance.

For the first time in James' short life, he felt real fear.

Before Andrew realized what happened, Katie had flung the door open and bolted into the fog. His heart raced and without thinking, he followed across the kitchen and through the door into the night. He barely saw through the thick fog but nearing the gate, he spied Katie moving past gravestones, towards a lone elm that stood some distance away.

"Katie! Come back!"

The fog swallowed his shouts, devouring them with an insatiable hunger. "What would Superman do?" he thought as he raced towards the elm. "Use your *super-voice*," he lifted his hands to his mouth and shouted again. This time he saw Katie turn around but knew she did not see him. She approached the shadow and its outstretched arms.

Andrew ran as fast as he could, stopping at the edge of the small cemetery to watch Katie fly into the embrace of the shadow figure. He stopped and squeezed his eyes into narrow slits, "use your *super-vision*!"

His vision expanded and he observed other shapes appearing out of the fog, surrounding Katie and the shadow that held her. He saw her face magnified and watched her expression turn to one of terror as reality awakened her from her swoon. Andrew heard the stifled scream, and with mounting horror saw other shadows converge upon her. Hands floated through the fog grasping at her delicate arms and shoulders. He imagined the sound of flesh being pulled from bone filling the air and being carried on the night breeze, but he couldn't be sure. Slowly, the thing that was Roger and the other "funny ones" converged on Katie as the thick fog blanketed them leaving only a twisted branch of the elm visible.

Andrew's terror and sorrow escalated to heights he had never before imagined, as he felt empty and powerless. In spite of his helplessness, he moved quickly through the cemetery towards the elm where he had last seen Katie alive.

He whispered to himself, "What would Superman do?"

Suddenly the ground yawned open and he fell into a dark, black pit. For a moment, the sensation of falling felt like flying and he thought that perhaps he really *was* Superman. Then his body crashed on to the cold, hard dirt of the open grave and blackness swirled, filling his vision.

His last thoughts before losing consciousness were how sad he felt for Katie and how sorry he was that he wasn't really Superman at all.

Daniel was the first to hear the scream. He turned to Brian and Sarah, his expression a mixture of concern and fear.

Brian looked to Daniel, "Did you hear that?"

Even in the glow of the moonlight, Sarah turned pale and moved closer to Daniel feeling for his hand. She found it and clasped it tightly in hers looking from one boy to the other for their reactions.

"It came from downstairs."

"We better get going then"

"What about the rest of the rooms up here?" Daniel looked towards the door leading to the hallway.

"We'll have to come back."

Sarah asked in a whisper, "We go together, right?"

FOUR IN THE HOLE

Daniel squeezed her hand. "Let's go."

James stood motionless in the center of the darkened room, his mind unable to make sense of the thing that was slowly shambling towards him. He was more frightened than he had ever been in his life; his mind had stopped; barely remembering to breathe, his world had come to a halt, reality ceasing to make sense as he watched the thing move closer.

He knew it had once been a person, of this, he was certain. It had been a young man. Perhaps, James thought, close to his age, perhaps a little older. Its hair was unkempt and covered its face. The fingernails were unnaturally long and translucent; they curved inwards like Fu Man Chu. It wore a funereal suit that had become moldy and tattered as if from years of neglect. Clods of earth fell off the sleeves as the thing moved towards him. As it passed the couch, the fingernails scraped against the fabric making a soft, scratching sound that seemed to fill the room. Its pants were torn and muddy up to its knees and James could see that chunks of rotted flesh were sloughing off the bone with a sick, wet plunk against the wooden floor.

He closed his eyes and thought he might be dreaming. The thought came to him that he was still on the school bus with the sun dappling through the trees and playing across the benches onto the face of his fellow classmates. He had dozed off and would awaken very soon. Roger, Kate or even Mr. Fishell would place a sure hand on his shoulder and rouse him from this dream. He would open his eyes and see the house that he barely called home, the mother whom barely cared about him, or the string of "uncles" whom seldom let a day go by without a lesson or two with a switch, a belt or a fist.

He squeezed his eyes open into narrow slits and saw the thing almost upon him, its gaunt, dried flesh stretched across its skull, smiling while exposing a maw of fang-like teeth. It stopped a foot from James who opened his eyes. They stood inches apart as they regarded one another: James, whose breathing had become labored and the thing, which continued to shed flesh from bone.

Standing outside the door, Jenny and Penny did not understand what was happening or what they should do. It was Jenny who screamed when the door had slammed shut as both of the girls saw James standing alone in the middle of the room. They turned to each other with the same question in their minds: who closed the door? Penny tried to turn the doorknob as she pounded her small fist against the heavy oak door panel but it didn't budge.

They each turned upon hearing footsteps approaching and felt relief as they recognized Daniel followed by Brian and Sarah running towards them.

"Girls, are you alright?" Daniel looked relieved to see the two of them.

"Yes, we are," Jenny answered.

"We're so glad you're here," Penny added.

Brian looked down the hall past the girls, "Where's James?"

The twins nodded towards the door. Penny's eyes started to tear as she told them how James was now trapped inside the room.

Daniel turned to Brian, "Let's get this door open. Ready?"

When the door flew open Daniel and Brian cautiously entered the room. James met their stare with a vacant smile and glazed eyes. He took a single step towards them, raising his devil's pitchfork in a silent gesture of contrition and pride. The thing's head lolled gracefully on the three spikes of the pitchfork, its decapitated body crumpled in a heap mere inches from where James stood.

"I think I killed it," James intoned in a quiet whisper. His smile grew broader as he let out a peal of laughter that echoed into the hallway and filled the empty house. James felt as though he would never stop laughing.

Daniel walked across the room and placed an arm around James' shoulder. James flinched and dropped the pitchfork, which fell to the floor with a clatter then a wet sound as the thing's head rolled into a corner of the room. James physically shuddered then closed his eyes and leaned into Daniel's embrace. They walked into the hallway past Brian who stood by the door with pistols raised in each hand. Sarah gently patted James on the shoulder as he walked past.

"I think I killed it."

"I know you did, buddy. It's okay."

"It told me things." James raised his head from Daniel's shoulder looking him in the eyes.

"You mean it talked to you?" Daniel eyed James suspiciously not knowing what his friend's present state of mind might be.

"No. It was dead. How could it talk to me?" James said this as if it were the most obvious thing in the world. "But I could hear it in my head, and I could see pictures of what it wanted to show me. I know it was telling me and showing me things."

"Like what?" Sarah looked at James curiously, cocking her head to the side with an expectant look on her face.

"How could it show you anything? What are you talking about, James?" Brian asked as he followed them down the hallway towards the kitchen.

"Shut the fuck up, faggot," James stared daggers at Brian who moved behind Sarah.

"Take it easy, James." Daniel's voice was low and reassuring, "What the hell was that thing and what did it do to you?"

James was still nearly hysterical from shock and he was exhibiting a wide array of mood swings.

"We stared at each other and I couldn't think of anything, then I started thinking of my shitty house and my shitty parents. Then all of a sudden I saw him," James pointed back inside the door, "the way he used to look. He was a kid, like us. Only he's older than we are. Maybe twelve, thirteen. I saw him fall off the roof of this house, and then I saw his parents come out and pick him up. He was dead. Then I saw him lying in a coffin at his own funeral. It was in the front room of this house. People carried the coffin out to the back yard and buried him out there. It was summer, only a few months ago. "

Everyone was quiet. James looked like he was deep in thought. Daniel eyed his friend with concern and suspicion while Sarah stepped closer to him and unconsciously took Daniel's hand. Brian stood behind James and made "crazy" gestures, outlining invisible circles against his temple with his forefinger. The twins looked pale and withdrawn and Jenny in particular looked as if she were going to faint.

James continued, "They buried him just past the garden in that graveyard right out there," his voice became more excited and high-pitched, "then it was black. It was black for a long time until I saw *his arms* punching out of the coffin and clawing at the earth. Then he was here again; tonight, in this house. The room I found him in was the room they had his funeral in. He used to live here!"

Daniel put his arm around James' shoulder and spoke very softly, "James, a lot of crazy stuff has happened tonight. But what you're telling us is that the dead are somehow coming back to life?"

"That's what he told me. Only some of them don't want to be back. Maybe most of them don't want to be back. He said being brought back to life is like someone waking you out of a deep sleep by lighting a firecracker next to your head. It's not nice."

"Why'd you kill him then?" Sarah asked.

"He wanted it. He said being alive like that was too painful. He also said there are two kinds of people brought back from the dead: the ones that don't want to be here and the ones that are mad about being here. He said to beware of the other kind; the angry ones."

The group reached the back kitchen and stood in the entranceway. The kitchen was empty. The only sound they heard was the back door repeatedly slamming against the crooked doorjamb.

Andrew lay in a silent cocoon of blackness. He felt like he had been there forever. In that place, there was no up or down, no sound and no pain. He knew he didn't belong in that eternal blackness, he hoped it was only temporary; but like being in a bad dream, it's one thing to be aware of dreaming, it is quite another thing to try and wake up from it. This was where Andrew found himself. He knew he wasn't dead, and he was sure he wasn't dreaming, he just wasn't sure how to wake up.

A quiet voice intruded at the edge of his dimmed perception. It was a woman's voice and had a familiarity to it that set his heart racing. "Wake up, Andrew. Come on, honey, I know you can do it, dear."

He recognized the muffled whisper as his mother's voice and he struggled to make sense of how she had found him. His head was still a cloud of blackness with no immediate thoughts taking shape in his mind's eye. The voice began to move something within him. As Andrew thought more about his mother's voice, the cocoon he found himself wrapped in slowly unraveled as he struggled to break free from its bonds. The edges of blackness gradually began to bleed away and he could make out the faint impression of his bedroom, its lines and colors coalescing into a more definitive shape as he concentrated on their form. He was so intimately familiar with his room and its objects that his heart sang out. He distinctly saw the morning light playing across the rocket ship patterns on the bedroom curtains as he heard footsteps approaching the door. He closed his eyes then opened them to see his mother standing over him next to his bed.

"Hey buddy; it's time to get up." She smiled and crinkled her eyes as she beamed at him. "Come on, buddy, time to go." Her smile grew and he began to feel a tension, a pressure building in his head as her image wavered, then blackness intruded at the corners of his vision.

He felt himself falling again, but not from a great height, it felt as if he were falling into himself, that his consciousness or spirit had found his body. For a moment, he glimpsed himself from a great height. He saw that he was still wearing his Superman costume and that his body lay quietly in an open grave. His essence flew, swirling towards the prone figure and he felt a tearing as if from the core of his being as the two; consciousness and self; became one again. He convulsed and felt the aches and pains of his corporeality as body and mind reunited into that unique presence named Andrew.

It took a moment to open his eyes and then to close them again, as he became conscious. He slowly moved arms, then legs but could not discern anything as being broken. He felt the insistent throbbing of a headache stubbornly taking root behind his eyes and stood up slowly shaking his head from side to side.

As his head cleared, images exploded through his mind. Recent memories of that day and evening seemed to have happened a million years ago. The day had started out like any other: his mother waking him up with a kiss and a smile, breakfast and the excitement of the upcoming Halloween party, his mother helping him to put on his costume and then waiting with an unprecedented anticipation for the school bus to arrive.

He smiled to himself at the memory of Mr. Fishell opening the accordion doors of the bus and whistling at the sight of the tiny Superman waiting on the curb. Dark memories began to intrude into Andrew's mind. He thought of James murmuring something mean as he walked past him to sit with his friend Brian. Darker memories intruded: the "funny" men chasing figures across the field and Mr. Fishell becoming something strange and scary as it stepped out of the car in the road.

Finally, he saw the image of Roger disappearing into the vines of the pumpkin field and returning as something else, embracing Miss Katie and then taking her away. He opened his eyes to stop the memories from taking shape but closed them tightly as his headache hammered against his temples with renewed force. Whatever was going to happen next would have to happen soon, and if this bad dream was going to end, he hoped it would end with the coming of day. Nothing scary ever happened in the day, it was only at night when the thing in the closet became real or when shadows took on strange and terrifying shapes. The daylight always cleansed away the evil in the world. Even as he thought this, something deeper inside him hoped it really was true and not something his mother would tell him to make him less frightened of the world and the evils that he knew existed and would always be there…waiting.

Holding an arm out to steady himself, he felt the cold,

damp earth against his fingertips. His eyes took in the four walls of dirt that enclosed him. He felt the curved wood of the casket beneath his feet and saw its broken lid gaping open to the sky. He raised his head towards the rectangle of stars above him. The sky was still dark but it was beginning to brighten, slowly turning from black to deep blue, and heralding the eventual dawn.

"Where are they?" Daniel turned to James and the twins with a look of fright and panic in his eyes. His voice was still soft but there was an edge of hysteria beginning to creep into his usually calm tone.

"How the hell should I know?" James' reply was terse but his face showed a surprise at how close he thought his friend was to losing it. James began to feel disappointed in Daniel. He also didn't really care where Andrew or Katie might be now. They could be dead for all he cared and a secret part of him hoped that this was the case.

Daniel walked with purpose towards the back door. He grasped the edge of the door before it had a chance to strike the jamb again and opened it as he turned to the group that was still assembled behind him.

"Someone has to look for them. Someone has to look out for them."

James rolled his eyes. Sarah stepped away from the group and strode towards Daniel. She stood next to him.

"Daniel," her voice was soft and measured, "what do you think you can do. They could be anywhere. They could be..." She looked down at the floor feeling ashamed of herself for sounding like James.

"Dead? Is that what you're trying to tell me. Forget about them because they *might* be dead? That doesn't sound like you, Sarah."

"No, you're right, Daniel. Katie would never just leave us somewhere," Sarah admitted.

"Screw them," James couldn't help himself and smiled.

Even before James said this, Daniel had made up his mind to walk out of the house and into the fog in an effort to find them. He didn't even think to be afraid. It just seemed to be the right thing to do. Daniel turned back towards the kitchen and stared at James from across the distance. "No, James, screw you." Then he turned and disappeared into the night.

Andrew watched the cottony fog gently roll past the aperture of his tomb. He heard distant sounds; night birds calling to one another, the wind whispering past tree branches and gravestones, and the disturbing moan of the living dead echoing in the distance. They seemed to be close but not near, still these new sounds had a chilling effect on him.

Even at his age, it was difficult to imagine the dead somehow animated and threatening, walking again amongst the living, a reminder of his mortality yet an unimaginable reality even at his young age. The dead should stay dead. They had no right to be amongst us. He thought of church and Pastor Thompson who would always talk of the Kingdom of Heaven. He never said anything about our world becoming a Kingdom of the Dead. There was not a plague or an event to rival this in the Bible. So what was happening?

He heard moans again in the distance and shivered. He pressed himself into a corner of the grave. Earlier, he had tried to climb out only to find himself too small to gain any purchase on the earthen walls and the dirt too damp and loose to hold his weight. He had never felt so frustrated and alone in his life as he did at this moment. He heard another sound coming from a short distance; approaching footsteps and then a familiar voice, "Andrew, where are you, man? Andrew, I know you're out here."

"Help, I'm down here!" he shouted, his heart suddenly pounding loudly in his chest.

"Andrew? Keep talking, I don't see you, but I hear you. I'm coming."

"Danny? Is that you? I'm down here in this pit. Be careful. Don't fall in like I did. I'm really glad to hear your voice. Please help me. Get me out of here."

Daniel's face appeared over the edge of the grave staring at Andrew with a broad smile on his face, "Are you okay, buddy?"

"Yeah, please help me outta here," Andrew replied. He

felt as if he was going to cry. He had never been so happy to see someone in his life.

Daniel extended his Louisville Slugger into the pit, "Grab on to this and I'll hoist you up."

Andrew grabbed the blunt end of the bat as Daniel pulled. Andrew used his feet to kick himself up the sides of the grave and in a few moments he was back on firm ground sprawled at Daniel's feet.

"Where's Katie?"

Andrew shook his head back and forth. "Roger got her. I'm so sorry. I tried to do something but I saw him take her and when I ran to stop him, I fell in there." Andrew pointed back towards the open grave. He felt like crying again but Daniel stopped him.

"We have to get out of here. Those things are still around here. I don't know where they are right now, but I'm pretty sure they haven't gone away."

Andrew's eyes watered as he looked up at Daniel, "You mean we have to go back to the house?"

"I think so. That's where I left James, Sarah, and the twins. It wouldn't be right to leave them with James.

Andrew laughed, "Yeah, you're right."

Come on Andrew, the sooner we get back to the house, the sooner we can get out of here." He put his hand on Andrew's shoulder and gently patted him on the back. "Keep an eye out for the dead guys, okay, champ?"

Andrew looked up at Daniel again and smiled, "Okay, boss."

***

The sky purpled and darkened in revolt against the dawning of a new day. As the wind gasped and sputtered, it gathered strength as it flew across the fields, past stands of trees, carrying no good news on this morning. A single vein of lightening silently flickered against the gunmetal grey of the sky, summoning a sudden fall of cold, hard rain. Night tarried longer, crowding out the dawn as the air turned graveyard-cold, and moans echoed through the valley like the caws of funereal night-ingales.

The ground churned and heaved as stiff dead fingers groped towards the surface seeking not light but life. To be dead was to consume the living for no other reason than it must be so. The things that earlier in the day had reposed in a somber sleep had been awakened. Angry at this intrusion of their slumber they now sought out that which they could not possess, but only in-gest; the life force of the living.

Hands sought purchase against the hard ground, ravaged elbows pistoned against cold dirt until a head half-covered with muscle and dead tissue emerged gasping for air out of a half-remembered habit, to avenge this uncertain and misunderstood disturbance. Wherever the dead had rested, this scene was re-peated a thousand-fold until shambling figures took their first uncertain steps towards the unknowing. They felt a comfort in action without forethought, malice without consequence, death without fear of reprisal. Seeing through dead eyes, hearing through deaf ears the newly formed mobs, regardless of their location, or distance looked for the living.

Tens, perhaps hundreds seemed to sense the lone farm-house near a patch of pumpkins and felt an essence that would satisfy their gnawing hunger: flesh that could be devoured, skin and bone that could be ripped and broken for some dark and un-knowable reason. They growled in unison and shambled slowly toward the solitary farmhouse that stood in the field illuminated solely by a violet moon.

***

Daniel dragged Andrew through the gloom towards the house looking over his shoulder again and again, feeling an in-surmountable fear that would not go away. Andrew for his part felt a new comfort yet wariness at being given a second chance, knowing how fragile the balance between day and night was. He whipped sidelong glances into the thickening gloom ready to scream at any intrusion, be it monster or man.

The two moved quickly and quietly beneath the violet canopy aware of the change in the sky and wondering why the sun failed to break over the horizon. The air around them changed from a moist, sweet-scent to the stench of rotted meat and clotted blood. Andrew wrinkled his nose and cast about for the origin of the offensive smell. Daniel turned towards Andrew and creased his brow in uncertainty. Andrew could see Daniel tighten the grip on his Louisville slugger as they both slowed to a dead stop.

Daniel sniffed the air, as the scent became stronger he tried to discern where it was coming from and where it was going. He motioned with his free hand for Andrew to crouch down close to the ground. As he did so, Andrew could feel his heart beating harder and faster as they both heard shuffling coming from their right.

The gloom thickened then as a thick quilt of fog quietly rolled into the woods like a tide breaking across a beach. Though the boys where no more than a foot from one another, each was enveloped in a smoky shroud rendering them blind to one another and their immediate surroundings. The effects were dizzying as Andrew and Danny became lost in the sudden fog. All sounds in the woods around them immediately ceased as each lost their sense of time and place and found themselves in a world of illusion and hallucination.

Danny violently blinked his eyes to try and clear them of the fog using his free hand to rub at them to clear his vision. All was smoky grey until his vision went momentarily black and then he saw stars. His eyes blinked involuntarily from the unexpected intrusion and when his vision finally cleared he found himself on a softball field. It wasn't a familiar field, he could barely make out a line of crooked trees hidden behind a haze in the outfield, but he could feel a hot sun on his face and he sensed the batting cage behind him.

Suddenly the scene became alive with sound. He heard a crowd cheering unintelligibly. As he surveyed the field, he saw that bases were loaded. He looked to the pitcher's mound and saw Mr. Fishell grinning through a ruined face, baseball cap set at a jaunty angle looking right at him. Danny turned behind him and saw the man in the hunter's jacket wearing a catcher's vest staring silently ahead.

Then Danny looked at his teammates on base. Each wore a softball uniform stained crimson from mortal wounds on various parts of their bodies. The first runner was missing his right arm; blood had soaked the front of his jersey a deep brown. The third base runner was a small boy with a deep gash through his shoulder and a gash on his neck. The second baseman limped expectantly back and forth on an impossibly twisted right foot. They were all looking at him to see what Danny would do.

Mr. Fishell threw the softball into his glove then stopped and spit on the ground. What should have been chewing tobacco juice stuck to the pitcher's mound in a bright red globule. There were teeth in the gore that rested at Mr. Fishell's feet. Mr. Fishell took the ball out of his glove and began his wind-up, throwing his left arm back behind his head at an impossible angle before letting fly with the pitch.

Time slowed like molasses. Danny felt perspiration rolling down his spine. The sun glinted off the trees and a sweetly scented breeze brushed his hair. All the while he could see the ball careening towards him at an impossibly slow speed as if he were batting a game on the ocean floor. He saw and felt the air move in front of the pitch towards him as he involuntarily grasped his Louisville Slugger and lifted it shoulder high and behind his body, the bat quivering ever so slowly in anticipation of its inevitable meeting with the ball. Danny eyed the ball as it neared, swung and felt the bat connect with nothing but empty air before leaving his grasp and bouncing on the ground. Danny could not believe it; he missed a slow-pitch as it gently curved away from him at the last moment.

He looked up at the pitcher's mound only to find it empty. He turned to the bases and was met with piercing bloodshot eyes and mocking grins. His vision went black and as he cleared his head he realized he was back in the fog. A pair of hands suddenly shot through the gloom and clutched at his throat. As

Danny stood there slowly beginning to choke he followed the hands to a pair of arms and finally to the mocking gaze of Mr. Fishell, their dead school bus driver.

Andrew felt the fog seductively envelope him and fell through it like a bird through a cloud. His vision blurred then blackened until a comforting weightlessness cradled his body and gently laid him down. He felt himself on the verge of sleep until he was jolted back to awareness by the gentle caress of his own bed. He was home again. He had no clue as to how this miracle may have occurred but his heart was bursting with happiness.

He looked around at his room and all of the familiar objects were there. His Superman posters, the Superman alarm clock on his nightstand, a morning sun weakly backlighting his rocketship curtains which hung across the robin's-egg window frame. Andrew clutched at the quilt and felt the softness and heat of it surround his face. He closed his eyes and smiled. Perhaps everything had been a dream. That had to be it. He fell asleep on the school bus and his dad picked him up out of his seat (as everyone probably laughed and made fun of him), brought him inside and laid him in his own bed until now.

Morning, how wonderful he felt now knowing in his heart of hearts that everything had been a bad dream. He shivered when he remembered the pit he had been stuck in, or when everyone had to run through the pumpkin field to escape those things. He was glad it was all over. He closed his eyes again and breathed a heavy sigh of relief and actually smiled to himself for the first time in what seemed like forever.

He heard the first footfall on the stairs outside of his room and felt a tingle. The second footfall seemed unfamiliar; he knew his mother's footsteps and those of his father. He knew them in his sleep. The third footfall sounded heavy and ponderous and he concentrated on the sound trying to find a reason why they were different. Was his mother carrying something heavy to his room? Was his mind playing tricks on him? He pinched himself to be certain he wasn't still dreaming. He involuntarily winced with the pain and decided he was indeed awake.

THE NIGHT WE DIDN'T GO HOME

It was when he heard the thing on the staircase murmur his name that he felt sheer terror. His name sounded as if a mad dog had slurred it out of its ungodly yaw. The sound had an animal quality to it and yet was human; just barely. Andrew drew the covers up to his face until only his eyes and forehead where visible, still the steps continued; excruciatingly slow; reaching the door and stopping.

The next moment hung like a still life as the doorknob began to move. First left, then right and finally left again, the mechanism unlocking itself and gently freeing the door. If Andrew could scream, he surely would have but the voice that uttered his name again froze his blood. It was just outside his bedroom door and it sounded huskier, almost liquid, as if one were trying to speak his name underwater.

Andrew momentarily brought the bed sheets up over his head and shivered as he heard the door slowly open and bang against the wall. Silence hung in the air as his breathing became more rapid and shallow; still he dared not pull the sheets back. Perhaps he wouldn't be noticed and the thing would see an empty room and turn back towards the staircase. Instead the heavy steps moved towards the bed, closer and closer until they stopped at the threshold of his mattress. He felt something grasp the quilt and sheets and tug it out of his hands with an unexpected force.

Andrew opened his eyes against his will and saw standing at his bedside Katie dressed in his mother's clothes. Her head rested at an impossible angle as it wrestled to stay attached to the rest of her body. Blood still gently oozed from the side of her neck as she gently cooed in her liquid growl, "Wake up buddy, wake up. It's time for school."

Andrew did not even have the strength or presence of mind to scream as he tore the bed sheets from the thing's hands and covered his head again hoping it might go away. Fingers of steel wrestled the sheets again from his grasp then quietly reached for Andrew's own hand. Its grip was that of a vise, death was in its eyes, and on its breath as it whispered, "Come on, buddy, be nice to mommy."

As Andrew fell through the blackness he regained his awareness to find himself surrounded by a shroud of fog while Katie's hand tightened around his own as she slowly led him into the woods.

Danny shook himself free of his hallucination and felt an insistent pressure on his neck. He moved his head only to be confronted with the torn and dead face of Mr. Fishell whose hands gripped tighter around his throat. Danny's blood ran cold as the ruined face slowly moved closer towards him, its jaws quivering, bloodied teeth grinding, drool leeching from the sides of its mouth.

In a panic Danny reached with both hands towards the ground looking for something to fight with. They brushed loose earth, rock and leaves until his right hand glanced over a long, hard object. He immediately tightened his grip on the Louisville Slugger feeling the weight of it in his left hand. The thing that had been Mr. Fishell snapped its jaws open and closed as its front teeth cracked with the force.

Danny felt his head being slowly pulled towards the creature's maw and he pulled back against the force as he brought the bat swinging upwards in a high arc over his head and into the head and shoulders of the thing. The force of Danny's blow stunned the creature that had been their bus driver and it released its grip as it staggered back from him.

Danny pulled himself into his familiar batting stance throwing the Louisville Slugger over his shoulder where it quivered with energy waiting for something with which to strike. The thing seemed to regain its balance staggering towards Danny snapping its jaws, growling and fixing its dead eyes upon him.

Danny waited for the thing to approach, squinted his own eyes as it bore down upon him then let fly with his bat. The Slugger cut through the air with an audible whoosh and connected with the thing's head as a crack of wood and bone reverberated across the fields. The thing's head flew off his body and into the dark morning sky; seeming to travel into the very heavens above them; as the thing's body crumpled to the ground;

lifeless and finally at peace.

Danny knelt close to the ground collecting himself as he breathed heavily; drinking in the cool morning air. It momentarily struck him that the events of the past several hours were unexplainable and unbelievable, he just killed their bus driver; he corrected himself, their *dead* bus driver. A swell of nausea rose from his core and he violently vomited onto the ground. Sweat poured off his forehead and he felt dizzy and disoriented.

In his mind's eye he replayed earlier events that now seemed to have taken place eons ago. He saw everyone sitting in the bus, driving through the countryside on a warm October afternoon. He could feel Sarah's hand within his own, radiating its soft warmth. He saw her smile and remembered smiling back at her. Katie and Roger were two silhouettes sitting in front of him. He could see Katie turning around and smiling at everyone, Roger laughing at a private joke he and Katie shared, the sun lowering towards the horizon and the comet streaking across the sky leaving a thin greasy trail behind itself.

Daniel creased his brow as he remembered the sudden fingers of lightening stretching out across the sky as if looking to grasp the bus and shake them all out of it, the crashed car and then the flight from the back of the bus to the house. Nothing after the comet seemed real seemed right. He felt the panic when Andrew had been lost and the elation of finding his friend and helping him out of the open pit, out of the grave.

The realization that Andrew was again missing jolted Danny out of his recollections as he scanned the fog around him. Where was Andrew? Would he find him in time? The idea that James was in the house with Sarah, Brian and the twins caused momentary worry but he quickly pushed it down and stood up, bat in hand and at the ready scanning through the fog for any sign of his companion.

Danny sensed shadowy figures shambling towards him in the fog but he quickly observed only one pair of silhouettes moving away from him towards the field. He could barely make out a ghostly figure seemingly floating above the ground but he saw that it was leading a small figure beside it.

FOUR IN THE HOLE

As Danny's vision clarified he could make out the red cape and blue costume of his friend Andrew. He yelled out Andrew's name and saw the figure holding him rear its ruined face as it let out a snarl of defiance. It was Katie, her grey dress stained with a cloud of blood, a large piece of her neck missing and her face caked with clotted blood from her neckline to her shoulder. It seemed to clutch Andrew's hand tighter as it hurried its shamble further into the fog.

Danny lifted his bat and moved into a trot following the figures as he continued to shout Andrew's name. As he neared, Danny could make out two other figures hovering near the thing that had been Katie: the first figure wore a red hunter's jacket. Danny recognized it as the thing from the roadside accident that had stopped their bus and claimed Mr. Fishell. The other shadow appeared to be a well-dressed man wearing a bald cap that now rested on its head in a comically askew manner. Danny's blood froze in his veins when he realized that it had to be Roger.

As the two figures moved forward towards him, he could see their dead eyes and the wounds that would have meant death to anyone but these things. Their gait was uneven and uncertain yet they remained undeterred as they drew closer.

Danny yelled again, "Superboy. Wake up. Please!" His voice was high and shrill, revealing the desperation and fear that he felt. As he looked, he could sense Andrew beginning to return to consciousness as his head slowly moved towards Katie's. Danny heard Andrew scream as he pulled his hand out of Katie's grasp. The thing that had held Andrew returned his scream, its timbre shrill and breathy as air passed through the gash in its throat.

"Andrew, I'm right behind you." He saw his friend turn, looking through the fog, searching for him. "Superboy. Over here!"

Danny could see that Andrew knew where he was and the relief on his face shone through the gloom. As Andrew ran towards him, Danny could see tears cascading down his cheeks. The ghouls could hear Danny as well and he saw them turn to pursue his friend. Hands moved through the fog and nearly found Andrew's neck, but he dodged them as he advanced forward.

Danny lifted his bat shoulder high as Andrew came upon him. "Run, Superboy, run as fast as you can. Find the others and get them out of here".

Andrew's face fell as he saw Danny and the bloodstained bat advancing past him into the fog. Andrew began to run towards the house, but could not help one last look over his shoulder as he saw Danny in his best batting stance waiting for the nameless silhouettes to converge upon him.

Andrew's tears flowed freely as he realized what his friend was doing for him and the others. He stopped and turned towards his friend who was now a safe distance away. Andrew could make out the things that had been Roger, Katie and the hunter leading half a dozen other shadows towards his friend. As Andrew looked, they converged on him.

Danny turned and yelled, "Fly away, Superboy. Fly away."

Fog rolled across the clearing as Danny became a blur; and Andrew watched silently while Danny let fly with a mighty swing of his bat scattering half a dozen monsters into the air. Andrew choked back a tear and ran towards the house hoping that Danny would be okay.

As Andrew ran, the fog slowly lifted revealing the looming shadow of the house. The facade grew in size until it filled his entire vision. He felt his feet on the front steps and gained the doorway as he finally stopped, gasping for breath; his entire body heaving with the cold as he took in great gulps of the cool air. He turned to grasp the doorknob when suddenly the door flew open of its own accord and a pair of thick hands grasped him roughly and pulled him in. His vision dimmed as he let out a scream.

***

The moon languished on the horizon as if to rest while awaiting the coming day. Its sickle-shape radiated a harsh sanguine light as it alternately hid and revealed itself in the rising mists from the surrounding fields. Impossibly, the moon's color deepened to a crimson then violet shade before disappearing below the western sky.

Across the horizon, its passing seemed to be echoed in the faint crimson light finally dawning in the east. An obsidian crow awoke and bleated out a jagged caw heralding the new day. Slowly, hesitatingly, night released its hold on the sky as daylight began to illuminate a new world revealing its ugly and terrifying secret. The first rays of sunlight barely penetrated the gloom of the countryside as pitted and bloodied faces turned to snarl at the new dawn.

***

Andrew found himself inside the house staring into James' cold, dark eyes. He was forcefully pushed into the back of the door while James gripped the front of Andrew's costume in his thick hands. The bright red "S" emblem had been twisted into an ironic question-mark as James stared and sneered at his hostage.

Andrew opened his mouth to speak, but James slammed him into the door to quiet him. He lifted an index finger to his lips whispering, "They're here." He giggled softly under his breath lifting his eyes and tossing his head over his shoulder towards the back of the house. "They're here," he whispered again and his giggling almost turned into outright laughter before he gained control of himself. His grasp tightened around Andrew's costume.

"Where is he," James spat out in a voice filled with menace. It wasn't a question; it was a preamble to a threat.

"Who," Andrew replied softly

James pulled Andrew towards him and then violently flung him against the back of the door again. "Who do you think, smartass?"

Andrew bit his lip and suppressed the urge to cry as he stared into that hard face. He feared the truth would bring

James' anger upon him so he wanted to be careful how he answered the question. Something fell in the back of the house and the sound of it caught Andrew's attention; he looked over James' shoulder and knit his brow. James continued to stare, awaiting an answer. Another sound drifted from the back of the house, like something walking into a wall or a closed door. Andrew knit his brow again and continued staring into the dark.

"You want to know what that sound is? They're here, buddy boy, they're in the house. While you were outside playing around, we bin' in here tryin' to keep these freaks from coming in. But you know what?" James paused as if waiting for Andrew to reply. "They got in anyway, and there's a lot of them and they're hungry. I bet they would just love to take a bite out of you." James pulled Andrew toward him again then once more flung him into the door. Andrew hit the heavy oak and crumpled to the floor.

"WHERE IS HE?"

Andrew could only look up from the floor as James towered over him. He watched helplessly as James' face turned beet-red, his ears nearly purple. Rage was written on his face and his hands trembled with rage. Andrew closed his eyes and resigned himself to wait for the first blow and then the successive blows that would probably end his short life. He didn't feel fear, he was too young to understand his own mortality, but he was frightened of the sheer brutality of the act that was to be inflicted upon him. He feared the pain, the blood, the hurt. He had never thought about the hereafter, what happens when it is all over. His father called it the "Big Nowhere", his mother called it the afterlife. These terms where vague and abstract and he couldn't conceive of a "maybe", his world was defined by concretes; someone hits you, it hurts; you fall off a building, you die. What dying meant hadn't occurred to him, it just meant you where gone.

Then a soft hand touched his shoulder and he opened his eyes. "Welcome back, Andrew."

It was Sarah's voice he heard, her hand he felt on his shoulder. He looked into her eyes and suddenly a night's worth of tears flowed freely over his cheeks. He stood up and held her tightly, thinking of Danny, of Katie and Roger and all of the things that might never be right again. Then he told her everything that had happened from when he fell into the pit to when he left Danny fighting for his life and he felt empty for the telling. Sarah held him close all the while, stroking his hair and patting his back; soothing him and calming him yet fighting back tears of her own. When he was done, she pulled him away and looked into his eyes saying thank you but meaning sorry. She took his hand and led him to a door very close to the front entrance of the house. Sarah opened the door and sitting on the dusty wooden floor of the small bedroom where Brian, Jenny and Penny and a dour James. Sarah locked the door behind them and sat him down next to her.

Andrew looked around the room and realized it had been a children's bedroom. There were faded spots on the walls where pictures had once hung; against one wall were two small twin beds and in the corner of the room was a long bench that had been a bright yellow toy chest but had now faded to a dull mustard color.

Everyone sat quietly wearing sullen expressions on their faces and fearful anticipation in their eyes. It was an unspoken fear of what could happen next to each of them.

Brian nodded to his friend and gave him a wan smile. "How are you doin', Andy?"

Andrew returned the nod and mumbled a half-hearted reply.

"Where's Danny?" James voiced again with insistence punctuating the quiet of the room. Andrew looked at Sarah who nodded back to him.

"He's probably dead or like those things out there. Okay?"

"He's dead because you're an asshole." James began to rise from his sitting position when Sarah turned around and glared at him.

"You better stay on that floor or so help me, I will make sure you don't get up for a long time to come." The intent behind Sarah's words left no doubt that she was not afraid of James and that she meant every word she said. He slowly sat back down on to the floor.

Brian glanced at James then Sarah before continuing, "What happened out there? You where gone for the longest time. And what happened to Miss Katie? Do you know?"

Andrew looked again at Sarah before turning to his friend, "Miss Katie is dead or she's like those things out there." He paused for a moment letting out a small sob before continuing. "Roger got her."

Jenny and Penny simultaneously turned to one another in disbelief.

"Roger got Katie," Penny said.

"Katie is with Roger now," Jenny said.

"Poor Katie," they both softly murmured in unison.

James turned to the group and voiced what all of them were thinking, "What are we supposed to do now. Just sit here and wait for those things to walk in here and get us? Because I am not going to become one of those monsters, I will kill myself or take as many of them with me before I become one of them."

There was an edge of panic behind James' words and everyone was staring at him in anticipation. They were waiting for James' temper to boil over or for him to do something rash but he continued sitting as he stared down at his hands.

Brian answered, "We need to get out of here and if we have to, we need to fight back. James is right, we can't just sit here and wait for those things to find us and they will find us. We need to leave this place and get back home. It'll be daylight soon and we can get out of here. I just know it."

"How do you think we can get out of here with those things all around the house, Brian?"

"We make a run for it James and take out as many of those things as possible until we are out of here and out of danger."

James snorted and gave Brian a hard look, "How? We walk through the front door and hope those things don't like sunlight? We hope those things get tired of waiting around for us and they just leave? How are we gonna get out of here?"

Brian stood up and smoothed his chaps with the flat of his palms then curled his right hand around the pistol grip of his six-shooter. He slowly walked over to the toy chest, all the while smiling at James then jauntily he cocked his cowboy hat towards him.

"You want to know how we get out of here?" Brian grasped the lid of the toy chest and flipped it open. The chest was full to the brim with toy rifles and pistols. "You want to know how we get out of here? We shoot our way out of here."

He turned to the rest of the group and smiled. Everyone shook their heads excitedly and began to stand up so they could get a better look at the arsenal that Brian had uncovered.

***

They gathered in front of the bedroom door, each of the children carrying whatever pop-gun, rifle or cap-pistol they could fit into their costumes or on their person. Sarah still wielded a weighted baton in her right hand, Penny clutched tightly to her scepter while Jenny grasped the ubiquitous Barbie doll in her small fist. James beamed while holding a metal Winchester cap-rifle, Brian held a Colt .45 cap-pistol in each of his hands; but left his other six-shooters in their holsters for good measure insisting that "you can never have enough firepower."

James impatiently looked towards Sarah who stood against the door with her ear on one of the wooden panels.

"What are we waiting for? Let's go already."

"Shhh, James, I'm trying to hear."

"Hear what?" James hissed. "Let's just go already."

"Fine, you go first." Sarah stepped away from the door, pushing Brian and Andrew aside and placing her hand on James' shoulder, pushing him towards the door. "Go ahead. You're in such a hurry, open the door."

James looked over at Sarah, his eyes beginning to cloud over as he grasped the doorknob.

"I hope there aren't any monsters on the other side," Sarah spat out.

James released the doorknob and walked back to his place in the rear of the group.

Sarah returned to the door and resumed listening for sounds in the hallway. The house was deathly quiet but with the new dawn all of them could hear the world awakening. It seemed to each of them that every bird in the world began its song as the air filled with the high-pitched whistle of starlings and the guttural cawing of crows. It was a sign that even with so much death around them, life went on.

Turning her head to look over the group she whispered, "Okay, I'm going to go out first. If it's all right, then we make a run for the front door. Understood?" She eyed each of them in turn then grasped the doorknob and gingerly turned it. It squealed in response as the door eased away from the jamb.

She slowly cracked the door and peered into the dim hallway observing only dust moots dancing in the rays of a newly-risen dawn. She opened the door far enough to squeeze through till she stood in the hallway. She peered through the dimness towards the back of the house but could discern nothing.

Hearing movement from where the kitchen was located, she thought it could be a mouse or rodent scurrying among the shelves. An involuntary shiver ran through her.

Then she turned towards the front door. It stood ten feet away from her. The entranceway was empty; but a cold, brilliant light surrounded the door frame; the sunrise illuminating the front of the house. Its light was so intense; it hurt her eyes to look at it. She walked slowly towards the front door, the floorboards groaning at her intrusion; stretched her arm out until her right hand found the cold metal knob.

In a moment she would have the door open and she could gather her friends and leave this suffocating house, all that was left to do was to turn the doorknob. A noise from somewhere within the house interrupted her concentration causing her to turn around and face the darkened hallway. Her body tensed as she recognized the sound of footsteps coming down the hall. At first she thought it might be one of the boys impatiently leaving the safety of the bedroom to follow her, but she saw nothing in the hallway ahead of her; and knew it wasn't any of her friends.

Her nervous system humming; she picked up the baton in both hands and positioned herself against the door in a batter's stance. Whatever was coming for her, she was not going to make it easy for them. The footsteps drew nearer echoing through the gloom of the house, emanating from deep within the recesses of the darkened hallway, and then just as suddenly, they stopped.

She stood against the doorway, peering into the darkness, her eyes slits as her chest heaved visibly and her body gulped in air with a heavy, audible panting. Every nerve in her body was ready to fight against whatever she knew would come at her from the darkness. In that brief moment she remembered Danny, how strong and alive he looked in the batter's cage, swinging two, sometimes three bats from shoulder to shoulder in preparation for his turn at bat.

Her body unconsciously corrected her stance so that she could put more power into her swing. In her mind's eye, her baton became the largest and heaviest Louisville slugger that could be made and even though her baton was slender and weighted on both ends, she imagined the weight of a heavy bat being evenly distributed in her hands and balanced against her shoulder. She felt the head of the baton crack against the door behind her and without looking instinctively knew that she had just taken a small chunk out of the heavy oak door. She was ready.

"Come on, you bastard, let's get this over with," she hissed into the darkness.

The thing lurched out of the darkness at a speed that surprised her. Its long stringy hair was matted with blood and covered its face. The smell distracted her momentarily as she fought the urge to vomit. It drew nearer, closing the distance between them in seconds, she took in small details, the long fingernails caked in dirt, the disheveled clothing matted in blood and stained brown from age, the torn pants and bare feet caked in grime and gore. She had one chance, could she stop it? The thing threw its arms out towards her, its long hair finally parting to reveal a face that was more skull and muscle than flesh. An eye lay on its cheek and its face was exposed muscle tissue and bone; the skin having been drawn back from desiccation. Sarah screamed as the thing clicked its jaws at her. She swung and felt the end of her baton connect with its temple; she followed through putting all of her strength into the blow. The thing crumpled to the ground in a heap.

Sarah had no time to ponder and no time to cry, she ran to the bedroom door and knocked loudly on it, James opened the door and met her gaze.

"Let's go, guys. Right now, RUN."

James was out the door and heading towards the front entrance followed by Brian, then Jenny and Penny and finally Andrew. James stopped short in front of the ghoul's body blocking everyone else behind him.

"We have to move this thing."

"Eeeewwwwww."

"What's that smell?"

Sarah came running up pushing Jenny and Penny aside. "James, take the arms, Brian the legs. Andrew, help your friend, and I'll help James. We have to hurry."

The four of them started grasping the limbs of the thing on the floor as Sarah looked over her shoulder down the dim hallway. Sweat was collecting on her brow as she grasped one of the things arms and pulled. She gagged as she felt the flesh slough off in her hands and fall onto the floor with a loud plop. The boys looked at her in disgust. Brian turned to face the wall and vomited painfully onto the floor.

"Hurry," yelled Jenny.

"Something's coming," added Penny.

Wet sounds slapping against the floorboards approached from the darkness of the house. Sarah reached over the body and grabbed the doorknob twisting it open and pulling with all of her might. The door opened an inch before stopping against the body of the dead ghoul.

"Boys, you have to help me."

James quickly leapt over the body and forced his hand

into the door opening, pinning his body against the wall, he pushed with all his might as Sarah pulled. Slowly the opening grew as the body was pushed away from the entranceway leaving a crimson smear in its wake.

"Just a little more and we're out of here," Sarah grunted as she continued to pull with all of her strength.

The wet sounds echoed in the hallway as Jenny and Penny peered into the dark. Jenny clutched her Barbie doll in her right hand tightening her grip on the small plastic figure. With her free hand she sought out her sister's fingers and grasped Penny's hand in hers.

A hideous ghoul leapt out of the darkness towards the twins. It wore shabby, blood-encrusted rags, while its feet were bare leaving bloody footprints in its wake. Arms outstretched, it held a silent scream on the ruins of its face as it barreled down the hallway. Jenny looked at her sister with concern but no fear. When the creature was almost upon them Sarah noticed it for the first time and involuntarily screamed. Jenny stretched the arm holding the doll up into the air and flipped it around so the doll's legs pointed forward like two small stilettos. The creature ran headfirst towards Jenny who shoved the doll's legs as hard as she could into the thing's eye socket. The ghoul dropped at her feet like a sack of potatoes. Jenny stared at her sister and smiled.

"Good one, Penny."

"Thank you, Jenny."

They both turned to Sarah, "Are you almost done. We have to go."

Sarah had almost fainted seeing the creature bearing down on the twins, but now she smiled.

"I think we're almost there girls."

James pushed the door open and the group was met with brilliant sunlight streaming through the doorway but beyond the sunlight lay a heavy fog that was starting to burn off in the new morning. Crows burst forth in their guttural song as Sarah tried to shield her eyes from the dawn.

"Guns out, lock and load," Brian yelled.

Everyone took a toy rifle, six-shooter or cap pistol and

held them at the ready.

"CHAAAARRRRGGGGGEEEEE!"

They ran into the new dawn with toy guns blazing. A dawn filled with brilliant morning light that hid from their view hundreds of zombies and eminent death.

***

The morning was much like any other autumn morning for Curvin and Mollie Hersh. Dawn meant leaving a warm bed, putting on work clothes and venturing out into the barn to check their cattle, feed the chickens and start their day. It was still dark when they left their cozy house for the barn, but cows needed tending and chickens needed caring. Curvin's dad had always told his son, "a farm doesn't take care of itself," and his dad would always follow with "if you start your day while the sun is up, you've wasted the best part of the day."

Curvin hated his father, but loved the farm and it was with his animals that he always felt his best; his wife, too. He loved the quiet of this time of day as well, but when the sun poked its head over the hills, the earth just woke up and sang. He loved it and this morning was no different. As the first rays illuminated the valley and sent long shadows across the fields, sparrows and starlings commenced their morning chorale. He stopped for a moment to consider their song. His wife had been outside at the pump filling a bucket with water when she burst in. He could see she was in an excited state.

"Curvin, I think I hear screamin', like children screamin'." Her face was pale and Curvin could see that she was clearly upset. "It sounds like its comin' from the Hofstedtler place."

"Hold on, mother, let me come out and hear what I can hear." He patted the cow on its haunches and slowly walked towards the barn door, wiping his hands on a rag as he went.

He stood outside the barn, head held slightly upwards listening to the day. He could hear the birds and now the occasional caw of a crow. His wife walked out of the barn to join him. She too held her head upwards as if looking for an invisible antenna that might help to locate and amplify the sounds she needed him to hear. She held a finger upwards pointing towards the Hofstedtler property, just next to theirs. They stood silently waiting.

"Are you sure you heard…"

A high-pitched scream cut him off as it sliced through the chill air.

Mollie Hersch went pale and contorted her face into a horrified yet curious gaze. Curvin wasn't convinced.

"Just some kids, Mollie. It was Halloween night last night, wasn't it?"

"Just some kids, Curvin? Screamin' blue-bloody murder even before the rooster crows?" Are you sure? You best be sure."

"Mollie, I could call the poli—"

Another scream pierced the distant field, this time sounding as if it were cut-off before it could reach its zenith followed by popping sounds like tiny firecrackers.

"Goddammit, Mollie. Stupid kids is all."

He walked quietly back into the barn to gather his herd and let them out of the barn for grazing. He was in their ten minutes when a frantic Mollie came running in looking more frightened than he had ever seen his wife.

"Curvin, you've got to come out. Something damn strange."

"What darlin'." He was starting to think his wife was acting like the boy who cried wolf and he did not have any patience for it this morning.

"You just come out of that barn. There is a strange child outside here."

Curvin scratched his head and let out a sigh. "I'm comin'."

He reached the outside of the barn moments later and looked around the yard. His wife was nowhere to be seen. Curvin scratched his head again and walked around to the other side of the barn but still could see no sign of anyone. He soon found himself back at the barn door when something deep down inside told him in a quiet panicked whisper to run and get away as quickly as possible; hide in the house, but do it now.

He dismissed his momentary panic and turned his attention back to his search for Mollie. He stood in the dirt yard looking around trying to decide what he should do next when he heard the cattle in the barn start to low in distress. He turned and walked through the sliding door into the cavernous building. The cows seemed to be huddled along one wall, a sight that struck him as very unusual. They were never very choosy about where to congregate and he had never seen behavior like that before. Then he noticed a shadowy figure standing near one of the stalls. It seemed to him to be a boy but Curvin couldn't make out much as it had its back to him. He began to walk across the length of the barn, moving cautiously towards the figure.

"Hey, kid," Curvin yelled across the expanse of the barn. "Hey, kid."

The figure slowly turned around to face Curvin who stopped and stood frozen in place. He realized that this must be the strange child Mollie had been warning him about. Curvin saw that the young boy wore a little league uniform as he watched it pick up a blood-stained baseball bat from the wall beside it. It placed the Louisville Slugger on its shoulder and raising its cap with its free hand, smiled at Curvin. It was a wide smile showing gleaming white teeth rimmed with blood; the bloodstains seeming to make the teeth flash that much more brightly. It was a smile that froze Curvin's blood and rendered him speechless.

The thing that was now Danny advanced slowly on the man and as he did, a figure dressed in a ghostly shroud appeared in the entrance to the barn behind Curvin. Brilliant morning sunlight streamed through the entrance creating an orange aura around the ghostly figure. She was followed by a little boy in a Superman costume accompanied by a small witch who delicately held his hand in her own.

Curvin's vision dimmed as more figures; some costumed, others barely clothed appeared in the doorway moving relentlessly towards him. He felt dizzy, frightened and sickened.

In a burst of brilliance, a final dazzling ray streamed through the entrance of the barn, momentarily blinding him. When the light abated, all Curvin could see were the stained and hungry teeth of a dozen children snarling and clicking their jaws at him. He finally found the strength to scream as his world turned red before fading to black.

ROADKILL COUNTING BOOK

BY PAT R STEINER

Tommy McGuire unclasped a sweat-stuck hand from the truck's steering wheel and used it to rub his temple. Blue and white lightning flashed across the windshield threatening to shatter the glass. Just beyond the hood, the twisting county road disappeared, in its place a white field of pain. The pickup swerved.

"Tommy?"

The hand leapt back to its former position at ten-o'clock and the endless blacktop reappeared. Tommy, feeling as if he'd been caught jerking off and not massaging the walnut-sized canker of twisted nerves, which had been slowly eroding the left side of his skull for the past...God knew how long it'd been, glanced sideways at Gail and murmured, "Yeah?"

"You okay?" She'd been asleep. Her ripe pregnant form leaned against the passenger door. A motel pillow rested between her head and the window glass.

"Right as rain."

"You want me to drive?"

"Naw, I'm good for awhile yet. Go back to sleep."

"Sure?"

No, he wasn't. Sure. About anything. The world had basically ended overnight. As his kid brother Cody used to say, all bets were off. *Used to*. Cody—always the hero—one of those in the first wave to volunteer. Cody, whose hunting cabin Tommy and his passenger now headed toward unsure of what the next day might bring.

He glanced again at Gail. A stranger, really. Another survivor trying to escape the inevitable. He'd picked her up two days earlier. She and her father had been hitchhiking along the interstate. Two days ago—back when the four-lanes were still safe to drive.

187

She'd fallen back to sleep, her face aglow in the afternoon sunlight.

"Yeah," he muttered. "I'm sure."

***

Gail was dreaming of Papa when the dog stumbled onto the road.

Tommy admitted to her later that he'd been dozing off; otherwise, he would have missed the poor thing entirely. As it was, she woke from one nightmare to another. Head snapped sideways by the truck's sudden change in direction, she opened her eyes to glimpse a clump of matted fur right before it vanished below the truck's hood. Next came that awful hollow *thunk* sound, followed by the truck's screeching brakes and an outburst of foul words from Tommy's mouth.

The truck came to a stop in the middle of the road, yet somehow the brakes continued to sound their high-pitched wail. It wasn't until Tommy reached over and grabbed her arm that Gail realized she was screaming. She flinched at his touch, her hands moving to cover her abdomen. Protect the baby. She had to protect her unborn child.

"Sorry 'bout that." Tommy raised his own hands, palms up. "I...I didn't see it."

The sudden hurt look on his face made her cheeks burn. She opened her mouth to speak, but nothing came out. Beneath her fingers, her heart pounded against her ribs. In her womb, its beating counterpoint. She swallowed past a dry throat.

He asked, "You okay?"

She managed a nod. The dream again. She'd been back on the off-ramp, Papa's last words no more than a haunted whisper on his lips. *That's your main task now, Gail. Live. You and the babe both. Keep her safe at all costs.*

Oh, Papa. So much blood. And those terrible men who'd hurt him—those creatures. An icy hand touched her spine. She wanted to ask him—*Tommy or her father?*—why? Why were

188

these terrible things happening? But her tongue continued to betray her. "Wha—?"

Tommy turned to stare out the windshield. "A dog...I think." He looked back at her, his green eyes mesmerizing. "I swear I didn't see it, Gail. Goddamn thing came from out of fucking nowhere."

The heat on her face intensified. If Papa heard such words uttered, he'd...but Papa was dead, just like everyone else she'd ever known or loved. She whispered, "Please don't talk like that, Tommy."

He blinked a few times real slow, and a cute furrow appeared on his forehead. "Don't talk like what?"

"You know...those cusses. God wouldn't like it if he heard."

The furrow deepened and a second row of tilled flesh joined the first. "Well, I certainly don't want to upset God now, do I?"

She nodded her head again and smiled.

See, Papa? This is a good man you've brought me. You said he'd come, and he did. Too late to save you, but he came for me. You should have seen him drive those monsters away...

***

Tommy laughed, slapping a frustrated palm against the steering wheel.

Right. God wouldn't like it.

He levered the gearshift to park and moved to open his door, but Gail stopped him with her voice. "Where are you going?"

"Out there." He gestured with a thumb. "I want to check to see if I killed it." He knew they should keep driving, get as many miles between themselves and *New Humanity* as possible, but the collision had him rattled. Gail's *God talk* hadn't helped matters either. "S'kay. I'll just be a minute." He glanced out all the windows in turn. There hadn't been any other vehicles since the gas station, and those had thankfully been unoccupied. For all he knew, he and Gail were the last two un-affected (infected?) people alive. A regular Adam and Eve. He smiled at her. "Besides, I've been driving too long. I need to stretch my legs some, get a breath of fresh air." He also needed to take a wicked piss.

She smiled weakly, but her eyes shone with fear. "Don't be long?"

"Sure."

"Promise?"

"Cross my heart." He didn't finish the childhood saying. Without a doubt, Gail wouldn't like the *stick a needle in your eye* bit. Nor did he hope to die.

At least not yet.

Tommy reached for the door again and hesitated. Since the world had turned to shit, every here-before inconsequential choice was potentially a life or death decision. Sure, his bladder was ready to burst, but they could cover another thirty miles before he'd piss himself. On family trips when he and Cody were younger, their father never stopped for a trivial inconvenience like a kid who had to pee. *Tie a knot in it, you pussy*, just one of many of their father's colorful expressions used to degrade and humiliate the brothers.

Screw this. He wasn't going to let a bunch of brain-dead high-tech zombies run (and ruin) his life. Grabbing blindly under the seat, he fumbled around until his fingers felt the cold kiss of iron.

***

As Gail watched Tommy scamper away from the truck, the chill in her spine returned in force. The iciness spread outwards, a heavy, wet blanket that made her nipples harden against her blouse. Her heart sank in her chest.

Oh, God. No. He was leaving her.

In a panic, she fumbled for the door handle. She yanked the lever up repeatedly before she remembered the door was locked.

190

"Please, no." He couldn't do this to her. He'd just promised.

Her fingers, slick and clammy with sweat, kept slipping off the tiny lock-release knob. When she next looked up, she saw Tommy—raising the truck's tire-iron like some kind of knight from a fairy tale—round the nearest tree and disappear. Not far beyond the tree, a derelict barn sat. Half-hidden in scrub and weeds, its gray timber and clapboard construction tilted at an obscene angle. It looked like it was collapsing in ultra-slow motion.

Had something in the barn caught Tommy's eye? Or someone? One of *them*...

"Please." Not Tommy, too.

She couldn't do this alone. The weight was too much. The unknown too overwhelming. She would kill herself first. In desperation, she managed to clamp her fingers around the lock-release and lifted. The resulting *click* was a light switch turning on. Her hands, already back on the door handle, paused. What did she mean she'd kill herself? If she died so would the baby. There was no greater sin.

Live, Gail.

Tears burning her cheeks, she forced her hand to release the handle. "Papa, forgive me."

When she could see again clearly, a jogging, smiling-faced Tommy was already halfway back to the truck.

***

Tommy felt light. Such a simple pleasure—taking a piss. He smiled to himself, turning his slow walk into an ambling jog. He spotted Gail in the truck and waved. When she didn't wave back, his smile faltered.

What now? He'd only been out of sight for a few minutes, doing his business behind the closest object offering any semblance of privacy so as not to embarrass her.

She looked pale, as if she'd seen a ghost.

191

No, not a ghost, he realized. A ghost would be a welcome relief. A ghost couldn't hurt you. Kill you. Eat your brains out while it replaced the gray matter with tiny machines that ran your body like a goddamn remote-control robot. No, a ghost would be a welcomed treat.

He ran the rest of the way back to the truck, his hold on the tire-iron transformed into a death grip.

When he reached her side, she lowered the passenger window. "I...I...thought..." Her eyes darted away from him back over his shoulder.

He understood. She'd thought he was going to split on her. Leave her out here. Alone in the middle of nowhere. To die. He felt like a complete shit. "Sorry 'bout that." He rubbed the back of his neck. "I really needed to uh...pee."

Her mouth opened wide and twin roses bloomed upon either of her cheeks. "Oh—"

Before she could say anything else, make him feel any more foolish, he blurted out, "I'll check on the dog, and then we can get out of here."

To his relief she nodded her head and rolled the window back up.

Now that he'd mentioned it, he realized he'd almost forgotten the damned thing. He hadn't seen it when he bolted for the tree, nor had he on the jog back. Hefting the tire-iron high, he turned once again toward the truck's front end.

What's the big deal? His foot kicked a random stone off the roadbed. So there's another dead dog in the world. Was killing it any worse than killing a man? No comparison. Not even close. Not by a long shot.

Not even if you knew that man was already good as dead.

***

Gail closed the window, leaned back and sighed. She should have known he wouldn't abandon her. She should've trusted him—Tommy, her savior. She watched him walk to the front of the truck, move next to the hood ornament and squat down. This time when he vanished she wasn't worried. She clutched the motel pillow to her chest and waited.

Her breasts ached more every day as she crept closer to the baby's due date. They'd always been small—her breasts— the boys at school used to call her *Snail Gail* as her nipples often poked out the fabric on her school uniform like two—

She clutched the pillow tighter. Those days were long gone, the boys in question now dead or turned into monsters.

Worse monsters.

But even jerks like Jamie Hollenbeck and Stephen Davis didn't deserve what may or may not have happened to them. *Did happen to them. Don't fool yourself, Gail.* At least back then—in the good ole days—her tormentors still had a shot at redemption.

She heard a soft *thump* from beneath her feet and jumped. (Tommy hitting his head against the floorboard?) She also peed a little, a hot trickle seeping into her cotton panties. This was another new and fun development as the baby rear-ranged her internal organs. *Make way, Mama. I need more personal space.* She giggled and felt another hot spray escape her.

She hadn't peed since the tiny Ma and Pa gas station back around lunchtime, and that had been ages ago. She'd sneaked off alone to the women's toilet while Tommy siphoned fuel from one of the station's underground tanks. She shouldn't have done that. One of *them* could've been in there. There hadn't been. But there could've—

Gail hissed and bit her lower lip as the baby did a flip in her womb and kicked outwards. *Gonna be an Olympic swimmer, this one.* She attempted a smile but it came out more as a gri-mace. Then the baby kicked again and she groaned.

She looked out the windshield and saw the tree with the dilapidated barn looming behind it. Then she saw herself squat-ting behind the tree, Tommy holding her hands so she wouldn't fall flat on her *dairy air* while she let Nature do what Nature did.

Oh, God. Tommy would *see her*.

Her face and neck flushed, but the urge to urinate over-rode any embarrassment. Besides, she could do this alone.

The truck door opened with a loud and rusty *creak*. Gail—mentally gathering her various body parts—shushed her bladder foremost and awkwardly hopped out onto the blacktop.

***

The truck rocked and lifted slightly above Tommy. At the same time, he flinched but managed to keep himself from another concussion. His head stung from where he'd smacked it onto the truck's underside when the dog had tried to take a chunk out of his hand. He glanced from the petrified and blood-matted dog to the shoes and cuffed jean-bottoms that suddenly appeared off to his side. "Gail. What is it?"

"Can't wait," the now dancing feet said. "Have to go." The *go* came out as a long whine.

Before he could so much as fart, the sneakers disappeared. The slap of their rubber soles diminished as Gail raced up the road. He craned his neck backwards and caught a glimpse of her from beneath the front bumper just as she dodged behind a tree.

His tree, he realized. *The Pee Tree.*

He glanced back at the panting dog. A thick pink froth coated its tongue. "Pregnant women." He shrugged. "Go figure."

The dog, a mutt if ever there was one, stared at Tommy with its dark eyes neither affirming nor outright rejecting Tommy's comment.

"Saving your judgment, eh? That's wise."

Gail should be fine. Let her do her business and they could head off again. They might even reach Cody's place before nightfall. If they didn't run into any more trouble.

"Trouble like you, buddy."

Reacting to the words, the dog skirted even further backward, wedging itself up against the truck's universal joint. Tommy couldn't tell how badly he'd hurt it. Blood, mud and grime covered its fur.

"And what'cha doing running out in front of me like that anyways? Hitchhiking not working out for you? Couldn't get anyone to stop?"

The dog's chest hiccupped. A xylophone of ribs played beneath the patchily grown fur there. Bloody drool hung from its lips. And that pinky froth...*internal injuries?*

Tommy inch-wormed closer.

The dog whined a high-pitched, squeaky sound. Like bedsprings in the middle of the night. Like a tea kettle setting to boil.

"Take it easy, Mister T. I'm not gonna hurt you none." *Excepting to running you over that is. And then there's the very real possibility I may have to put you out of your misery.* Although he'd left the tire-iron behind, balanced up on the front bumper. He crawled another inch forward. "Other than that though, I'm pretty harmless."

But that wasn't true either, was it? What about Gail's father? Back at the interstate off-ramp. Look at what he'd done to the man. *Had* to do. If Tommy believed in a god, he would've said God had left him no choice in the matter. Gail's father was dead...or would have been soon enough. He'd been infected, sure as shit, the change happening right before Tommy's freaked-out eyes. What else was Tommy supposed to do? It was a mercy killing, pure and simple.

"But you ain't buying that particular load of crap, are you, Mister T?"

The dog whined again, that bedspring, tea-whistling whine, but the tail made one hesitant thump.

"Nope, no sir, not by a long shot. Better try to sell your shit-ware elsewhere Tommy McGuire. I'm not about to become another slab of road kill for you to tally up in your damned counting book."

Another thump of the tail.

At least the dog's spine wasn't broken then.

Tommy reached out with his open hands and hesitated. The last time he'd tried this particular maneuver the dog nipped at him. Might have taken off a finger or two if he hadn't flinched and knocked his blasted head against the truck's oil pan. Would've served him right though. A smattering of Karma. The Universe balancing out and such.

He wiggled forward and a squishy lump dug into his flesh just below his left breast where the road pressed up against him. He thought it was a stone, but then remembered the candy bar. Twisting onto his side, he managed to unbutton his shirt pocket and slip out the chocolate bar. Back at the station, besides acquiring (stealing) gasoline, he'd also ransacked (there you go, that's better—no more lies, eh?) the place for fuel he and Gail could use.

The bar was squashed from his caterpillar impersonation, but the dog wouldn't care.

"Do you, Mister T?"

Using his teeth, Tommy tore the wrapper down its length, but before he could grab it, the bar slipped from the smeared waxy-paper and hit the road like a dog turd. The sweet aroma of chocolate mingled with the reek of truck grease and dog. Tommy's stomach growled.

Better me than you dog, he thought. He needed to gain the dog's trust. Either that or he could leave the animal be and hope not to run him over (for the second time) when he and Gail high-tailed it out of there.

And speaking of Gail—what was taking her so long? Come on, woman. Shake the dew off the lily, already.

Mister T's panting grew louder as he eyed the pancaked chocolate bar.

Tommy picked it up and waved it in front of the dog. The dog's head followed the movement. "Looks good, eh, Mister T? It's all yours, buddy. Go on. Take it." He held the bar motionless. "Now, not my fingers, mind you. I pity the fool who tries."

Mister T took a hesitant step toward the offered food. Tommy spotted a dog collar with tags. "So, you're somebody's pet then, eh, Mister T?" Or *was* someone's pet. Once upon a time. Past tense not-so-perfect.

The dog took another step, sniffing the air around Tommy's fingers as if sensing for hidden traps.

"Come on, Mister T. There you go, boy. Nobody's gonna hurt you. Eat up. It's good for you."

He thought he remembered hearing one time or another about how dogs weren't supposed to eat chocolate. His father had never allowed him or Cody to have a pet when they were kids. He recalled Cody asking the old man once. *And who you suppose will end up picking up all the dog crap?* his father had replied. *Me, that's who. Forget about it. Go outside and play with your fucking selves.*

Tommy's hand trembled, lowered an inch, before he recovered. "Come on, Mister T. I promise I'm not going to hurt you."

Mister T's eyes darted from the bar to Tommy. The eyes seemed to say, *Cross your heart?*

"Yeah, sure."

Hope to die?

A snail of drool splattered upon the road.

"Okay, okay already. Hope to die."

Mister T inched closer to the bar and Tommy's outstretched hand. He felt hot dog breath on his fingertips.

Stick a needle in your eye?

For whatever reason, Mister T sounded a lot like a young Cody. Tommy's lips thinned. "You bet, brother."

Tommy barely felt the transfer as the dog moved with a slow and delicate movement, grabbing the bar lightly with his teeth.

He grinned. "We got us a real Miss Manners here."

The etiquette lesson was forgotten however once the bar was in the dog's mouth, as Mister T gobbled the candy down in two bites.

"Atta boy! There you go, Mister T." Tommy laughed.

The dog whimpered and leaned forward, nudging Tommy with his nose. Tommy laughed again, feeling a weight lift from his shoulders. First, taking a leak, and now giving a dog a treat. The Big Bad World might eat you up without warning, but simple pleasures still existed. Far and in-between, but still...

FOUR IN THE HOLE

A barrage of raspy, chocolate-and-dog-breath smelling licks covered Tommy's face. "Hey, ease up there, pal. There's more where that came from up in the truck bed—"

Gail's faraway scream seemed to come from another world.

***

The boy didn't immediately run away when Gail screamed. His lower body concealed behind the barn, he stared at her with dull eyes. She'd just about finished peeing a couple seconds ago when she spotted him *peeking* at her from around the barn's tilted corner, the barn, not more than a short stone's throw away, down the roadside embankment. Any remaining water in her bladder had evaporated at her startled cry.

Startled cry? She snorted. She could still hear her so-called cry echoing off the surrounding woods. She was surprised the crows roosting from the top-most branches hadn't flown the coop at the sound. The boy, his hair, maybe blond beneath a layer of dirt and crusty grime, continued to stare at her blankly, not moving. He had to be under ten years old. He had that little boy look about him: the large eyes, small button nose, a touch of baby fat visible upon his cheeks.

Come on Snail Gail, don't be such a ninny. It's just a little boy. She called to him. "Hey there, honeybee."

The boy pulled back until only one eye remained visible, a bit of fuzzy cheek and that mangy, unwashed, and undoubtedly lice-inflicted hair.

She took a step forward and stumbled, but reached out to the old oak tree for support. Its rough bark bit at her palm. Glancing down beyond the bulge of her buttoned blouse she glimpsed her rumpled jeans and panties wrapped round her ankles.

"Oh, my." Her cheeks flushed.

He'd seen her peeing. No wonder he didn't want to budge from his hiding place. She'd probably scared the bejeezus out of him.

Unless, he wanted to see...

She knew from sad experience boys were that way. Wanting *it* all the time. She wondered at what age those nasty thoughts started to occur. As young as ten?

The boy's face returned in full. A slight wind worked at the once-upon-a-time blond hair.

"Well, aren't you a regular Peeping Tom?"

Saying the name Tom, she arched her head around the tree trunk. She thought she could see the soles of Tommy's boots from beneath the truck's shadowy underside. Did Tommy want to do *it* with her? Even with her pregnant and ready to pop? The warmth on her cheeks spread; her neck tingled.

No. Tommy was a good man. A pure man. He was above such carnal urges. He was her knight in shining armor. Chivalrous to a fault. Look at how he had tried to save Papa. Almost getting himself killed in the process. No, not her Tommy. Tommy was *different*. Special.

Unless he thought she was ugly.

That would be bad. She wanted Tommy to like her.

The baby kicked in her womb. *Stop woolgathering, Mama.*

Gail looked back for the boy, but he had disappeared behind the barn. She grunted.

Not yet angry, no, not really, but more disgusted—at herself, or the boy? And better yet, which boy in particular?—she bent over to pull up her panties and jeans.

She managed to pry the unruly clothing up to her knees when she lost her balance for the second time and for good. In less time than an eye blink, the hard-packed ground reached up and smacked her. Hard. In even less time, sharp stones and sticks raked at her exposed belly as she slid-rolled down the roadside embankment. She screamed again, inwardly this time, since she couldn't catch her breath for a real honest-to-goodness shout. It all seemed unreal, silly even, as if this were happening to someone else, not her, not uppity and ugly-as-sin Snail Gail.

She couldn't tell which way was for heaven when something inside her tore and a renewed hot-gush of wetness splashed between her legs.

***

Tommy glanced at the tire-iron as he ran toward the oak tree. It was the interstate off-ramp all over again. Except, this time he didn't have a gun and extra ammo. He berated himself for not searching the gas station for more than food rations. Country stores like that always had weapons stashed behind the counter. The steel bar grew slick in his grip. He grabbed it tighter, daring it to slip from his fingers.

He would have forgotten the tire-iron entirely if the dog hadn't barked. Mister T.

Gail's scream had been like one of his father's wake up calls. *Hands off your cocks, boys, and onto your boondocks. It's reveille.* Tommy couldn't believe how fast he'd scurried out from beneath the truck. Nothing at all like his current nightmarish slow-mo trudge. In his haste, he'd almost scalped himself on the truck's exhaust, had in fact gotten a nasty burn on his forehead from the still-hot pipe. He had taken a few frantic steps toward the oak tree when a short-yet-sharp dog bark stopped him dead in his tracks. Cranking his head around, Tommy had seen Mister T sitting by the truck's front bumper. Right behind the dog, the tire-iron dangled from the bumper's shining chrome surface.

Forget something, Big Bro?

Tommy would have slapped his forehead right then if it didn't already sting like a royal son-of-a-bitch. As it was, he'd dashed back to the truck, snatched up the metal bar in one hand while ruffling Mister T's head with the other, and turned again toward the tree.

The still so-very-far-away tree.

This was a nightmare. His legs, sluggish, didn't want to move. Each time his work boots slapped blacktop, the upward pressure drove his leg bones painfully into his hip sockets like twin pile drivers. Inside his skull, his clenched teeth felt ready to crack.

Gail hadn't screamed a second time. Or if she had, he hadn't heard. The blood pounding in his ears was deafening. He didn't know whether this was good news or bad.

He forced his legs to move faster, and miracle of miracles, the tree grew larger. Its gnarled limbs seemed to beckon Tommy onward. *Put some speed in your legs. You're running like a girl.*

Gail was nowhere in the tree's vicinity.

Had she gone to investigate the old barn? He'd thought it a deathtrap, a card-tower construction just waiting for someone to bump the table and trigger a fatal collapse. As he reached the oak (and still no hide nor hair of Gail) Tommy was positive the nearby barn's lean looked more pronounced than when he'd relieved himself not more than a few minutes ago.

He paused to catch his breath. The sharp tang of ammonia hovered around the tree's roots. A second later, he realized the smell was urine and that he stood in it, the acorn shells and sandy soil underfoot splattered with pee.

When he stepped sideways, he noticed the piece of ripped blue fabric.

It hung like a pennant from the broken branch of a roadside dogwood. Loose threads sprouted from its torn edges. The bright blue cloth was a shattered sky fragment against the green foliage.

Gail had been wearing a blue shirt.

Looking closer he noticed other signs of disturbance—more bent or broken branches, small rocks recently overturned, marks in the soil—as if someone had fallen—

"Gail!"

Without a thought for his own well-being, Tommy leapt down the ditch face, leaving the hanging piece of shirt waving in his wake.

***

At first, Gail thought the boy called her name, but that was crazy thinking. The boy was one of *them*, and *they* did not speak. Oh, no, *they* had better things on their minds than wasting their breath on mere conversation.

If they even breathed—what use was breathing for the living dead?

Gail would have laughed if the next contraction hadn't grabbed her insides at that moment and gave them another great big friendly hug. *Oh God, the baby. Not here. Not now.* Her body felt like a giant toothpaste tube, and that tube's owner was determined to squeeze every cents worth out of his purchase. She squawked at the pain.

At her cry, the boy leaned forward and cocked his head sideways. To her mounting horror, he opened his mouth and mimicked her—although his call was drawn out, more of a slow building *Kraa-AWK*.

Another shout. "Gail!" Closer this time.

The boy's grin soured. His dull lifeless eyes turned toward the roadside ditch from where she'd crawled—on scratched hands and bleeding knees, her jeans a half-shed snakeskin caught upon her sneakers—before she'd collapsed in the barn's shadow. She didn't know why the boy hadn't attacked then but had followed her as dutifully as a puppy dog. He'd left barefoot impressions in her trail of amniotic fluid.

Then she remembered Tommy.

How could she have forgotten him?

She wanted to warn him, but the Giant took a firm hold of her spine with both his hands and s-q-u-e-e-z-e-d. She managed a half-garbled mewl before gave up. She was going to faint, pass out like she had at the off-ramp. Life was too terrible. Too painful to deal with. She needed a time-out.

The boy leered down at her and grunted. A second later, he sniffed like a hog and licked his blackened lips.

She closed her eyes and began a prayer. *Dear Heavenly Father...*

It didn't seem possible, (or fair) but the pain grew worse. Through gritted teeth, she tried to breathe as the books said she should.

Close by, the cursed boy continued to mock her. "Woo-woo, hee-hee, woo-woo, hee-hee."

Why hadn't he killed her right away? She'd been dazed after the fall. Knocked silly. Her first thought when she focused upon the boy leaning over her was that he'd been eating black licorice. His black gums and lips. The stained teeth. Then she noticed the emptiness in his eyes and finally understood: he was one of *them*. She'd been a fool. Pure and simple. Snail Gail, as slow as molasses in January. As slow as a...snail. The boy could have easily fallen upon her exposed body. Ripped her throat out, but he hadn't.

Yet.

Oh, God, what was he waiting for? Why did he continue to torture her with his hellish mimicry?

The contraction reached its peak and diminished ever so slightly. She breathed easier. The baby gave a weak kick.

That was it, wasn't it? *Hell*. This was all the Devil's doing. This was the End Times. The Book of Revelations. Judgement Day had befallen Mankind.

Why would God do this to her?

To her baby?

She heard a shuffle of running feet and then, "Gail! Jesus fuck."

She opened her eyes to see an out-of-breath Tommy brandish a flaming sword high over his head.

***

Tommy couldn't figure out why his kid brother stood over Gail like a horny preteen ready to spew a load of cum in his jeans, or why Gail would drop her drawers for him in the first place. She hadn't even bothered to remove her pants all the way. His eyes traveled up her legs to a dark patch of pubic hair. The thick hair was clumped and slick with dampness. His eyes darted upward, over her basketball of a belly and landed on her face, which seemed to glow. Had they already done it then? He lowered the tire-iron.

"What the hell?"

The boy—obviously not Cody—backed away, snarling like a cornered animal. He appeared to be heading toward the barn only a few steps away. Tommy imagined a rundown farmhouse somewhere behind it. A derelict henhouse-

"Kill it!"

Tommy looked back at Gail. Her eyes shone with the same fury he'd witnessed in his father's baby-blues every time the old man had drunk himself into one of his particularly foul moods. "Wha—?"

"For Christ's sake, kill it!"

Tommy knew he wasn't always the sharpest tack in the bunch—Cody was the brains of the brothers, the one who'd gotten the good grades at school, the scholarship to West Point— but Tommy should have made the connection sooner: the boy was a zombie. New Humanity had moved *Up North*. No place was going to be safe. He and Gail were on a hopeless quest.

"What in the double-dutch fuck are you waiting for? Kill it before it kills us. Before it kills my baby!"

Hearing Gail swear startled Tommy. A sheen of sweat covered her exposed skin. Cuts and scrapes that he hadn't noticed before marred her legs and belly. She groaned and pressed her head backwards against the ground. A single leaf and bits of sand were stuck to the lower side of her jaw.

Jesus H. Christ. She was having the baby. Right there and then.

The zombie boy took another step backward. His dull eyes slowly shifted from Gail to Tommy. He made weird wheezing sounds. *Hoo-hoo. Ha-ha.*

Laughter?

Tommy shivered, raised the tire-iron, took a step toward the boy, but hesitated. The zombies at the interstate off-ramp hadn't shown this much...life.

Something wasn't right.

No shit, Sherlock. If you haven't noticed, *nothing* is right. The world is one left turn after another-

This time he startled himself. "Shut your stinking rat trap!"

At his shout, the boy turned and ambled out of sight behind the barn, his strange laughter slowly fading with him. From a nearby treetop, a crow cawed.

Tommy lowered his arm and let the tire-iron drop. It fell to the ground with a deadened metallic *clunk*. "Don't loose it now, Tommy McGuire. Keep your head on straight." Gail needed him. The baby needed him. He could do this. Trying to remember any movie he and Cody may have watched where a woman gave birth, Tommy turned his back on the ruined barn.

Gail, her knees now up, lay panting on the ground before him much as he'd witness Mister T doing not that long a time ago. *The panting part, not the giving birth.* Tommy snorted and decided to further lighten the mood by asking, "Hey, Gail. What do you think of the name Bosco Albert? B.A. for short."

He barely had time to register the moving shadows behind him when icy cold fingers yanked back his head and something sharp tore into his neck.

***

Through eyelids opened mere slits, a fascinated Gail watched the four demons approach the unaware Saint Thomas. A part of her knew she should be worried. She hadn't a clue as to why exactly. All she knew was that the situation before her was so very *very* intriguing. Romantic even. *Whyever* had the crusading saint shown the first demon mercy to begin with? He'd even dropped his flaming sword after the hell spawn slunk away into the darkness. And now the creature had returned— with more of its evil kind no less!

A dull ache made her cringe. She felt as if she'd eaten some bad food, her stomach hurt so, yet she couldn't remember what she'd had for breakfast that morning. She'd better warn Papa though. He could be such a baby when he got sick. *The*

Trotskys—that's what he called a bout of diarrhea. Oh, how he moaned and groaned. Such a baby.

One of the taller demons—Gail suddenly realized that just like with Noah and the Ark, the demons came in two's; one pair was tall, the other short, although all four looked oddly similar in appearance. Anyway, one of the tall demons was sneaking up on Saint Thomas, who happened to take that moment to smile at her with his heavenly face all aglow. He had such beautiful green eyes. And that smile ... oh, how she loved it when he smiled at her like that. It made her feel tingly all over.

The ache became more persistent. She pushed it aside. *Later alligator, I want to see my hero vanquish these, his latest foes.*

When he still didn't notice the quickly closing demon, she grew a little concerned. Surely, he sensed the approach of evil. She could smell the rank odor of decay from where she lay.

The ache became a sharp pain centered down near her private parts.

Definitely the Trotskys. She would need to find a bathroom and soon-

Gosh darn it to heck.

She'd missed it. Her hero had spoken to her, and she hadn't heard him over that damned panting dog. What did Papa think? He knew she was deathly afraid of dogs. Why would he bring one into the house?

She turned her head sideways and spotted the pooch. It sat not far away watching the scene unfold much like she did—another spectator. *A hound from hell.* That's what it was all right. Although with its tongue flopping from it its mouth like that, it looked almost silly.

Nothing to be afraid of there, Snail Gail.

When she glanced back, the demon was in the act of kissing Saint Thomas. Her heart thudded in her ears. The pain became unbearable.

Tommy didn't look to be enjoying the embrace, but still...

No! You can't have him. He's mine alone.

With a great deal of effort (and a whole bunch more pain added to boot—she didn't know such pain was possible) Gail propped herself onto her elbows and shouted, "Leave him alone, you hell-spawned bitch!"

The exertion proved too great. Her words ringing in her ears, the world once again started to spin. She lay back flat on the ground and moaned. When she opened her eyes next, the darkening sky was filled with fuzzy, dancing gray dots.

How strange and wonderful, she mused. She'd already forgotten what had made her so upset although she heard carnal animal grunts from not far away. Her eyelids grew heavy. She blinked and an envelope of silence surrounded her. *Ah, that was better.* It couldn't have been that important. Surely, she'd remember if it had.

The gray dots vibrated with a rhythmic pulsing.

They're beautiful. So very very pretty.

At peace, Gail watched in awe as the dots brightened, then shifted into a pure and brilliant white.

***

Tommy struggled to pry the teeth from his neck while his mind shouted in revulsion. Oh shit, shit, shit. He was dead. Dead. Road kill dead.

From a great distance, he heard Gail spew another round of profanities and thought *God wouldn't like that Gail.*

He continued to stagger under his attacker's weight. He knew he would collapse soon if he didn't do something. Swiveling his hips he planted his feet firmly upon the ground and drove an elbow sharply backward. He felt the impact, the sudden give of soft flesh, followed by a satisfying *grunf.* A sickening stench filled his nostrils, but thankfully, the teeth released their hold.

Tommy propelled himself forward and turned to face his attacker—*attackers*, four zombies stood at irregular intervals around him and Gail. The closest, a woman, was the one who'd attacked him. *Killed him.* Blood—*his blood*—dripped from her chin. Dark red splatters stained her flower-patterned housedress.

The boy was the next closest. Tommy glanced for and spotted the dropped tire-iron beneath one of the boy's mud-crusted feet. Beside the boy, an even younger looking girl stared with rapt and no-doubt ravenous hunger. Long blonde tresses hung limply from her skull. A middle-aged male zombie stood not far behind the youngsters. He wore farmer's overalls and those knee-high rubber boots his father would've called shitkickers.

Rubbing his bleeding neck, Tommy suppressed a laugh. A family. A goddamn fucking zombieified family. He imagined their Christmas Family photo. *Season's Greetings from the Living Dead! This year Pa ate his four-hundredth brain while little Susie May gobbled down her very first...*

The woman, the mother—where in the hell was Grant Wood when you needed him for a portrait?—raised an arm and wiped her mouth off. When the arm lowered, a blood-coated toothy grin greeted Tommy. She hissed and made a move toward him.

Tommy did the first thing that popped into his head. He raised his hands and hooted. Feeling like a fool, he quickly added, "Whoa, whoa. Hold on a second there, lady."

It worked. The woman paused. Behind her, the boy copied Tommy's owl call, while the little girl raised a hand and absently twirled her hair with an index finger. Tommy swore he saw something crawl from her ear and drop to the ground. The man, *Pops Zombie*, stood mute, staring off at the nearby treetops.

"A-huh. That's right kid, *hoot-hoot*. Mister Owl."

The woman's gaze shifted down to Gail and then back at Tommy. He sensed an intelligence lurking beneath the dullness, an intelligence that the off-ramp zombies hadn't shown.

The boy kept up with his damned hooting. To Tommy's amazement and horror, he raised his arms, flapped them, and began to stomp around. Beneath his dancing feet, the metal bar shifted.

The zombie woman's head snapped toward her son. She hissed a second time.

The sound made the hair on Tommy's body stand on end. "Take it easy, lady. The kid's just having a bit of fun."

The eyes returned to glare at Tommy. That evil intelligence looked much closer to the surface now.

What the fuck was going on?

Tommy's neck stung where the woman had bitten him. He didn't want to die this way. He wanted to live.

Near his feet, Gail mumbled something.

Beautiful?

What in the hell could she possibly think was beautiful about the moment? Very soon now, zombies were going to feast upon them. Her baby, most likely served as dessert. *Baby's first birthday cake. Baby as birthday cake.* The world was a sick place. Then again, maybe it was better this way? Going out now. Proper nourishment for a poor zombie family.

Gail moaned and the woman's grin widened. Then licking her black lips, she went toward Gail.

This time Tommy didn't hesitate.

Lunging forward, he knocked the woman sideways and away from Gail. He hit the ground and rolled until he bumped into the hooting boy. Then, with a quick movement that surprised him, he snatched up the tire-iron and struck violently outwards with its beveled edge.

The steel tip bit deeply into the boy's throat. The boy staggered backward and the maddening hoots stopped cold. A surprised and confused look crossed the boy's face.

Tommy felt surprised himself. And revolted. At himself. Before he could stop himself, he yanked the tire-iron free—black oily goo oozed from the wound—and swung again. This time the metal bar tore into the boy's cheek. Tommy heard and felt teeth shatter and when he pulled back, chunks of the boy's flesh hitchhiked a free ride on the tire-iron.

The boy fell to his knees, but turned his head up at Tommy. "Hooo?" A skull grin peeked out from the gash.

Not Cody. Not Cody.

Something inside Tommy broke—a barrier that had kept the insanity at bay until then. Spittle spraying from his lips, he shouted, "Say, Mister Owl, how many licks does it take to get to the center of a zombie pop? A one? A two-hoo..."

No, this boy wasn't his kid brother. This boy was a zombie who would kill him if given the chance. Tommy wouldn't take that chance. *No way, Jose.* You put a rabid dog down, plain and simple. You didn't let emotion, or worse yet, morality come into the picture. No second guesses. No guilt.

Almost blinded by his falling tears, Tommy jammed the tire-iron straight into one of the boy's eye sockets.

"...A tha-three."

The organ burst with a sickening *pop.*

Tommy kept pushing the bar—deeper and deeper in the boy's skull. The boy's body went rigid, began to convulse—a fish tugging at the end of the line, in this case a heavy test made of good old American steel—before it turned limp.

"Nnn-not Cody."

The boy's head slipped from the brain-lubricated metal bar, and the body slumped to the ground.

Tommy's lungs felt ready to burst, but he didn't have time to regain his breath. He looked up to see Ma Zombie.

She'd regained her feet. Dark hatred burned coldly in her eyes. She screamed and rushed him.

Tommy, now deep in the throes of madness, smiled at her—gritting his teeth. He readied himself, raising the bar high over his shoulder and shouted, "Batter up."

The first swing wasn't a homerun, but knocked Ma Zombie's head sideways, leaving a deep dent in the side of her skull. She quickly recovered, kept coming toward Tommy, her arms outstretched, her fingers, claws raking the air in front of his face. Tommy swung again and again, but the mother wasn't a young boy. She was made of sterner stuff.

He kept swinging, his mind on the verge of blacking out.

When she finally relented to his blows, her bashed in and shattered body looked like a Mack truck had run her over. Repeatedly. Tommy—a sharp pain stabbing his lower ribs, his shoulder muscles burning with acid—screamed at her prone form, "Yer out! Yer out! Now stay the fuck down."

He fell to his knees beside her, the boy's body not far away. One of the mother's arms reached out as if—even in death—to comfort her child.

Through stinging eyes, he looked up.

The man and girl had disappeared. Back behind the barn? Back to home sweet zombie home.

Why?

Why hadn't the twosome attacked while he'd been busy with the mother? Nothing made sense.

He heard a whimper and craned his neck around, sure that the two remaining zombies had tricked him somehow. But no, the noise had come from a dog—his dog, Mister T. He made an instant connection: *Mister T had once upon a time been the zombie family's pet dog.* He imagined the little boy playing with the dog; playing fetch or something like that. The boy so happy and full of life. He saw the mother come to the farmhouse door, call to the boy that his lunch was ready. A peanut and jelly sandwich with a handful of Fritos on the side.

Tommy was somehow positive that had been the boy's last meal, or the last *human* meal before the change. He could even smell the peanut butter.

Oh, God. What had he done?

Mister T whined again and Tommy finally noticed Gail lying beside the dog.

Shit. Gail. The baby.

Her chest rose and lowered. She was alive. Another fainting spell then? He'd never seen anyone actually faint before in real life. At least not until the off-ramp when Gail had dropped like a dead weight right before his eyes.

That must be how her mind coped with the unbelievable. He would need to check on her soon. See how close the baby was to...being born.

Jesus. What kind of life would the kid have?

He turned away from Gail and Mister T to look at the boy, the boy who he'd thought had been his brother. Cody. If only for a moment. Then the mother. The damn bitch had fought Tommy until her last—breath?—was whacked from her body.

He lowered his head. It felt so heavy. Too heavy to hold up.

How could he have done this? This wasn't who he was. Bits of what looked like blackened cottage cheese coated the tire-iron that rested on his thighs. Gathering his remaining strength, he flung the metal bar away. Then he leaned over and puked.

Stomach bile drooling from his lips he pleaded, "No more. Please, no more. I'm sorry. So sorry. I didn't mean to. I didn't want to..."

Another whimper sounded, this time right beside him. He heard a snuffle of breath and felt a cold nose brush his cheek.

***

Papa looked funny. He had a small round hole in the center of his forehead. It looked like a third dark eye. She told him so.

He sighed. "Gail...Honeybee."

"What, Papa?"

"You can't keep doing this."

"What, Papa?"

He raised an eyebrow. A black tear dripped from the dark eye. "You know very well—"

"Really, Papa." She crossed her arms over her chest. "I have no idea what you're talking about."

Why did Papa always have to be so serious? Even Jesus had fun from time to time. Look at the wedding feast in Canna. At his mother's suggestion, the Christ had turned water into wine.

"Don't lie to me, young lady. And better yet—don't lie to yourself."

He'd been acting this way so often lately. Well, ever since she'd become pregnant. But that wasn't her fault. Not entirely. After all, it took two to tango. She thought of Stephen Davis's bare chest, her fingers running through the thin trail of hair that pointed like an arrow from his belly button down to-

Her face grew warm.

"There you go again. Off into your little fantasy worlds. Gail, Honeybee. Life is going to eat you up."

"Ha. That's funny Papa. I seem to recall you..."

More black tears fell from Papa's third eye. "Yes?"

She shook her head. "Nothing. I don't know."

She felt a stabbing pain from her womb. Felt her body lifted. Carried. Jolts of movement. Jolts of pain. Someone speaking her name over and over.

"Papa, why are you doing this to me?"

He smiled sadly. His gums were black as if he'd recently eaten black licorice. "I'm not doing anything Gail. This is all you."

She felt frustrated. Angry. Afraid. "What do you mean?"

"I can't help you anymore. I have to go."

"No! You can't leave me here alone."

And where exactly was *here*? She finally looked around and noticed her childhood bedroom. Papa sat upon her bed. Pink and purple unicorns decorated its comforter. Movement caught her eye. Out the window where the backyard should have been with its swing set and clothesline was instead a rolling landscape of towering pine trees. Behind their black silhouettes: a setting red sun. The sight made her nauseous. She turned back to Papa, but Papa wasn't there anymore.

In his place was a man she knew she should know sitting behind a steering wheel. He looked so serious. Like Papa. His clothes were filthy—caked and splattered with black stuff. He stank too. *Pee-yew*. To high heaven. She wanted to laugh, but a gnawing, stretching pain, sprang from her tailbone, tearing its way across her privates a second later. She moved a stiffened hand *down there* and felt wetness on her fingers.

The baby!

How long ago had her water broken? When was the last time she'd felt the baby move? Oh God, something had to be wrong with the baby. This couldn't be normal.

She looked back at the driver and a name came to her lips. "Tommy."

FOUR IN THE HOLE

***

Tommy felt a momentary wave of relief flood his body. Gail had finally regained consciousness; had spoken his name. Gail, back with the living...with the still living. His neck itched where Ma Zombie had sunk her teeth into his flesh. He reached up and scratched the angry wound while he imagined the tiny *zombites* working their way up into his brain. Replicating there like a virus...

He shook his head. "Hey, Gail. Glad to see you're awake."

"The baby?"

He'd left her upper body leaning against the passenger door, the motel pillow, once again in place between her head and the glass.

"I think we still have some time. I...I...uh, looked."

Before he'd picked her up and carried her to the truck, he'd checked to see how *far along* she'd been. Or at least that was the terminology the TV shows always used. Mister T hadn't been happy about the wait. The dog had whimpered and danced about the whole time Tommy maneuvered his fingers—wiping them off as best he could first on a somewhat clean section of his undershirt—into Gail. It was the strangest thing he'd ever done. Well, besides killing zombies, but those violent acts were being tallied-up in a whole other book.

He pushed the guilt away. "You're not...*open* enough yet."

She repeated, "The baby?"

His middle finger was the only digit that had been long enough. He'd been able to feel the tiny opening along the back of her—*What? Cervix?* He'd kept it there until he felt a tiny pulse beat against his fingertip.

"It's fine."

She'd reclosed her eyes. "She."

Tommy blinked. "Huh?"

"It's not an *it*, but a girl."

Tommy re-gripped the steering wheel. "Oh, right. Well, *she* seemed okay."

He glanced into the rearview mirror and then looked over his shoulder into the truck bed. As soon as he'd managed to get Gail into the truck, Mister T had jumped into the bed. Tommy had taken a moment to rip open a few more candy bars for the dog and spread out an Army surplus blanket. Mister T, now curled up in the blanket, raised his head and stared at Tommy.

He said, "I could feel her heart beating through her...um, head."

He then nodded his own head in acknowledgement to the dog.

A second later, Mister T returned to his former position.

Good dog, there. Gail will need someone for company...

He turned back to Gail. Her eyes were closed. By her quiet even breathing, he knew she'd fallen asleep.

***

Tommy's words didn't embarrass Gail. She was glad he'd been there for her when she most needed help. That he was there for her now. Life was hard enough. It was nice if you could find someone to share it with. Why then, even those bad moments didn't seem so...so bad. A feeling of peace spread over Gail and she drifted off to sleep.

***

"There's evolution at work for you, boy. Adapt of die."

The truck's headlights marked the bloated deer corpse lying along the roadside and then passed it by. Tommy swiveled his head, checked the animal off in the counting book, and faced forward again.

All three Tommys had been hearing Father's voice for some time now.

Yes, *three* Tommys.

215

FOUR IN THE HOLE

He'd turned into one of Gail's goddamn triumvirates. His ghostly reflection in the rearview mirror chuckled. "Three of me for the price of one. Buy now. Offer ends soon."

The speaker was Tommy One. He who drove the pickup truck through the night in the hopes of reaching Cody's hunting cabin before his passenger delivered her baby. And before he turned into a certified brain-dead zombie.

Tommy Two was Young Tommy. Or Memory Tommy. He was the one who listened to the old man speak, while tallying up corpses in the Road Kill Counting Book.

Tommy Two (and thereby Tommy One when you got right down to it as memories made you who you were, didn't they?) was being slowly devoured by the third Tommy.

Evil Tommy.

Zombie-ified Tommy.

Tommy One dug fingernails into his itching neck. A hornets' nest swarmed beneath the skin all the way up to behind his ear. He forced his eyes to stay focused on the road ahead while he wondered how many memories he'd already lost.

No way to know was there?

Except he *could* tell. He felt *less* of himself. He was slowly and steadily *shrinking* as the miles piled up. His identify. Tommy One. Original Tommy.

"Will the real Tommy McGuire, please stand up."

***

The counting book had been Cody's idea. Tommy glanced into the back of the station wagon where his kid brother snored. He leaned forward and asked the back of Father's head, "How much longer before we get there?"

There was their latest new home. This time a little shit-hole called D'Lo.

Question: How low can you go? Answer: D'Lo, Mississippi.

Pulling in a favor from a fellow former Marine, Father had landed a maintenance job at the town's only attraction: a water park.

"We'll get there when we get there," his father replied.

Tommy flopped back into the wagon's middle seat. He shouldn't have asked. He pulled out the pencil stub from the spiral notebook in his lap, opened the notebook, ran a finger down the list until he came to *deer*, and made another tally mark.

"Five deer," he said, mostly to himself, although somewhere far away and in the future, Tommy One nodded his head.

He and Cody had quickly tired of the ABC Game. And since Father insisted on driving the *scenic route*, taking county or state highways whenever possible—the License Plate Game was dead on arrival. Then Cody had spotted the weirdly scaled animal lying along the gravel shoulder. Tommy had never seen an armadillo before.

And The Road Kill Counting Book was born.

Father thought the idea sick at first. "What the fuck's wrong with you boys?" being his first response when an excited Cody hooted for joy as they drove by a blood-smeared and flattened furry corpse that turned out to be their first deer. He warmed up to it though after the large black body of a panther showed up not more than twenty miles later, stretched across an intersection where the old county highway crossed a gravel road.

And now the old man was talking science.

Would wonders never cease?

Tommy dared another question. "What did you mean?"

Tommy didn't think Father heard him, or was ignoring him as he often did. But then Father cleared his throat. "Think about it. You've heard *it's a dog eat dog world*, right?"

Tommy nodded even though Father wasn't looking.

"Same deal here. All these dumb as shit animals don't got a chance against us humans. They sashay their furry asses up to where Mother Nature meets the pavement and—*whamo-blamo-splato*—Road Kill City." He slammed a palm against the steering wheel for emphasis before he added, "Unless, of course, they got enough brains in their tiny skulls not to try to cross said

217

blacktop when two tons of American made steel is blaring down upon them. *Adapt or die*. Damn good motto to live by too, now I think on it."

"Road kill?"

"That's what people call'm. Heard folks down hereabouts even eat'm. *Southern-fried road kill*." Father's eyes latched onto Tommy in the rearview mirror. "Hey, how does *bar-bee-cued* possum sound to you, boy?" He smacked his lips together. "Yum-yum. A real *deli-fucking-can-see*."

Tommy smiled back at Father and licked his own lips together in mimicry. "Ha, that sounds good—"

* * *

"What sounds good?"

The voice startled Tommy. He leaned forward and stared at himself in the mirror. "What are you talking about?"

"Don't know," the dull eyes replied.

"Well then, shut up and give a guy a little peace, will you?"

"Sure thing."

He leaned back. "We should see it any minute."

The turnoff for Cody's cabin. Tommy scratched the top of his head. Had he gotten fleas from Mister T? He never should have stopped for the damned mutt. Served it right for walking out into the road.

He muttered, "Dog eat dog."

Beside him, Gail stirred. "Tommy?"

Like the dog, he'd picked her up along the way. Not that he could exactly remember when or where it had been...

A sudden rage filled him. "What the fuck now! Can't you see I'm driving?"

She cringed and pulled away. "Sorry, Tommy. But I think it's time."

"Time for *what*? If you have to pee, tie a knot in it. I'm not stopping until we make it to the cabin."

The cabin was the key. The cabin was important. He had to get there at all costs.

"The baby."

Baby? Tommy turned and looked at his passenger more closely. Vague images flitted across his mind like ghostly shadows. She looked ready to burst. He swallowed. "Did I...I mean am I the..."

"Tommy, what's going on? You're joking, right?"

Tommy had no clue what was happening, but thankfully, the truck took the moment to round a small curve and he spied the familiar gap in the trees. He slowed the truck to a crawl as the chain crossing the gravel drive came into view. Cody used the length of chain to *protect* his property. Wired to the chain's sagging middle was a sign that read: NO TRESSPASSING. He pulled the truck over to the side of the road and stopped, slamming the gearshift into park as the truck rocked on its springs.

Now, that was a joke. The chain wouldn't stop anyone. Neither would the sign for that matter. All a trespasser had to do was walk around the chain. And why even bother to go that far—he could just step right over the goddamn thing. Tommy chuckled. The chain was Cody *marking his territory* as clearly as a dog pissing on every tree in its yard.

Tommy wasn't sure whom he spoke to when he said, "Made it."

***

Gail didn't like the way Tommy was acting, but for the moment, she had bigger concerns. Like getting inside the cabin before they baby did a nosedive from her privates onto the ground. Not that that was possible—Tommy had thankfully redressed her before he carried her to the truck.

Tommy—at the moment guiding her by the arm as she *waddled* toward the cabin's door—mumbled a barely audible, "Well, what did you expect?"

Once again, she let him be. He'd saved her life enough times over the last few days to earn a bit of slack.

The dog—Tommy called him Mister T for whatever crazy reason—trotted ahead, leading the way down the moonlit path. His claws—*toenails?*—made telegraph-like clicking sounds on the stone pavers.

Gail wanted to tell Tommy to hurry, but she didn't think she could go any faster. She bit her lips as the urge to poo almost overwhelmed her. She knew it was the baby and not a number two.

"Sleep."

"Wha—?" He'd startled her, but at least he wasn't mumbling.

He turned her so she faced him. His eye sockets looked like twin caves. "I was falling asleep."

She made a move toward the cabin. "We can both rest after I have the baby."

"No, damn it!" He squeezed her elbow. "Don't you get it? I was almost asleep when-" He jabbed an angry finger toward the dog.

"No, Tommy, I don't understand. And you're hurting me."

He looked confused, but loosened his grip a little so it didn't bite into her flesh.

Ahead Mister T paused and turned to look at them as if to ask, *What's the holdup, folks?*

"If I'd only been a little more alert, none of this would have happened."

Gail finally realized he was talking about hitting the dog. "An accident. They happen all the time. You can't beat yourself up about that. Look, you got us here in one piece, didn't you? Even Mister T there. You could've killed him."

The dog thumped his tail at the name.

Tommy shook his head, raised his face to the moon and laughed. The sound broke her heart.

***

It was near pitch black inside the cabin. Gail quailed in fear. Some of *them* just had to be waiting for her in the dark. She just knew it.

Holding her hand—*God, he felt so cold*—Tommy led her through the darkness to a corner by a window where a rickety bed rested. She gratefully collapsed onto its mildew-smelling quilt.

The moonlight-bathed window cast his profile in silhouette. He muttered, "Better get the generator started."

Since the talk about the accident, he'd been more *there*, but now his voice was distant again. Lighter. As if he spoke from far away and not right next to her. He turned, but she stopped him, grabbing his hand. *My goodness, he's as cold as ice.* "Um, could you help me with my jeans? And panties?"

He grunted as he slipped, first her pregger-pants, and then her underwear, down her legs and off her feet. Afterwards, he stood over her. His body swayed.

He's tired, she realized. Dead on his feet. A light breeze might knock him over. She instantly felt terrible. Ashamed. He'd done all the driving while she napped the day away. He was the one who fought off those demons... My, God. She'd never even asked him how he had managed that. She knew she'd been delirious at the time. Seeing angels and demons. Well, a solitary angel: her Saint Tommy. She patted her swollen belly. Somehow, in the coming days, she would make it up to him.

She thought he'd actually fallen asleep standing on his feet when his whole body shook. His head tilted toward her and he asked, "Anything else?"

Yes, she would make it up to him. Do something *nice*. Nothing extravagant—their new life wouldn't have luxuries, the cabin gave testament to that. Yet she would find *something*... something simple only she could do which he would appreciate. She spoke meekly. "No, Tommy."

Without another word, he turned and marched woodenly across the floor and out the door. A few seconds later, she heard scrambling sounds as he moved around outside.

Voices, too.

He was talking to himself again. An argument by the sound of it.

A noise at the door startled her, and she turned her head in time to see Mister T click-walk into the cabin. The dog hadn't come in with her and Tommy, almost as if he wanted to avoid Tommy. *Well, no kidding, Snail-Gail.* Tommy had run the poor thing over. The dog might be road kill right now.

Mister T trotted up to the bed, offered her his cold nose, made a short circle and flopped to the floor with an exhausted huff.

She closed her eyes to the dog's quiet panting. "Everyone's tired. Me, too. But—"

A contraction hit and she knew the time had arrived.

Mama, here I come. Ready or not.

Through the pain, she glanced once more at the doorway. It glowed, an eerie milky rectangle. She gritted her teeth and said, "Thank you."

***

In the moonlight, the terrain behind the cabin took on a dreamlike quality. The last time Tommy had been here was two hunting season's ago, but then a good foot of snow covered the ground.

And then Cody had been alive.

"White snow. White moonlight. Tit for tat, what'ya think about that, Jack?"

He looked up at the moon and hooted. The familiar call disturbed him. He stumbled but kept to his feet.

"Not funny."

"So don't laugh."

The shed—a reconverted outhouse once Cody installed indoor plumbing inside the cabin—stood in the same place at the wood's edge. "Oh, really? What a surprise!"

"Shut up."

"No, you shut up."

"Make me."

He undid the hook-latch and yanked the door open. A memory of Father sawing the crescent moon vent into the door came to mind before it vanished, a puff of smoke. Inside, still in shadows, the portable generator sat bolted atop the old double-seater. A ten-gallon gas can rested right next to it.

"How'ya doing neighbor? Pass the Sears-Roebuck, why don'cha?"

He took a step inside but leapt backward when his foot touched what he first thought was a timber rattler. But then the snake rematerialized for what it was: the thick electrical cord that ran the power to the cabin.

He heard hissing laughter.

"Eat me, why don'cha."

"Don't tempt me, big boy. Youse look'n mighty tasty lately. But then again, the way you been smelling..."

He raised an arm and sniffed his armpit.

"A bit ripe?"

"You think?"

He stepped back into the shadowed interior, unscrewed the generator's gas tank cover and set it aside. Next, he picked up the gas can and started to pour its contents into the generator.

"You know what I think?"

"That the gas is probably half water?"

Liquid poured out from the overfilled tank and gas fumes filled the former outhouse. Tommy set the gas can back down and redid the tank's cap.

"No, not that. *You know...*"

He pulled the generator's choke, primed the fuel pump, and switched the key to ON.

"Don't go there again, buddy. I told you: leave her alone. She's off-limits."

"But she looks so utterly *scrump-chew-us.*"

He gripped the manual start and pulled. The generator turned over but didn't catch.

"Cheap bastard, Cody, could've at least bought an electric start."

"What good would that do, dumbfuck?"

He paused to scratch under his chin. "Oh, yeah. I didn't think of that."

"That's right, *you* don't think. But you *know* what I think."

"Stop it. I warned you. Leave her alone!"

He yanked on the pull start repeatedly; the generator sputtered a few times, but refused to start.

He slapped his forehead. "Fuel."

He'd forgotten to open the gas shut-off valve. He quickly turned it to the proper position, pulled, and this time the generator sprang to life. He let it warm up before he pushed in the choke. Then bending over, he picked up one end of the power cable.

Dark blood glistened on the back of his hand. He'd cut a knuckle starting the generator. He lifted the injured finger to his lips and licked.

"Then what about the baby?"

***

Inside the cabin, two things happened at once: all the lights went on, and Gail pushed a final time, giving birth to her baby. Laughing and crying at the same time, she dragged the baby up to her chest. She'd worry about the umbilical cord and the placenta later. For now, she desperately needed to know her baby lived.

Slimy, blue colored and splotched with blood, the tiny girl looked more like an alien than a human being. What was worse—what was worse than worse, what was utterly horrifying—was that the baby lay motionless.

"No, no. No."

Mister T, who paced about the bedside, started to whimper.

Gail's panic almost got the best of her then, but she forced herself to calm down. There was still a chance. A good chance. If she kept her head about her. *Silly-nilly Gail, need not apply*. Yes. Yes. This happened from time to time. The books said so. But what was she supposed to do? She felt the panic raise its ugly head again and squelched it flat.

"I can do this. My baby *is not* dead. She just needs a...a kick start."

Using a finger, she cleaned out the goop that filled the baby's mouth, and then, like out of a bad dream, she grabbed the baby by an ankle and lifted her. The pain shooting upward from her privates was intense, but she didn't stop. Praying and then saying, "I'm so sorry, baby, I'll never hit you again in your whole long wonderful life I swear it!" she slapped the baby's backside.

The baby's body jerked in her hands and Gail almost did drop her, but she quickly lowered her arm when the baby—*your daughter Gail*—sucked in a great big breath, her very first breath. Gail thought she would suck in forever, breathe in every atom of oxygen the world contained, but then her daughter, a precious gift from God, released that pent-up potential life, and loosened a loud and beautiful cry.

***

Tommy plugged in the electrical cord and bent upright as light from the nearby window stabbed out onto the night. Tired from fighting himself, tired of everything, yes, even living, Tommy turned, leaned his back up against the cabin wall, and let gravity pull him down to earth.

He'd fought off the other Tommy in his head vying for control. Yet he knew it was only a temporary victory. Other Tommy would be back. For good.

He pressed the back of his head up against the wood planking. A chuckle shook his ribs. No, not for *good*. For evil.

He sensed death, smelled it upon his skin, tasted it upon his lips. So cold. He'd never felt so could in his life. He chuckled again and something loosened inside his chest. He coughed; spraying thick rotten clumps of what he thought must be parts of his lungs. He wiped his mouth on a sleeve and let his head droop between his raised knees.

Oh, yes. Very soon now, Cody's *zombites* would kill him and then Zombie Tommy would take over.

Would any of his original self remain? Aware of what he'd become? He hoped not.

A high, loud wail broke through into his troubled thoughts.

Gail's baby.

He squeezed his eyelids tight and felt the last of his body's warmth trickle down his cheeks.

Congratulations kiddo. Happy birthday. Welcome to the world. This messed up world that's gonna eat you up alive in no time at all.

He pounded his head against the cabin. Again and again. He wished to shatter his skull. Reach inside and mash up his brains. Feel the gray matter squish between his clenched fingers.

By now it wouldn't be gray matter though, would it? The stuff upstairs would be black. *Black as sin* his father would've said. And it wouldn't even be his brain. The technology that had killed his brother and spawned this so-called *New Humanity* would've already consumed most of his brain, replacing each cell with corrupted nanotech hardware.

Adapt or die? He'd rather choose death. And by-the-way, thanks for asking. Yet no one *was* asking him. He'd have to do it himself.

Cody had weapons in the cabin. Hunting rifles, shotguns, the Old Man's service revolver—a Smith and Wesson .38 Special. Except, they were locked inside a gun cabinet and Tommy didn't know where Cody kept the key.

Was it that he *didn't know* or because he *couldn't*?

Had the zombites eaten that particular memory like so many others he sensed lost? *Road kill memories*, run over, left dead along the roadside as life passed him by. As life passed. Ended. He felt where memories should have been, but couldn't quite bring them back to conscious level.

It didn't matter anyhow. He'd have to go *inside* the cabin to even make an attempt at breaking into the gun cabinet, and he didn't trust himself not to hurt Gail. Or the baby.

Maybe that's what Zombie Tommy was waiting for? Let Tommy (by his own decision) walk into the cabin, and then *he* would take over...

No. He couldn't chance it. He would go into the woods and keep walking until he came to the gorge where he'd shot that ten-point buck. The drop had to be at least a hundred feet. The fall might not kill him—*ha*—but even Zombie Tommy would have a royal bitch of a time climbing out.

Having made his decision—likely, the last decision he'd ever make—Tommy raised his head.

Concealed by the shadow of the nearest tree, someone stood watching him.

Tommy's breath caught in his throat. He wanted to shout, to warn the person to stay back, but the figure took a step forward and the moonlight revealed his features.

"Cody."

"Hey there, Big-Bro. How's it hang'n?"

***

Tommy wanted to rub his eyes like a cartoon character, but his hands and arms refused to budge. They lay lifeless at his sides. In fact, every part of his body from the neck down felt numb, distant. He tried to wiggle his unresponsive toes and managed a long, wet raspberry of a fart. A rotten stench rose around him making his eyes burn.

The figure that looked like Cody walked forward. "Dying sucks the big wazoo, don't it?" He even wore military-styled fatigues. A tilted beret. Combat boots. "But believe me when I say, it'll get better."

"Not Cody."

The man that couldn't be Cody smiled with his brother's familiar shit-eating grin. He pointed a thumb at his nametape, which Tommy could clearly see read MCGUIRE. "Says otherwise here."

"Dead."

"*Was* dead. Past tense."

227

"Not...possible."

Not-Cody hooted. "*Right*. Like all the shit that's been hitting the fan lately don't seem impossible. Come on, Bro. Everything is fucking possible. You just have to have the balls to make it real."

Tommy's tongue joined the revolution, betraying him. "Nnnn—"

Not-Cody squatted in front of Tommy. His eyes, less than a foot away, glowed with moonlight. He looked just like Cody...except the skin color was off. Freckles or dark splotches covered his cheeks and nose.

"That's right, my main man. *Nnn-nnn*-New Humanity." He smiled again. "Buy this man a cigar, boys. We have ourselves a winner here."

Another bout of swamp gas escaped Tommy.

Not-Cody waved a hand in front of his face. "And *whew*, a cigar would be very welcome at this moment." A second later he sighed. "Oh well, can't have everything." Swiveling on a heel, he turned and plopped down next to Tommy. He patted Tommy's knee. "I swear it's going to be okay, Bro. I'm here for you in your time of need. Funny that, eh? I'm finally the one who's looking out for you."

Tommy turned his head the tiniest degree toward his visitor. This couldn't be his brother.

"Sorry to disappoint you, but it is me."

How could he—? Did he read minds?

Not-Cody tapped the side of his head with a scabbed knuckle. "It's like I said: New Humanity. We *are* the future. We are *One*."

He spoke with the intonations of a TV voice-over actor. Tommy wanted to reached over and choke the imposter.

Not-Cody chuckled. "Ever the doubter, I see. Pops named you right."

I'm imagining all of this. Not real. Like the other me's. This is the zombites trying to rub it in before they kill me off for good and take control.

228

"Zombites? Cool name. I'll have to suggest that to the top brass—well, I guess, if *I* know, then they do, too."

See, that proved it. Not-Cody was just another version of Tommy Three. A different mask, but—

"Come on, Bro. You don't have much time left. Let a dead horse rest already."

Tommy's breaths became more shallow. He felt light-headed. Couldn't focus his eyes.

"Listen to me, Tommy. All right? I'm being serious here now. Dead serious. Haha, sorry about that, you know—old habit die hard and such."

Tommy had to give it to the zombites: they had Cody down dead to rights. Tommy felt a moment's victory. *See, you bastards, I still have my sense of humor. Can't take everything from me.*

"You nailed it on the head there, Bro. We don't want to—not if you don't want to."

Gibberish. What game was this imposter trying to play now?

"No games, Tommy. You're almost beyond the point of no return."

Tommy's eyelids felt heavy. They lowered halfway then stopped. Stuck in place like a broken window shade. Inside his chest, his heart gave a hiccup, stopped, and then started up again with a slow, irregular beat.

Dying sucked all right. He had to give that to his tormentor.

"I can get rid of the zombites for you."

What?

"It might kill you—haha—but, yeah, I can do it. Try, at least."

Delusions. Deathbed, wish-fulfillment-

Stop thinking for a second, all right?

Cody had been right inside his thoughts. In between and overlapping. The feeling had been unsettling. If this was how it was going to-

"Please, Bro. Just listen for a sec."

Fine. I'm all ears. Or all mind.

"Things went wrong—"

Ha. Now that's a good joke.

Another burst of Cody sharing his mind, but this time Cody *squeezed*. Tommy's heart skipped another beat. He tried to still his thoughts. *Oooommmmnnnn.*

"You always were a smart ass."

Better a smart ass than a dumb ass.

The squeeze this time felt like a giant boa constrictor had decided to make his brain lunch. Tommy thought one more word: *Uncle.*

He may as well listen. What else could he do?

"There's always a risk when you make a big leap," Cody said. "Set-backs. Shit goes wrong. You make adjustments. Work out the kinks and such."

Tommy forced his mind to stay blank, which wasn't very hard now that he thought about it. He felt mostly blank as it was.

Cody continued as if choosing to ignore Tommy's latest thoughts. "What happened as far as I know was that the *controlled* part of the experiment turned out to be not-so controlled. To make a long story short: you're so-called zombites got out of the lab somehow. Spread like a plague. You know the rest."

Oh, and how he did. A flash of a female zombie reaching toward her zombie son.

"Turned out the gestation period for these suckers is a lot longer than anyone figured... But by then of course every host was dead..."

An unwanted side effect. He thought of the mother zombie again and realized that was what had been different about her and the boy—and the father and daughter too come to it. The zombites were in the process of changing them even further, not satisfied with only killing them, but taking over their brains and bodies and turning them into these...*things.* A thing like Cody.

"There you go, Bro. Bingo. Hit it right on the head."

You mean brain.

"Yeah, right. Zombies. *Eat brains.*" A pair of hands rose in Tommy's peripheral vision. Not-Cody laughed before he continued. "That was another unfortunate side effect. But don't you get it? That showed the experiment worked."

This hallucination was taking its fucking time. *You said something about getting rid of the zombites?*

"Yeah, yeah, thanks. The new me is just so stoked about all of this. You wouldn't believe the shit we can do—"

Tommy whipped a mental middle finger. The beating in his chest was long and far in-between.

"Sorry, Bro. Here's the deal. I'm giving you a choice. *We're* giving you a choice. You can stay the course and I'll help you through the transition period, or I can attempt to reverse the zombites."

No shit?

"No shit."

With what was left of his brain, what was left of his self, Tommy weighed the decision. Most likely he *was* delusional. Hadn't he been for the last few hours? Reliving moments from his life and then having them dissolve; wiped out, run over as if he'd never lived them. As if he himself had never even lived.

But then again, maybe this really was Cody. It made a kind of twisted sense. If New Humanity was of one mind that explained how Cody kept showing up in his mind. That had been Cody trying to reach out to him. It explained how Cody knew to come to the cabin.

Bullshit. This had to be all in his mind.

But...

What if he still had a chance? To live. What if this really was real?

Okay.

The man Tommy prayed really was his brother said, "What's that?"

I believe you. But I don't want to be like you. I choose to remain the way I am. The way I was. Screw your New Humanity. I'd rather be fucking road kill.

"Hey, I respect your choice, Bro. I had a feeling you'd go that route. Old School forever. Not a problem. Just a fair warning though. I'd stick to the boondocks for a while yet. Stay away from the cities and such. Not every one of us is as laid-back and good-natured as your kid brother is. You get me?"

Yeah, I get you, Bro. New Humanity same as Old Humanity. Now get the fuck out of my head.

"You kill me, Tommy."

At some point, Tommy's eyes had stopped processing signals to his brain, so he only felt it when Cody leaned over and pressed his cold lips against his own.

And no promises that'll you'll be the same as before. Some of your memories may be gone forever.

Go ahead, Tommy thought. *I'll take my chances. If this is even really happenin—*

Okay, here goes.

The pain was excruciating.

Right before Tommy blacked out he felt Cody separate from their final kiss and heard his brother say, "And by-the-way. Congrats, Tommy. You're going to be a great father."

***

Gail's milk let down as a thick fuzzy blanket that slowly spread its warmth from her breast where the baby suckled, down her aching stomach, and out to her extremities. She rubbed her baby's cheek with the side of a finger.

She.

Gail would have to decide on a name soon.

Thomasina sounded ever so sweet.

Whatever name Gail eventually decided upon, she knew deep down in her heart her baby was the most beautiful thing she had ever seen in her life.

She sighed in contentment.

Life couldn't be any better.

She glanced toward the closed door. Well, it might be a tad better if Tommy were there. She wondered again, what was taking him so long. The cabin's electric had been on for what seemed like hours already.

Maybe he was embarrassed.

He needn't be; she'd managed to slip herself and the baby beneath the bed's quilt, first disposing of the placenta and umbilicus beneath the bed.

Luckily, she'd found a pocketknife in the nightstand drawer. She saw herself tying the chord in a simple knot and using the knife to cut...Papa would've been so proud of her. She'd also taken the time to hobble across the cabin and close the door.

The night had become cold. Winter wasn't far off. The cabin had electric but no heat. A neat pile of firewood was stacked beside the cabin's wood burning stove. She wondered if she had enough energy to build and start a fire, but from below the bed, Mister T made satisfied lip-smacking sounds.

She scowled up her face. "Ugh, gross."

Papa would have scolded her. *Life eats life, Gail.* Thinking of her father, a momentarily pang of grief settled inside her chest, but as Baby Thomasina continued to suck, the grief returned to that of joy.

Life was good.

Papa would've said that too. Had in fact. Many a time.

Gail yawned and closed her eyes.

***

A sound at the door woke her from the dream.

Below the bed, Mister T growled.

Gail glanced down at the sleeping Thomasina and then at the door. The moon had set while she'd slept. Outside, the hum of the generator sounded erratic as if it ran low on fuel. The cabin's lights flickered.

The door squeaked open revealing a yawning emptiness. "Tommy?"

Mister T's growls intensified, scaring Gail.

"Is that you?"

Out from the porch came a scuffling footstep.

"Tommy? Please say something if that's you."

Still snarling, Mister T crawled out from beneath the bed. His fur stood on end.

"Tommy. This isn't funny."

She'd been dreaming of summer. She remembered that distinctly, could still feel the sun's heavy warmness pressing down upon her skin. Thomasina had been in the dream, a babe of six months already able to crawl. The two had been lying upon a blanket spread across vibrant green grass. Tommy had been somewhere nearby, working. She recalled the slow, repetitive strike of an axe cutting into timber. Thomasina was picking the pedals off a dandelion with thick, chubby fingers. Yes, there'd been that too. How could she have already forgotten? An innocent smile had lit her daughter's features as she studied the yellow flower. So beautiful.

Gail glanced down at the sleeping newborn—*is* beautiful. Will be beautiful.

She struggled against her fear, the unknown facing her. She wanted to feel that dreamlike splendor so light and free, not this cold and sterile fear that gnawed her so.

Please, make this go away. Make everything good again. Clean again.

"Please."

The generator, an unthinking manmade machine, didn't care about her fears or her hopes and dreams; it took the moment to give up the ghost and the cabin went dark.

The doorway revealed a dark silhouette framed by starlight.

"Tommy."

Another scratching scuffle as the figure moved inside the cabin and closed the door.

Gail moved to protect Baby Thomasina, but Mister T— whose growls scared Gail almost as badly as the dark figure— stopped his hellish calls, and she paused with her hand resting upon the child's soft skin

Holding her breath, she listened.

The next sound she heard was the repeated *thump-thud-thump* of the dog wagging his tail.

The unthinkable has happened. The dead are walking!
Humanity's fragile thread may be reaching its bitter end.
Individuals and groups struggle to survive…some at any cost. Will there be anybody left?
Or, is this just…

The Ugly Beginning?

Book 1 of the *Dead* Series

DEAD:
REVELATIONS
THE SECOND
BOOK
IN THE 12 PART
ZOMBIE EPIC

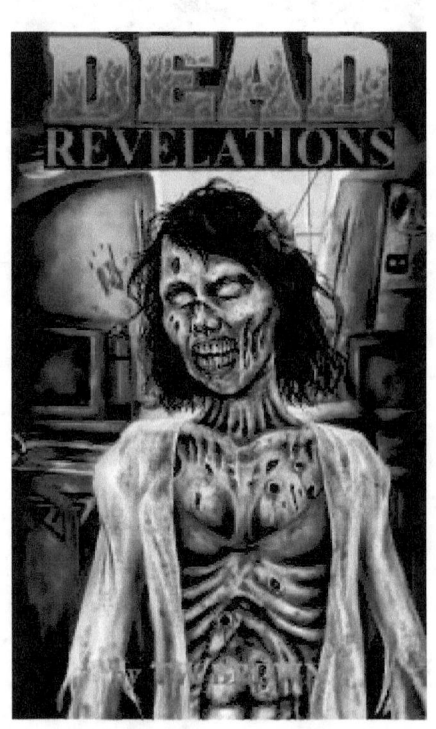

THE DEAD WALK!

Samuel Todd is a regular guy:
...Failed husband...
...Loving father...
...Dutiful worker...
...Aspiring rock star.
He had no idea if anyone would care, or take the time, to read his daily blog entries about his late night observations. But what started as an open monologue of his day-to-day life became a running journal of the first-hand account detailing the rising of the dead and the downfall and degradation of mankind...

Meredith Gainey is a survivor...and determined to retain that status as the zombie apocalypse wipes out most of humanity. Unable to accept an existence behind walls and fences, she finds herself in constant danger...and she wouldn't have it any other way.

**Look for Zomblog: The Final Chapter
coming August 2011**

The legions of the undead continue to grow.
First Time Dead proudly presents a host of brand new names to the genre pantheon.
Each writer contained herein might be the next "it" writer on the rise…the one to watch for. You never know where the next Romero, Kirkman, Brooks, Keene, or Wellington may emerge to scare and entertain the masses.

Our matched set anthologies
Available Mother's Day and Father's Day 2011

It has been said that women are the "gentle" sex. Apparently, not all of them got the message. Within the pages of this anthology are a dozen zombie tales by women who will help you discover why they say something else about the ladies: **Hell Hath No Fury...**

"Ladies first" So say the gentlemen.
This is the companion anthology to Hell Hath No Fury...Inside, you will find an undead bakers dozen that will remind you of how dark and desolate the minds of men can truly be. Vowing not to be upstaged by the dark musings of their female cohorts, the men offer up a usceral, gore-drenched collection that strives to prove... **Chivalry is Dead**

Slip into the skin of common men and women and experience the horror through their eyes. Follow the Zombie Apocalypse from its initial stages to the brink of the abyss, and over…into the pits of an unthinkable Hell on Earth. Tune into your local radio stations for the latest updates or stay here and follow the story as it unfolds on…

Eye Witness: Zombie

A Man of Letters
by Eric   Pollarine
A Soldiers Lament
by Patrick D'Orazio
Blackout
by Amber Whitley
Childish Things
by William Wood
Feral
by Rebecca Lloyd
One Nation Undead
by Mike Harrison
Shear Terror
by Chantal Boudreau
That Ghoul Eva
by Marianna Mann
and more

MayDecPub.com/*e*-LIT

LOOK CLOSELY
THESE ARE DRAWINGS, NOT PICTURES

To have your pet art done
Contact Denise @
dlbrown@maydecemberpublications.com

MAY DECEMBER
Publications

**The growing voice in horror and
speculative fiction.**

Find us at www.maydecemberpublications.com

Or

Email us at contact@maydecemberpublications.com

www.ingramcontent.com/pod-product-compliance
Lightning Source LLC
Chambersburg PA
CBHW050925120626
46552CB00001B/41